Publish and be damned
www.pabd.com

Josef Sope

Maurice Aldridge

Publish and be damned
www.pabd.com

First published in Great Britain 2004 with pabd.
The moral right of Maurice Aldridge to be identified as the author of this work has been asserted.

Designed in London, Great Britain, by Adlibbed Limited.
Printed and bound in the UK.

This novel is a work of fiction and the characters and events in it exist only in its pages and in the imagination of the author.

ISBN: 1-905059-26-4

To Christine, Oliver and Wendy,
the best family a man ever had

Chapter 1

Jangle of keys in the dark. Electric light explodes in my eyes. -- "Hurry up and get over to the exercise yard, you!" -- The warder glares in at me.

"Here we go again! You've forgotten my therapy, haven't you? Today's my day for shock treatment, remember?"

He came in and stood looking down at me stretched out on the straw mattress. -- "I haven't forgotten anything, sonny. Your therapy's been cancelled. You're going to have to be a brave boy and cope without me from now on. Believe it or believe it not, the ministry's washing its hands of you. They reckon that, after all these years of loving care, you're either beyond redemption or a reformed character. You a reformed character? Fucking idiots! They should have asked me! I'd have told them! Anyway, they didn't so there we are. You're being tried for life with all the rest of them. Who would have believed it, life for you of all shits! You slimy bastard! Heaven help the human race is all I can say. Now, get your fat arse off that bunk while I'm still in a good mood!"

We'd come to know each other well over the years. I was his special responsibility. He fed, watered and bedded me, knocked me around -- as long as I was chained up -- and, every tenth day, escorted me to the treatment centre and back again, walking or on the stretcher. Familiarity had fostered mutual contempt and now that tobacco had corrupted his lungs and his heart had begun to fail, he'd grown frightened of me. -- "You mean to say I'll be free again for a few years, free to go where I like and do what I like without you always there, riding on my back?"

"As long as I don't have you up on a charge, which I easily could. Go on, clear out of my sight while your heart's still a-twitter."

"Ok, if you say so but I can't possibly leave without saying goodbye. No hard feelings, my old pal. You were only doing your job and you did it very conscientiously, I must say." -- I stood up, stretched invitingly before him and offered my hand.

Can you believe it? The bastard clasped my hand with genuine tears in his eyes. -- "Thank you for that, sonny! You'll never know what this means to me. I'm sorry if I've had to be a little harsh on you now and then, I really am. I only wanted to help you, that's all. The truth is, you've always been like a son to me -- you and your little ways! I'm going to miss you so much!"

"Same here, Fred honey." -- I tightened my grip on his hand, kicked him in the crutch then beat him around the head with his own revolver till he collapsed unconscious on the floor. Lovely sight, so much blood! I thought about hanging on to the gun but decided to get rid of it. Nothing much in the pockets, some cash, cigarettes, matches, a ballpoint pen. The pen made a nice hole in his left eardrum but I chose to be merciful and leave the other. It was enough to take the cash, unclip the keys from his belt and leave, locking the door behind me. I dropped the gun and keys down the sewer and was walking away to freedom when I heard the shrill of his panic whistle sounding behind me. -- "Oh shit!"

--- * * * * * ---

First light in the exercise yard and soldiers sorting us out, the haves from the have-nots. A corpulent major seemed to be in charge. -- "Those of you who have proof of identity, on the right, the rest of you on the left. Move along and, you there, stop that blasted pushing!" -- In fact, I wasn't pushing, just on my way round to join the top set but before I could fall in line, he prodded me up the arse with his baton. He was flourishing a list. -- "And who do you think you are, boyo?"

"Can't say for sure, major. It's been a long time. You wouldn't credit what I've been through."

"I'm not interested in what you've been through. What's the name? Well? Oh, come along, I haven't got all day! Let's have a look at your papers."

"That's the problem. Nothing in writing arrived, you see. God knows why." He snorted, showering me with nasal spray. -- "Don't worry, boyo, it's obvious who you are."

"Is that so?"

"Ask anyone with eyes to see. You're the ubiquitous Joe Soap, aren't you? Rings a bell, does it?"

"You being serious?"

"Little Joe Soap, that's who you are, Mr Nobody. So now we know why you haven't received identity documentation. You don't have an identity worthy of the name. Common as shit, you are, a grain of sand, a number and nothing more. Alright, get over there and lose yourself in the mass of humanity where you belong. -- You heard what I said. Don't stand there, move!" [Spun around and caned once, twice across the back of the legs]

In front of all those people! My balls told me to give him a thrashing but my brains said leave it for another time and, as usual, they were right. Without at least a knife, physical responses were out. -- "I recognise that, as a mere major, you have no say in such matters but I have to tell you I don't understand what is going on here. Me, a mere number? That's never right! I've always been -- well, for want of a better word, a celebrity. Something's wrong here. -- And why are you lot grinning? Take a look. I'm as good as any of you, head and shoulders above most. Why should you have status and not me? If there hasn't been a cock-up somewhere along the line, this is all a plot. They're trying to take away my birth-right. A dead dog could figure that out."

The fat major gave me another stroke with his cane. He was in a hurry to get the job over and gallop down to the officer's mess for breakfast. -- "Ok, ok, that's enough! I've let you have your gripe, Soap. Now just do as you're told before I have you put back in the cage for good."

"One thing I will say," I told him and the grinning goody-goodies, "there'll be hell to pay for this. I'll get this lot sorted out and once I do, I'll be sorting a few people out as well." -- Several of them smiled sympathetically and one or two looked embarrassed but, otherwise, nothing but sniggering and haughty stares. I marched away and stood in the front row of the masses to wait.

It took for ever for the proceedings to get under way and, several times, I could have sworn I heard a distant whistle. However, before anyone bothered to react, the governor and his cronies appeared on the balcony to address the multitude. -- "Alright all of you, quieten down and listen carefully to me. The time has come at long last for you to be discharged. We, in the ministry, have done all we possibly can to reform, re-educate and generally bring you up to date with life as it now is in the 21st century. The rest is up to you. In a few minutes, you will be starting out on the road to reincarnation and what sort of road will that be? Not a level road, nor yet a straight one, that I promise you. You will have much to think about and much to do because in effect, your journey will be a trial, a trial by ordeal, and its purpose will be to discover how fit you now are to walk yet one more time through the valley of the shadow of death. And what will this ordeal be like? It will be a lot like life, of course. For a few," [wide smiles for the haves] "The select band who already have status, it will be a first rate opportunity, the chance to develop strength of character, learn the ropes, acquire social graces, amusing eccentricities, make friends, build up influence where it counts, get, in short, both feet in the door of life. For those of you at the top of the tree, it will be one long summer stroll provided only," -- His face hardened for an instant. -- "They behave as anticipated and follow the advice they are given by the ministry. In which connection, it is always prudent to remember that privileges bestowed can be taken away. The proudest sheep can become a goat, in other words. -- Now, what of the rest of you?" [sour face for the goats especially me] "Well, you'll have to survive on a diet of hope and that's it. For a tiny minority among you, blind chance will bring undeserved rewards, a winning lottery ticket or something of the sort, or else they will manage to hoist themselves out of the mire by their own boot-straps. For the vast, overwhelming majority, however, the road ahead will be as your lives will be, a vale of sorrows, characterised by poverty, ignorance, exploitation, blood, sweat and -- you've got it -- tears. -- My advice to you all, sheep and goats alike, is-- however you find it, Heaven or Hell, give it all you've got because it's for life and you won't get a second chance. Win the stamp of approval and you'll run again in the human race with the remote possibility of reward in Heaven. Make a mess of things and it's the worm-bank or Hell-fire for eternity. We at the ministry have dealt the cards, it's now up to you how you play them. -- Right, here's the drill. Those on the right will be taken by coach to the central bank where they will receive counselling and be provided with that staff of contemporary life, credit. They will be issued with a bank card, silver or gold according to rank and or influence. Guard that card with your life by the way if you want to be sure of your rightful place on the ladder. From the bank, card-holders will be taken or else make their own way to their assigned departure point. -- Now for you characters on the left. You will be marched from here to General Discharge where you will be given an identity number and told what to do next. -- I take it there are no questions. Speak now or for ever remain dumb." I raised my hand. -- "Who the hell was it who decided which of us should be the sheep and which the goats?" "You, is it?" -- The governor's chins wobbled scornfully. -- "I might have guessed. However, since you put the question – with your usual lack of respect, I might add -- I'm the one who decides and I do so on behalf of The Minister."

"And which minister would that be?"

"And which minister would that be, he says. My minister, sonny, and yours too, His Excellency, The Minister of police. Ok? I might add that your particular case-history made pretty depressing reading. If you plan to survive at all, my best advice is, keep your eyes down, your mouth shut and never leave off praying for a miracle. Not to put too fine a point on it, the powers that be around here do not look upon you with affection. Satisfied?"

Satisfied! Of course I wasn't satisfied. The fart! What right did he have, standing up there like the pope surrounded by hangers-on and sneering down at me as if I were already on fire? I pulled a face but said nothing.

"No more questions? -- Very well, carry on, no belly-aching, no fighting, no monkey-business of any sort whatever. Anyone making trouble will be automatically disqualified. -- The trials commence --" -- The governor makes a show of studying his watch, Some flunkey produces a starting pistol, points it at the clouds. -- "from right-- now!" [Bang]

At the sound of the gun, the sheep trotted away, most of them positively bouncing with joie de vivre, and I was herded off with the goats to General Discharge, a lowly cattle shed with trestle tables down one wall where we were supposed to queue for numbering. Not me though. I wasn't going to be reduced to a set of digits, minister or no minister. I simply ignored the proceedings, leaning against the wall by the door with my hands in my pockets. Just as well because that was how my first break came along. A luxury coach containing a whole flock of sheep swishes by and draws up a hundred yards or so further on where it waits for the prison gates to open. I slip out of the shed, stroll up to the passenger door, roll it open and climb aboard. There's a momentary silence among the sheep but otherwise no reaction. I slip into the empty seat beside the driver. -- "Sorry I'm late, driver. Had to go to the loo."

"That's ok, governor, no problem." -- The gates swing wide and we're on our way, speeding down hill in the direction of the central bank.

--- * * * * * ---

One of many advantages in being me is I'm up to speed in just about everything that counts. As we pulled up, I thanked the driver for the safe journey, stepped down onto the pavement, strode up the steps and into the bank as if I owned the freehold. The place was packed, packed but hushed and orderly as if everyone knew they were at a grand party but didn't know what was expected of them. I stood awhile in line for service but, when a woman journalist started moving along the queue with her notebook, it seemed only prudent to go to the loo. When I emerged a few minutes later, there were several more newspaper people but they had no interest in the world and his wife. They were swarming around two men, one in a banker's suit, the other in naval uniform, who were escorting the loveliest girl ever was to the doors. Aristocratic, she was, petite and hair so blonde it glowed in the light. There was a particularly bright flash as someone at the back of the crush took a picture and, turning her head, she looked straight at me. The impact was seismic. My pulse broke into a gallop and from deep down, sensations rose up which I had pretty near forgotten. I started forward but too late, she was being shepherded through the doors, down the steps and into a stretch limousine.

--- * * * * * ---

Ages later and the queue long as ever and the way the clerk behind the desk was operating his computer, any hopes of finding someone who could give me a lead on the blonde in the limousine had gone.

He was 100 percent goat—flesh, that one, labouring away at his ant-work as if the universe depended on him, entering, deleting, giving up then starting again, wandering off to ask for guidance, coming back, restarting, consulting his handbook then stamping everything in sight. We seemed to be moving at inches an hour but at least it gave me the chance to size up the situation. The big challenge, of course, was going to be identity. Like everyone else, I'd have to give my name and produce that wretched document. For a while, I considered picking the odd pocket in the hopes of finding papers but decided not in case there were security cameras. Maybe, I could -- what, say I was acting for John Smith, the well known quadriplegic? What about saying I'd been sent round by Number 10? Not a chance, even this goat couldn't be that stupid. There was nothing for it, when I finally got to the counter, I had to rely on my personality alone. -- "Do you mind speeding up, I have a life to live." -- God, what breath, enough to paralyse a rat!
"Want a card, do we?" [Plague breath wafting across the desk]

"Want, no, need, yes -- and today if that's not going to cause mental melt-down."

"Now, you just calm down, Mr. I'm going as quick as I can. Ok, what's the name and I will need proof of identification."

"The name's Josef, spelled J o s e f, Sope, spelled S o p e. As for proof, I'm afraid I've lost it."

"Lost it! Where for God's sake?"

"If I knew that, I wouldn't be standing here without it, would I?"

"Joe Soap probably would. How did you get on at counselling?"

"Counselling?"

"That's what I said, counselling—financial management, insurance, getting into the right firm, ditto for clubs, schooling for the kids, retirement, funeral arrangements and whatever. You should have had your identity document with you when they took you through all that stuff."

"So that's what it was all about! Well, I did speak to someone but, before you ask, I don't remember who and I definitely wasn't asked for any identity document."

"Really? How remiss! Was it a gentleman who spoke to you or a female?"

"Impossible to say."

"How about the office number, then, do you remember that much?"

"Let me see -- there was a 1 in it and -- and a 6 but -- um, no, sorry."

"Oh dear!" -- He sighed and plunked a touch-pad down in front of me. -- "One of those, are we? Press down on that a second, if you don't mind."

"May I ask why?"

"To issue the card, Mr, I have to check out your credit rating and in order to do that I have to look up your record and, since you have no proof of identity, I shall need your prints. Follow me or would you like me to go through it more slowly?"

"Will I get a shock, touching this thing? I'm highly sensitive to electrical stimuli."

"Of course you won't. Just hurry up, I'm busy. -- No, not with your knuckles, Mr Sope, your fingertips."

"A sense of humour is a joy for ever," I informed him and gave an extra press for luck. Lady luck was not impressed though. My prints processed and whatever, friend Halitosis sat staring at his screen. -- "Now here's a thing! The name you've given me and your prints don't tally. In fact, according to our data, you don't have status at all. In other words, you're not credit-worthy. I'm sorry but all we've got on you is that you're provisionally booked for accidental conception, date and location unspecified. Who …?"

"Accidental conception! What does that mean, for crying out loud?"

"It means you won't be expected and probably not wanted either. Most working-class pregnancies are like that according to our data. -- What I was about to ask was, who sent you to the bank?"

"And why do you need to know that?"

"It looks like there's been a clerical error, that's why. Your file is virtually empty. I don't know where you got this name, Josef Sope, from but you should have been taken along to general discharge. Only people with status are entitled to credit and you don't seem to be one of them. I'm afraid I'll have to speak to the manager."

The manager! Things were really getting serious. -- "I guessed something like this would happen. The governor was saying only yesterday how inefficient all this computerisation is. He sent my data

through ages ago. I'd better go back and check it out with him."
"In with the governor himself, are we? Well, there's no need to disturb him. If he sent the data, all I need to do is ring his secretary. Which batch were you in?"
"How the hell should I know? I simply followed instructions. The governor said to come round here and that's what I've done."
"You don't seem to know much about anything, do you, Mr Sope? Let's try another line then. How about the coach number? The driver will have the batch number."
"I didn't come by coach. I walked."
"Walked! And you in such a hurry! -- Ok, there's nothing for it, I'll have to refer your case to the manager straight away. Hang on a minute." -- He turned his back on me and started whispering into his phone.

There were piles of stuff on the desk, including a cardboard box half full of blank credit-cards, blank but for their border of gold. The clerk was in deep conversation so I reached over and helped myself. No Hanging around after that, out the door, down the steps and away. Thankfully, no security alarm, no sign of police, nothing.

--- * * * * * ---

I've always been an optimist and, once clear of the bank, it wasn't long before I'd decided that things were looking good in spite of the start. I'd avoided goat-hood for a time at least and I had a gold card. Without that magic number, I couldn't draw on it, of course, but so what? Lots of success stories in life are little more than smoke and mirrors but they're applauded just the same. I could always try flashing the thing or maybe find a no--hoper to buy it at a price. Certainly, even the suggestion of class would create quite a stir if the metro was anything to go by. Such squalor! About half a million steps down into the bowels, endless escalators out of order, miles of tunnel-walking in the semi-dark, sardine-crowds, hot winds, tone-deaf buskers, dirt, dust, gales of stink, more hot wind, rattle, roar and, at last, a litter-strewn platform with evil-looking rails running away into the dark and fifty thousand other recycles trying to shove each other over the edge. When the train arrived, I couldn't find a seat, of course, and would have missed getting out at the first stop if I hadn't managed to shoulder through a gaggle of refugees and climb over a wheelchair. Surfacing was pretty much the same story in reverse, more hot winds, motionless escalators, walk-tunnels, an idiot plucking at a harp which would have sounded better stringless, an Everest of steps and out onto the street.

--- * * * * * ---

After the metro, I wasn't expecting good cheer, certainly not the scene rocking and rioting like dear old Sodom and Gomorrah. Even so, I'd anticipated something more people-friendly than the stench and bedlam of a modern metropolis, hordes of people and traffic, high-rise depression, boarded up shops, ethnic restaurants, people hanging out in cardboard boxes, a dog trying to have it off with a tomcat, humans selling newspapers. It was all so drab and unwelcoming, I had to wonder if re-entry into the human race was such a desirable goal for your everyday nobody. Surely, an image of God deserves better than this. Maybe I should do something about it, devote myself to improving the lot of the masses, become a revolutionary, even go into politics.

The miserable lot of the under-class became more and more remote, of course, as I got further and further away from the station and entered the superficially refined world of the financially credit worthy. The buildings spaced out. I became aware of the blue sky, lots of trees, doves cooing and a cheeky breeze bowling a small crowd of leaves ahead of me. One way seemed much the same as another so I followed. We made good time, past the hotel de ville -- a minimalist drab-slab in glass and concrete -- through more and more urbanisation on the creep and, eventually arrived in a leafy suburb teeming with swank cars, horseboxes and blue rinses parading the poodle. The leaves led me past a mock Tudor pub -- Morris-dancers prancing about on the green -- village church with electric bells a-pealing, turned into the botanical gardens and frolicked away among some rosebushes. I wandered around for a while inspecting what was on offer, courtesy of the rate-payers, neat flowerbeds, fountains, headless statues and whatnot. None of it appealed and so I ended up feeling sorry for the middle class as well. Definitely, I told myself, something dramatic must be done about the human state. "It will be my duty to put my talents at the service of my fellow sufferers and inspire a new understanding of the concept of human dignity."

Disenchanted with the system I may have been but I did have an amazing piece of luck while poking about in the botanical gardens -- a roll of banknotes stuffed behind a pipe in the loo -- ransom money obviously. Well, I told myself, as children learn at school, exchange is no robbery. That must be right because otherwise most captains of commerce would be in prison. -- I put the cash in my pocket and the blank card behind the pipe. If the kidnappers weren't satisfied, then some ill-starred hostage would have to take what was on offer. I'd done my bit by giving up the card.

I was washing my hands when a grotesque slopped in, easily six foot, bull-necked and curtain-rings in his ears. He pushed past me in a cloud of sweaty feet and into the sit-down with the pipe. A few moments silence then he was out and rushing into the closet next door. Being pressed for time, I didn't bother to dry my hands too well.

My next stroke of luck was even more fortunate and probably only just in time -- the exit and a sign pointing East and bearing the inscription "Flight for Life Launch Centre -- half a mile".

--- * * * * * ---

They say pride comes before a fall. The same can be said, I think, of high expectations. Like everything else I'd experienced so far, the Flight for Life Launch Centre turned out to be something of a jaw-dropper, a small aerodrome with, it seemed, nothing more hi-tech than a few windsocks and what looked like TV-masts dotted around the place. We did have a rocket, of sorts, a phallic construction in white with Homo Erectus emblazoned on its side, its motors running and the crew going up the steps, but that looked more like a prop for a TV commercial than the real thing.

Bet your life it will be VIPs and invalids first, I told myself as I elbowed my way across departure and toward the front of the queue for boarding. Too bad, there'll be cops galore after me by now and this lift-off could well be my only hope. -- "Excuse me. -- Do you mind, I have to attend to a heart patient. -- Kindly let me pass, sir, madam."

"Do you find it absolutely necessary to barge about like that?" -- Jesus! Right in front of me, that blonde!

"Good God! It's you! -- I am sorry! I was trying to get past." -- What a beautiful creature! the bearing of a princess, a miraculous figure, blue eyes and that hair! -- I was suddenly aware that my mouth was open.

"What's the matter with you? One minute, you're trying to walk over me, the next, you're standing there staring at me with your mouth open. If you really are some sort of doctor, you'd better carry on or you'll arrive too late." -- I swear that voice would have silenced the dawn chorus.

"It's just so strange running into you like this. I was longing -- hoping to meet up with you one day but I didn't dream it could happen so soon."

"And the heart case?"

"Oh, he'll be alright. I should say by the way that I'm not a qualified doctor. I do, however, have a great deal of experience in resuscitation techniques and I'm always ready to put my experience at the service of others. As I came in, I thought I saw a gentleman in trouble but I see now I was mistaken. -- I really am sorry I knocked into you by the way. I don't usually behave so badly."

"I'm surprised but glad to hear it. Didn't I see you in the bank earlier?"

"You did indeed. You and your party left before me. -- Isn't that your car waiting over there? Look, the admiral or whatever he is is waving."

She pursed her lips. -- "Oh Hell! -- Look here, whatever your name is, just run across and tell them to go. Say I've made up my mind and I'm not changing it, not for anybody or anything."

"And you? You won't disappear while I'm gone?"

"Perhaps, perhaps not. Now, kindly do as I ask before the admiral decides to come over himself."

I rushed over to the limousine. The officer with all the gold was scowling as if to say he'd had as much as his pride could swallow. -- "Why have you been sent, young man? What is going on here?"

"No idea. She says you can go. Apparently, she's made up her mind

-- whatever that means -- and she won't be changing it no matter who says so."

"Says that, does she? Well, we'll see about that. Here," -- He took an expensive-looking envelope from a pocket and handed it to me. -- "Be so good as to give Lady Victoria this and you may tell her that I would prefer her to give me her answer in person."

I flew back again. -- "He told me to give you this. An immediate reply is required in person."

She grimaced, tore open the envelope, skimmed through the letter then, ripping it up, scattered the pieces in the breeze. The vast expanse of limousine executed an abrupt turn and vanished in the mediocrity of morning traffic. She watched it go but said nothing.

"Well," I said, feeling distinctly redundant, "Quite a dump, this, is it not? I'd have said it's more like a strip for microlights than a launch centre. That spacecraft looks pretty primitive as well if you ask me. -- Is there anything else you would like me to do? About the admiral, I mean. I took in the details of the car so it should be easy enough to find out where he's gone."

"I don't wish you to do anything, thank you. In fact, I don't intend to discuss the matter with you in any way. It's not your affair. -- What's wrong with the rocket?"

"What's right with it, you mean."

"You know, it isn't done to tell a lady what she means. Anyhow, this one means exactly what she says. To repeat, what's wrong with the rocket? Are you one of those clever people who work with engines or something? By the way, why should you be so anxious to meet up with me? Was it because of all the fuss they were making in the bank earlier?"

"I think you know the answer to that one. Incidentally, was the admiral being sarcastic when he referred to you as Lady Victoria?"

"Why should he be, don't I look like a lady?"

"And I'm sure you know the answer to that one too, my lady. As for the rocket, I just think it looks a bit Heath-Robinish. You've only to take a look at the name. Says a great deal, doesn't it?"

"Not to me, no. I never was interested in Latin. Translate for me if you will."

"If you really want me to -- the English might be 'The Coming of Man' -- depending how you want to read it, of course."

"Well, I have to admit that there could be problems with it. It doesn't even look like the Coming of Man will be big enough to me. Just look how many we are now."

There certainly were plenty waiting to get on board and what a crowd we were! The majority were obviously irredeemable goats, down in the mouth and out at elbow over the whole thing, some already bowed and bleeding in anticipation of life. On the other hand, there were plenty of sheep as well and some looked like they were very high fliers indeed, up to their armpits in savoir faire, golf-bags, skis, cameras galore, even a few star-charts. -- "From the look of some of our goaty friends," I observed, "they won't be unhappy if they do miss the launch."

"Goaty friends? Oh dear! I have to tell you that I find that sort of remark totally unacceptable. We're all humans, some more fortunate than others but none of us sheep or goats. We each have our strengths and our weaknesses but we're all entitled to self-respect and the respect of others. Low birth is clearly a handicap but it must have its advantages too. At least it leaves one free to go one's own way, I imagine. Anyway, from what you say, I take it you're one of the so-called fortunate few."

"Why else would I have been in the bank this morning, to rob the place?"

"You could easily have been for all I know. After all, there must be some reason why you're in such a tearing hurry to get off the ground. Are you in trouble already?" -- She patted my hand. -- "I do apologise. I shouldn't have asked you. It's not my affair, is it?"

The engines on Homo Erectus had been building up for take off and suddenly they were really giving it stick, maybe not the roaring thunder-and-lightening stuff to lift a few hundred tons clear of gravity and bounce them round the galaxy, but enough to blow out your eardrums.

"Even if you are in a hurry, you won't be leaving now," Lady Victoria's lips said. "Look, they've closed the gate."

"Doesn't matter," -- I had my mouth just about pressed against the curve of her ear, the golden hair brushing my nose. -- "To be with you for a few minutes will be worth a thousand lives."

"What are you saying?"

"I'm saying I love you, Victoria."

"Oh I give up! I can't hear a thing."

"3, 2, 1, zero, lift off." -- We were enveloped in acrid exhaust as Homo Erectus left the ground with a blinding flash. Victoria clutched my hand and, as the sound-waves from the rocket's engines rolled over us, I put my arm protectively around her shoulders. We stayed that way for a good half minute.

"Well, the Coming of Man might have been small but it was pretty powerful stuff," she said, the roar fading into a distant rumble. "What now, do you think? There's no point in standing around here. Would you care to act as my escort for an hour or so?"

Would I just! Without a thought for the morrow, I leaped onto her hook, swallowing everything right up to the float. To hell with life! I was bound for Paradise.

Chapter 2

We left the Flight for Life Launch Centre and headed for town via the stockbroker belt. The air was alive with the cooing of doves and, as we walked under the glorious trees, high branching and broad trunked, Jacaranda blossom bunching around their fingers like blue mistletoe, I knew I'd been right from the start. I was really special -- either that or to be at the bottom of the pile could be pure Heaven.

"Fancy something to drink?" Victoria asked, stopping to read an advertisement on a litter-bin. "I wonder what The Phoenix Arcade's like -- "Convenient for the waterside development" -- whatever that may be -- "The Nest, pool deck" -- Could be amusing. What do you say?"

I fingered the money in my pocket. It really was quite a wad. -- "I say yes to absolutely anything you suggest. Let's go."

"Alright, lets. What's your name by the way?"

Dark clouds suddenly moving in from the East. -- "I'm afraid I can't tell you that. At the moment, I'm travelling incognito. The military refer to me as Josef Sope, I believe. Not too flattering, is it?"

"The military? Do tell me more. What are you, a terrorist or something, a spy even? I knew there was something extraordinary about you from the moment I set eyes on you."

"How perceptive of you! I'll have to disappoint you though, I'm afraid. I'm no cloak and dagger man. The military are only marginally interested in me and that's because I'm out of favour with this awful regime, nothing more. Anyway, for the present, it's better that my identity remains a secret."

"And you say that's not something! You must tell me more. Which regime are you talking about? I didn't realise we were under one."

This was hardly the best topic to start up a loving relationship and, if I'd had any sense, I'd have laughed it off and moved on to safer ground but, as so often, my sense of self—importance dictated otherwise. -- "Perhaps someone in your position, my lady, is not as keenly aware of the true political situation as the common man. Social privilege is like a single malt, excellent for keeping the spirits up and reality out."

"And perhaps you don't know as much about people like me as you think you do, Mr Sope. Anyhow, you haven't told me, what did you do to make yourself unpopular with the powers that be?"

"Nothing at all. I am out of favour simply because of my political views. -- I didn't mean to offend you by the way. That's the last thing I want to do."

"That's alright, I wasn't really offended. It's just that having a title and all that doesn't necessarily shield one from reality. Like everybody else, I have my own cross to bear and I can tell you, it's a heavy one. -- Anyway, what are these views of yours? They must be very persuasive if they threaten the stability of the state."

"True, unless in-fighting and corruption have brought the state to the brink of political, moral and economic collapse. Once that situation has been reached, the slightest breath of criticism may well be seen as a violent wind of change. In fact, my views aren't particularly revolutionary. They're just the views of the man in the street, Joe Soap if you like, reflecting nothing but common sense and that's why they alarm those in power. I'm unpopular because they see me as representing the ordinary man and it's the ordinary man they have to keep chained up. I believe in the rights of man, equality of opportunity, the freedom of information and natural justice. In short, I'm a democrat."

"Good for you! Tell me, do you write your own speeches or learn them by heart?" -- She gave me an angelic smile which said in effect I was a clown. -- "I do apologise. I simply can't take pomposity, that's all. I find it quite suffocating and there's so much of it about! Anyway, I agree with you. You're not a revolutionary at all, just one of the vast majority and, as long as that's all you are, you'll be safe. In fact, I'm probably more of a revolutionary than you are at heart but I'm forbidden to become involved in politics of any kind and, above all, I have to avoid negative publicity. Still, there shouldn't be too much danger of that even if you are in trouble. We're only going to have a quick carrot juice or something together after all."

--- * * * * *---

The mink-and-manure-belt gradually petered out. Tall trees gave way to small ones, small trees to street lights, and doves to car horns and the scent of blossom to the smell of diesel and warm tar macadam.

Before long, we were well and truly snarled up in the roar and rush-about of progress. As for The Phoenix Arcade, that turned out to be one of those multi-story shopping centres which claim to have everything the human heart could possibly desire all conveniently under one roof - - convenient provided you go around in a helicopter or an armoured car. We had neither so it was a case of pedestrian roulette, dodging destruction in frantic dashes from island to island while knocking back a cocktail of carbon dioxide and burning brake pads. Eventually, we made it to the complex and took the elevator to the pool deck, all glass, sunlight and in-flight mood-music.

The Nest itself was one of those vaguely Mediterranean cafes, outside tables under plastic palms, warm beer, sweet wine, thin cappuccino and a mile-long menu with effectively two choices, pasta or sugary cake. Lady Victoria couldn't possibly be kept waiting so I ignored the mid-morning queue and grabbed the last table from under the noses of two elderly shoppers. -- "What do you think you are, young man?"

"Faster than you, granddad." -- We settled down beneath a dusty palm, knees close enough for comfort but not for pleasure. -- "What's it to be, coffee?"

"Not for me, thank you. I don't use stimulants. I'll try a carrot juice, thank you. -- Where did you acquire this nasty habit of pushing by the way? I do wish you wouldn't, apart from anything else, it's awfully embarrassing."

"Now it's my turn to apologise. Sorry! -- One carrot juice and a cold beer, Senorita." -- The waitress was a real breath stopper, stunningly endowed and with an adventurous, Latin American face. If I hadn't already met the only girl in the universe, I wouldn't have settled for beer.

"And kindly bring the paper," Miss Universe called as Big Boobs went off. -- "Why are you staring at her like that, Josie?"

Josie! -- "I was just thinking what might have been but, thankfully, is not."

The drinks and paper arrived some minutes later, not riding high on Senorita's tray, thankfully perhaps, but on the bay window of an aging fairy in a nose stud.

Lady Victoria commandeered the paper and once I'd read my side, that left me isolated and -- well, increasingly stressed. After all, I was anxious to make progress and she'd already shown signs of fidgeting about the time. Added to that, of course, there was the little problem of being on the run. -- "Do you realise," I said from my side of the newsprint, "I still don't know what to call you. What is the convention, Lady Victoria or My Lady? I had to skip the etiquette class, it clashed with political science."

"Victoria will do." -- She didn't bother to come out from behind the paper.

"Victoria! I am honoured. That makes me feel very special and that's something I really, really enjoy. As we're to be friends, may I call you Vicky? I could boast about that to my grandchildren – if I have any."

"No, you may not." -- She moved off the society and gossip page. -- "Well, all quiet on the press front at the moment, thank Heaven. -- I say, listen to this -- "Security forces today succeeded in capturing the notorious terrorist, the self-styled Phoenix, and all but two of his followers after a prolonged siege of his mountain hide-out. In past months, The Phoenix has claimed responsibility for numerous acts of terror against the people in his attempts to overthrow the legitimate government. He and other members of the sect are currently undergoing questioning. A spokes-person for the ministry said this morning that the public should be on the lookout for the terrorists who remain at large and should report their whereabouts immediately to the police. One is described as Middle Eastern in appearance, the other is a white, European male. They are both fanatics, highly dangerous and believed to be armed. They should on no account be approached directly."" -- She gave me a very straight look. -- "Thinking about that, it really is odd that anyone should have to go around incognito just because they think like any other man in the crowd. Tell me the truth now. Are you the missing, white European they're looking for, yes or no?"

As so often, vanity threatened to get the better of me but common sense prevailed, thank the lord! -- "Not guilty, I regret to say. The mob who run this set up have thousands of enemies and they're edgy. I'm just a peaceful dissenter, not an active freedom fighter."

She sniffed. -- "If you say so. -- Why does your friend call himself The Phoenix by the way? The Phoenix is something to do with Jesus, isn't it?"

"So is he, perhaps. Anyhow, he's no friend of mine. I know nothing about him. In fact, I hadn't heard of The Phoenix till you read that out."

"You hadn't heard of The Phoenix?"

"The bird, yes of course. The myth is that he recreates himself every five hundred years in fire and he's supposed to represent the grace of Christ. That's common knowledge. But I know absolutely nothing of this terrorist they're holding, poor devil."

"Poor devil? Well, maybe. -- Let's see now, want to know the weather? They say unstable and threatening a hot wind this afternoon with the possibility of rain later." -- The sunlight falling through the glass roof onto her hair gave it a glow which just about choked off my heart. I asked myself how it would feel against my face on the pillow. -- "Oh do stop staring at me, Josef. I simply loathe it when people do that. -- Not much more in this. Like a read? Apparently, the market is uncertain what with the security situation and yet another crisis in the government etc. The experts tell us it would be unwise to commit oneself at this stage."

"That's alright, you hang on to it. The last thing I want right now is to blot out the view."

Behind her, separated from us by only a couple of tables, the window of a jewellers was a jumble of glittering trash, earrings, bracelets, ropes of paste pearls, silver trays, a wall plate with the Chinese willow-pattern in glowing enamels, . . .

"Isn't that frightful kitsch?" -- Victoria was draped sideways in her chair, staring at the plate. -- "Imagine going into the breakfast--room to be greeted by the sight of that! What shocking taste some people have!"

"I don't find it shocking, I love it. The girl reminds me of you."

"What a thing to say! I'm not Chinese!"

"Of course not. You're nothing like each other in appearance but, she's a princess too and somehow perfect. Just look at the way she's floating over the bridge, that hair streaming out behind, leading her lover up the one side and down the other so fast the moon has hardly time to blink."

"I do wish you wouldn't try to be so clever. What are you really wanting to say?"

"Did I say anything clever? I don't remember."

"You said she was a princess too."

"Did I really say that? If I did, it is kind of true. It's your presence, you see. You have a natural grace, a regal quality about you which I find a little daunting and at the same time hypnotic."

"Is that so? Well, I'm not a royal and, frankly, I can't see why I should want to become one. Would you?"

"I believe that some are born to be great and others have greatness thrust upon them. -- Going back to the plate, I suppose you know what the picture represents."

"Two kids running over a humpback bridge in the moonlight? Presumably, they're off to have fun or maybe they're running away from someone, defying the wishes of her family or his even."

"Spot on! He wasn't thought good enough for her. The picture represents the flight of love from the shadows into the light, from limbo, if you like, to life. In a sense, those two are like us, about to enter a new life."

"I wouldn't know about that but how do you know about old Chinese stories?"

"Could be that I know it from a previous life. I might have been the princess's lover for all we know."

"But you're not Chinese either. In looks at least, you're a Westerner, a typical white European male."

"As you say, typical and politically uncomplicated. Anyway, West, East, what does it matter? We all spring from the same seed after all. We live, we die, if we have to, we go round again and, though appearances may change, we stay the same fundamentally. At each new birth, formative experiences from our past lives are prgrammed into our psyche. That's how I like to think of it, anyhow."

"Then you shouldn't. We're not mere computer programmes. We can think for ourselves and some of us are prepared to act independently as well."

"That certainly seems to be the case as far as you're concerned. Even so, the important thing is, programmed or not, we are of the past as well as the present. When two people are truly meant for each other -- which is not always obvious at first -- it's virtually certain that they were together in some other existence." -- If only I could have photographed the look on her beautiful face!

"I would prefer to change this subject if you don't mind. -- What do you think of that bracelet, there, to the left of the plate? Very pretty isn't it, even though it's obviously cheap trash. That combination of diamonds and moonstones gives it a child-like quality, a kind of innocence which I find charming and a little sad. If only growing up weren't so brutalising!"

"It shouldn't be for you. Anyway, moonstones are obviously for the moon and diamonds for the stars, in other words, everything one could possibly desire. Would you accept the bracelet from me?"

"Heavens! You really are ambitious, aren't you? We only met an hour ago and you're offering me the moon and stars already. Sorry but I can't accept casual gifts. I'm not for sale nor for rent -- not at this stage anyway."

"But I am and the tariff is close to zero."

"Then you must raise it. What costs nothing is rarely valued. If you're not careful, you'll be on the market for an eternity. -- Oh, look at those pigeons. See them? Over there above the window. They don't seem at all worried about being inside, do they?"

There were two of them, perched on the piping above the vast window with its panoramic view out over the town, plump birds with knowing eyes and their feathers slicked down as if they'd just come on duty. The way they were looking round, craning their necks to take everything in, you'd have sworn they were watching us all. I stood up to get a better view and saw why they weren't worried about being indoors. -- "I can tell you why they're not worried. They aren't real. What you're looking at is a pair of security cameras."

"Cameras! Oh God!" -- She sounded and looked panic stricken.

"If you look carefully, you can just make out the cables. Don't get upset though. We should be sheltered over here by the palms."

"I hope to Heaven you're right. The last thing I want at this moment is to be filmed. I mustn't be, it could be a disaster!"

"It's alright, relax. You're not on film, not yet anyway. -- On another subject entirely, was the admiral a close friend or just an escort? I remember he was with you in the bank."

She hadn't recovered from the shocking thought that maybe she'd been filmed in my company and it made her aggressive. -- "Look here, Mr Sope, I don't want to have to tell you again, my affairs are not public property so either change the subject or say goodbye."

There was a pause in the piped music, one or two seconds' silence, then it flooded back, light as soapsuds and inspiring as airline aerosol. -- "I didn't mean to pry. I was just wondering if I would be good enough to carry on acting as your escort for a while. In this setup, one doesn't know what's round the next corner and, if I say so myself, I do have a gift for finding my way around."

"No thanks. I'm more than capable of looking after myself. While we're on the subject though, there is one small thing. Since you know Latin, be so good as to explain this." -- She fumbled about in her dress, produced her bank card and handed it across. -- "What does that mean? There, at the bottom."

It certainly was some card! Double gold border and beautiful italics. -- "Lady Victoria, Mary, Elizabeth Hunter-Jones; class- 1A+; credit— unlimited; Destination--Bingham Hall, Surrey, England; time and point of departure—classified. [ceteris paribus]"

"England used to be quite a country, I understand, a green and pleasant land of the free, even freedom of speech at one time." -- I took time to memorise the details.

"And I would hope that's still the case."

"Well, it certainly should be for you. Bingham Hall sounds like some address!"

"You weren't asked to comment. All you have to do is say what the Latin means."

"Sorry, I'm sure. The Latin is to be read, 'everything else being equal'. It's a let-out clause, a formality, only there to cover all eventualities. You of all people can ignore such things."

"I see. Eventualities such as what?"

"Good lord, I don't know, anything -- not you failing to qualify, of course. That can never happen. It's a legal bolthole, a hedge against -- well, you name it, a car smash, assassination, revolutionary justice, things like that. It's only there to protect The Minister."

"The minister?"

"Number 1 around here, His Excellency, The Minister of police."

"Number one! I can think of a few people who wouldn't be too happy to hear you say that. Tell me, this Latin, is it on yours too? -- What's the matter? You do have a card, I take it."

I took a deep breath. -- "At this very moment, no, I do not."

"But why ever not?"

"That's a private matter. I'd prefer not to discuss it and certainly not out here."

"Does it have anything to do with you travelling incognito by any chance?"

"Possibly."

"Hmm! I knew there was something going on. Why wouldn't they issue you with a card? Not just because you have a mind of your own and a liking for speaking it, surely. Has your credit been withdrawn or what?"

"I thought we weren't going to discuss it. Would it make any difference anyway?"

"Not to me, why should it?"

"Why indeed! Anyway, since you're obviously desperate to know, there was a clerical error in my file." -- Why the hell am I giving into her like this, I thought. I'm every bit as entitled to privacy as she is. -- "It's nothing serious, just a careless mistake. In place of a credit card, they gave me a whole stack of cash. The card will catch up with me later."

"And what was this so—called clerical error?"

"Hang on, I thought you were all for personal privacy. I don't know why I should tell you anything. -- Oh alright! It was simply that some clerk misread the governor's report and failed to assign me the correct status. Naturally, I filed a complaint and now the whole thing's been referred back to The Minister."

It sounded fishy and obviously smelled that way as far as she was concerned. -- "And I thought you said it was nothing serious! -- Oh, do look at that strange character over there. See? That Arab behind those palms. -- No, not there. Look, in the robe. He's staring at us or rather at you. Who is he, the other one who got away?"

Behind the artificial trees and only yards from where we were sitting, a young man in Arab dress was standing on the walk-way. He saw me look and signalled me to go over.

"If you want my advice," -- Victoria stood up. -- "you'll be extremely careful how you choose your friends in future. I certainly shall be, very, very careful. Goodbye and thank you. Don't worry, I can look after myself."

"And, if you want my advice, my lady, you'll sit down and stay put. Those cameras are waiting, remember. Anyway, it looks like something's about to happen and we must be prepared. Ok, I'll report back in a minute or two."

Even before I came up, the smell told me what the Arab was up to. He stank of petrol. -- "Look," I said, "If you're going to set fire to yourself, do it somewhere else. Go on, clear off! It's got nothing to do with me. I don't know you and I don't want to."

Close to, he looked terribly young, eighteen at most. -- "But I know you from way back, Joe. The Phoenix said I would find you here. He commands you to guard this with your life. Keep it hidden, bury it if you must. If they find out you have been entrusted with it, say that you lost it. Whatever else, do not allow yourself to be taken with it on your person." -- He drew a chain from his robe. It carried a small, crystal phial.

"But what is it?" -- The phial gave off a strange fragrance which filled my nostrils, momentarily fading out the smell of gasoline.

"Brother, count yourself blessed above all others. You are being entrusted with the holiest of relics known to Man, The Christ Phial, which holds the true blood of the risen Christ. Guard it well!"

"So, you really are some sort of Christian! I didn't know Christians could be as mad as you lot obviously are. Anyway, you can count me out. I've nothing to do with you or your so—called Phoenix. Who is he anyway? I'm not interested in getting …"

"We're not mad and you'll do as you're told. My master, The Phoenix, is your master too as he always has been. You, I, all of us must carry out his orders no matter at what cost."

"But…"

"There's no time to talk now. It will have to wait till we meet again in paradise. In a moment, there will be a huge explosion. Many will be killed and you must not be among them."

"But who is this madman you call The Phoenix? He's nothing to do with me and nothing to do with Jesus Christ either. Christians don't go round killing innocent people just to protest."

"As I say, we will talk again when we meet. Now, leave the area. -- No! Do not touch me, I've been washed with holy water. Just do as you're told and remember that the master puts his trust in you as must we all."

"You say I mustn't be among the dead. Well, I will be if you go ahead with this because I'm staying right here in front of you, ok?"

"In that case, we will all have died for nothing, me, you, all these innocent people and, of course, that young lady you're with."

"Come on, Victoria, it's time we left. Hurry!"

As I spoke, the public address blasted through the building, annihilating a dummy-sucker's version of For Elise -- "Emergency! This is an emergency message. An individual wanted by the police has entered the complex. Clients are instructed to stay calm and not to attempt to move from floor to floor or vacate the building without authorisation. The elevators have been deactivated and all exits sealed. Clients are required to cooperate fully with the authorities. -- Emergency! This is an emergency message.…."

Pandemonium! Even before the message had time to run through once, the pool—deck erupted. People pushing and shoving to get through the locked fire-doors or running from one useless elevator to another, falling over each other to stab dead call-buttons, shouting for the management, screaming at each other, everything but keeping calm. The only point of serenity seemed to be the Arab, a thin column of smoke rising from a cigarette between his fingers. He pointed to the jewellers' door for me to go inside.

The shop was empty save for the owner, an old lady with a still beautiful face. -- "Close the door, Madame, there's going to be one almighty bang any second." [Slam -- snap]

"I wondered when you two would be in. How's it going out there? Is there anything you need?"

"The whole place is about to go up and cover's all anybody needs right now. You two lie flat behind the counter. There'll be lots of glass flying around and God knows what else so whatever you do, keep your heads down."

"But, Josie, what about you?"

"Me? I'm going to round up as many goats and sheep as I can. He'll hang on for as long as possible once he sees me."

Run out and grab a couple of kids, bundle them inside, out again and yet again, three, four times till there's quite a flock of us on the floor, some safely behind the counter but most not, including me. There's a lot of panic and wailing at first but Victoria is a ministering angel and soon everyone quietens down to wait for the worst.

The first rumble of advancing blades away to the East, then the roar and whistle of army helicopters hovering overhead. On the other side of the glass, the young man moves his lips in prayer, cigarette smoke ascending from the hand, out-stretched as if to bless. One second, two, a last nervous glance toward our window and the hand drops. Flames roar into life, leaping up the chest and he is lost in a pillar of fire. A stupendous explosion. The windows burst, splinters flying across the shop in a storm of razor-glass and metal. Miraculously, we take only one casualty, me. Lying by the door, I'm struck in the forehead just above the left eye by shrapnel. A brief numbness then the flesh burning as if under the branding iron.

For minutes, we all lie there staring out at the pool deck. Below the lifting smoke, an avalanche of debris, twisted furniture, body parts, blood up the walls. There is no trace of the bomber, only a solitary sandal.

"Come, you two, we must get out of here," -- The old lady points to a narrow door at the back of the shop. -- "I'll go ahead. Come on, come on, follow me!"

"Don't worry, I'll be right behind you." -- I slip the phial on its silver chain over my head. How gently it rests on my chest! For an instant, that strange perfume floating upward, mingling with the smell of desolation. I pick up the moonstone bracelet from the floor where it lies among the remains of the willow-pattern plate.

Gallop down what felt like a good two hundred steps, most of the way in darkness, and emerge at the rear of The Phoenix Arcade. There's a lot starting up, fire-engines, ambulances, police cars, photographers, every sort of busybody, but we manage to get away unnoticed. There's a difficulty though. After a hundred yards or so, it becomes obvious that the old woman intends to stick with us even though she'll slow us down. I try tact -- "God bless you for what you've done for us, Madame, but from here we must go on without you. It would be a disaster for you to be caught helping us."

It takes a few blocks but, eventually, we manage to give her the slip by dodging round the back of a stand-up loo, crouching in the ammonia haze till her head bobbed past then cutting back the other way. I keep a lookout as we run off but she's nowhere to be seen. In fact, except for two helicopters spinning away to the North, we seem to be alone.
"Your forehead, Josie!" Victoria said, turning round. "You've been burnt!"

"It's only a flesh wound, nothing to get excited about. Maybe it's my red badge of courage or something. -- Hold out your wrist. This is for you."

Even now, she drew back. -- "I hate to offend you after what you've done for me but I did mean what I said earlier. I never accept casual gifts except from family or the closest friends. I'm so sorry. And you were so wonderful!" -- She held out her hand but only for me to shake. -- "I'm afraid it's goodbye from here, Josef. As with the old lady, I shall have to go on without you now. It's the media, you see, the media and … and everything else."

Chapter 3

The roar of two motorbikes coming up behind, speeding toward us side by side, the riders low over their handlebars, perched behind, men with cameras at the ready.

"That's all I need!" -- Victoria runs off. -- "A pack of press hounds!" I spurt after her. -- "Cut down that street, down hill's got to be the way to the river. Good luck!" -- I throw myself down across the road. The heavy bikes race up, front wheels lifting, seesaw over, blasts of heat fanning my neck and legs. Screeching of tyres into the distance as the riders battle for control. I leap up and run down after Victoria.

Down a narrow alley, sunless and smelling of dustbins and last night's restaurants, past a wine-bar full of late-morning drinkers and cigarette smoke, a quiet road and, beyond it, a towpath and the river. -- "It's alright, My Lady, you've got rid of them for now at least. Come on, let's grab a boat. You'll be safer on the water."

Victoria stopped but not simply to get her breath. -- "You're making this very difficult for both of us, Mr Sope. I've tried telling you gently but you simply won't listen. After what happened back there, I just cannot afford to be seen in your company ever again so please stop following me. Our relationship, such as it was, is at an end. I, of all people, am not in a position to get involved with you or your problems, running away from the police, photographers and God knows who else. I am not a terrorist and I've no desire to be identified with one."

"As a matter of fact, I'm not a terrorist either but we'll let that pass. I can understand how you feel but it's not that simple. For better or for worse, you left the arcade with me by the back door and in one hell of a hurry and that could be enough to ruin you. This is a police state, after all."

A stretch limousine went by and slowed down ahead. The effect on Victoria was enormous and instantaneous. -- "At last! Once again, goodbye, Mr Sope, and good luck!" -- The car pulled into the side and waited, its tinted rear window glinting in the sun. She sprinted towards it, her hair ruffling in the breeze, but it whined past her in fast reverse and pulled up beside me. -- "Hello there, Mr Sope!"

What a shock! And what a powerful, bassoprofundo, a voice to make the guilty tremble! And my name, every Tom, Dick and Harry seems to know it! God! I wonder if it's the bank manager -- or The Minister himself! It's certainly not The Phoenix. He'll be in a torture hospital, poor devil! -- I kept going straight, ignoring the shadowy figure beckoning from the back seat.

"Don't look round, My Lady. Ten to one, he spells big, really big trouble. Just walk on and pretend you haven't noticed anything. The first hire boat you see that looks like it can stay afloat, jump in. I'll keep you covered for as long as I can."

It wasn't far before, at a bend in the river, the road and towpath parted company. I don't know why but I couldn't resist turning round and giving a wave. The car hadn't moved. It still sat there, windscreen flashing in the sun, the faint shadow of exhaust behind.

--- * * * * * ---

There were moorings in plenty along the towpath but nothing ready to sail -- launches under their covers and battened down, houseboats which would never go anywhere, what looked like a police launch, a magnificent Chinese junk with a golden dragon for her figurehead, her mast hung with red lanterns and flying a pink flag in the shape of a pig -- some river restaurant! -- empty water, more houseboats -- one rocking up the neighbourhood with its ghetto-blaster -- a gaggle of water-skiers, a few dinghies, one, two catamarans with masts shipped, a decrepit punt and, at last, a for hire notice.

Victoria came, saw and was immediately conquered. Not me, though. It wasn't Thunder-bird that put me off. On the contrary, she looked like a brilliant speedboat, dazzling white and low in the water, her long bow rising and falling in the river-flow, obviously mad to be off and mixing it with the elements. The no-no was the beautiful youth lolling in the stern, Tuscan eyes and dressed in little more than an outsize Rolex and suntan. He read the look on Victoria's face and summoned her over. -- "The Signorina want a ride?"

"Don't answer! He's not suitable for a lady in your position. You need someone less, shall we say, likely to attract publicity."

The lady wasn't listening to me, of course. As for the Tuscan dream, he raised expensive eyebrows in my direction as if to say I had no business being on two legs, shrugged and held out his hand to help her aboard. -- "Luigi's pleasure, Signorina."

The thought that I should push him into the river streaked through my mind as I followed on behind but I didn't try. By the look of him, friend Luigi would swim better than a dolphin -- and probably bite twice as hard. I did manage to tramp on his bare toes though. -- "Sorry about that, boy. Good thing I'm not wearing heels!"

"Does he have to come as well, Signorina?"

"I'm afraid it looks that way for now at least. I do hope you don't mind."

"Whatever you want, Signorina, you have. He can come if you insist. Where you want Thunder-bird to take you, Venus Island? With Luigi, we go as far as you desire. It will be my pleasure."

--- * * * * * ---

We used to be told there's an old devil in the underworld by the name of Charon, a ferryman, green with age and ugly as sin. It's his job to ferry the souls of the dead across the Styx to Hell. Not a pleasant crossing, of course, what with Charon's whip, the screaming and wailing of the passengers and the stench but at least smooth enough. This trip was another story entirely. -- "Hold tight, Signorina!" -- Luigi standing with the tiller between his legs, flicked the ignition key, the roar of a modified airplane engine, and Thunder-bird was on her way, her bow lifting as she fought to get airborne. -- "Trust Luigi, Signorina!"

Only a hundred yards out and we're thundering over the water in our own force 8 gale, spray blotting out the banks, Lady Victoria's hair streaming out like a water-nymph's.

"You were mad to get yourself into this!" I bellowed in her direction as we tornadoed past a rowboat, damn near tipping out its owner. -- "Your little friend's up to no good. If he's not a Mafioso, out to kidnap you, he's probably a sex maniac or even a TV journalist looking for a programme."

Thundering down-stream for a short distance then swinging around in a stomach- heaving hairpin, we blast up-river, smashing through our own wake, thump, thump, thump. Luigi standing in water as Thunder-bird dug her stern in, then clear of the turbulence and settling down to a smooth power boat charge up-stream.

"Happy now, Signorina? You love ride with your Luigi?"

"Yes, Luigi, yes, yes! It's mad, absolutely wonderfully crazy!"

He screwed the throttle wide open, lifting the bow even higher. -- "You have stunning figure, Signorina! It make a man's blood sing like a bird!"

"No need to pose for him, woman! He'll be taking pictures next."

We blasted past a group of fishermen, sending their floats bobbing madly, our wake slapping the banks, onward another half mile then, swinging round a bend, came in sight of Venus Island about two hundred yards away. No sign of people on it, no sign of anything but rocks, bushes and a gigantic yew close by the bank. Luigi cut the engine and, bow dropping, we swooped in on a soft glide. -- "Maybe you jump out and tie us up." He indicated the mooring-rope coiled up at my feet.

"Tie up to what?"

"To what? The tree of course. You do know how?"

I tried to leap over onto the bank but the pole which Luigi was using to keep us alongside mysteriously lost its hold. As a result, I landed up half in the river, letting go the rope. [Blurred vision of someone vaulting over me] Luigi had us tied up in seconds then stood grinning down at me struggling to pull myself onto the bank. -- "Here, take my hand, I help you. -- Sorry about that! Did I tread on your fingers? Not big problem I hope. Here you come, up!"

I sloshed my way up to the tree. What do you know! At a gap in the foliage high up, something sparkling in the sunlight. It could only have been the lens of a powerful camera. I went back to Thunder-bird. -- "Before you get out, Victoria, what do you make of that? -- Up there, about thirty feet, someone's taking pictures. See that thing shining up there?"

"Where, man? Show me!" -- Luigi made a great show of circling the tree several times, his head tilted back. -- "There's no one up there. I think you seeing things or maybe there's a bird's nest that's all."

"I know what I saw, a camera trained on us. Come on, let's go up and sort him out. He won't get far, not with the two of us."

"But there's no-one there, I promise you. You make mistake, that's all. Probably a magpie's nest or else your brain still mixed up after you fall in the river."

"What's the matter, boy, scared you'll get a nose-bleed? There's only one of them. -- What do you say, My Lady?" -- She didn't answer, too busy admiring Luigi from the boat. -- "I'm sure this is a trap," I said. "Someone's spying on you and it looks like I'll have to climb up and sort him out on my own. When I've done that, I think I'll be off, ok?"

"I'd rather you just went anyway. I don't need you. I'll be fine. Luigi says it's alright and I know he'll look after me. Thanks for everything."

"If that's what you want. I'm not bothered. Here, take my hand." -- I stretched across but she didn't need help from me. Speedy Luigi simply picked her up and swung her onto the grass. -- "You like to swim, Signorina? We go behind there, see?" -- He pointed to a house-size rock about fifty yards off. -- "The water perfectly calm there, deep also but crystal clear. We dive together right down onto the bed. Come!"
"But I haven't brought anything. Beside, I can't swim."

"No problemo!" -- His beautiful teeth flashed playfully. -- "Your faithful squire, Luigi, look after you. Nobody see, no reporter, not the gooseberry here, nobody at all. The biggest and best camera my papa sell in his store never reach behind there."

They ran off, leaving me alone with Thunder-bird and the tree. A moment later, the sounds of their laughter and water-pranks came floating up to my listening ears. -- "You ungrateful bitch, Lady bloody Victoria! No publicity! They'll make a block-buster out of this and serve you right! I don't care if you get aids! -- Now, how the hell do I get going, take the boat? As if I would!"

As much to vent spleen as inflict damage, I sent several fair-sized stones rattling into the branches of the tree but the cameraman refused to show himself. All I succeeded in doing was to hit a black and white bird. It practically fell out of the tree, stabilized a few feet above the ground then seesawed crazily off across the river. -- 'Sorry about that, brother, but you're not the first innocent casualty today. -- If only I could fly, be a spy in the sky! -- Now, there's a thought!"

What a specimen that yew was! No churchyard tree, this, watching over death, limbs cramped and twisted on a diet of rot and coffin ooze. It could have been the tree of life, at least sixty feet tall and heavily magnificent in an ancient, mythological way -- just right for surveying the nether world.

Not going to be easy to get started, I thought. Nothing much to hang on to -- but wait. What's this? Just look at these! -- Burnt deep into the yew's side, a series of holes, regularly spaced, extending up into the lower branches. I put my finger into one, right up to the knuckle, but couldn't touch the bottom. -- Someone's fixed up a ladder here way back, had a tree house probably or a hide. Perhaps I can make use of that, ram a stick in here -- and here -- then up there. -- "Hi there, peeping Tom, I'm coming up to gouge your eyes out!"

It proved to be more of a battle than I'd expected, getting up the first part, but once I'd made it into the lower limbs, the rest was simple branch-stepping. No sign at all of the photographer, more's the pity. -- "Come on, show yourself, you coward! It's alright, I'm not really going to blind you. I only want to share the lens." -- I climbed to where two giant branches crossed and, still finding no-one, perched there and took a look out over the island. The little Tuscan wasn't exaggerating. The ground must have dropped very steeply on the other side of the rock because, even from that height, it was impossible to see into Luigi's hideaway.

"Perhaps if I edge out a little, the picture will become clearer. Hold steady, old tree, I'm about to put my life to come in your hands. -- Damn!" -- My shirt snagged then pulled free. Three foot from the trunk, four, another, yet again, half a dozen further still, the branch bending ever so slightly and there's me having to stretch up a bit, another yard, the foliage quite sparse out here almost in thin air. What's that I can see down there, someone by the rock? -- Just a shadow by the look of it but no …

The branch does not break. Dipping in an elegant curve, it casts me off, slowly at first, scrabbling and clutching, then there is nothing to hang on to and I am airborne. -- What a landing! My backside spongy numb and scrapes on both hands. -- "Hell! And I'm sure I've heard that yews are dripping with poison. Well, that's what trash like you get for trying to spy on the upper classes at play, Josef fucking Sope!"

About ten minutes of buttock-rubbing and wound-washing later, Victoria came back, radiant, her eyes shining. -- "You still here? Oh well! Luigi won't be a moment. -- What on earth have you been up to, wrestling with a bear?"

"If you really want to know, I fell out the tree."

"You don't say!"

"I had to go up and sort out the movie-maker."

"But you didn't find one, did you? Luigi told you there wasn't anyone up there."

"But he was wrong, there was a cameraman. I eventually spotted him on the ground, creeping about by your rock. That's how I nearly killed myself, rushing to climb down and grab him. Too bad! More than likely, he's off the island by now and heading for the news-room. We must go after him straight away. There's not much chance we'll catch him but you never know. -- What's little Cupid playing at, restringing his jockstrap?"

Beautiful women like Victoria Hunter-Jones of Bingham Hall hardly need the gift of speech, their body language says it all. -- "You actually saw someone by the rock? When, what were they doing? Come on, tell me for God's sake, tell me!"

"I can't tell you any more than that. Where's your little friend, we can't hang around here like this."

I could literally see the blood drain from her face. -- "You're just trying to frighten me, aren't you? There couldn't have been anybody, Luigi said there wasn't and …and he knows his way around here."

"I bet he does. Come on, we're wasting time, we'd better get back into the boat. I'll give Mr Luigi a couple of minutes but if he doesn't pitch up, too bad, we'll have to go after the movie-man without him. And just to add to our troubles, it looks like we're going to have that strong wind you read about to cope with. Come!"

She was badly shaken but said nothing, simply climbed into the boat and sat with her back to me in her old seat, her face buried in her hands. What a pathetic creature compared with the daring, everything-to-the-four winds playgirl who'd sat in that seat on the way down and, in some ways, that was how it should have been. I probably wouldn't have been all that sorry to hear her weep but, of course, she didn't. She didn't even look round when I stumbled climbing in. As it happened, I wasn't hurt that much although I did give my left hip a crack on the ignition key and damaged the throttle. There were to be dramatic consequences, however. The modified airplane engine grabbed its chance and thundered into life. For about ten seconds, the rope held while we built up a tidal wave astern then parted and we were off, white water streaming out behind us in a widening vee. Back on the island, a frantic bellow, then splash and Luigi was swimming after us. No good, though. Even his iron man, Olympic crawl wasn't up to it. Thunder-bird was her own mistress, wild, exultant and definitely unstoppable.

For some distance, Victoria kept on staring straight ahead but eventually, she was forced to look back. -- "Sope! Luigi's trying to catch us, you fool, turn off the motor! Turn the thing off, you're leaving him behind!"

"You just tell me how!" -- I had to shout at the top of my voice with the wind blowing straight in my face.

"What is the matter with you, Sope? Turn off that motor! Luigi's drowning!"

"Sope now, is it? Well, I'm afraid Sope can't do anything about the bloody motor. The key's wedged in the bloody ignition. He's not drowning by the way, more's the bloody pity!"

"We must stop! The accelerator! For God's sake, do something, Josie, please!"

"Well, well! Josef, Sope and now Josie! I'm sorry but the throttle is damaged. -- Look, if I could do something, believe me, I would but I cannot."

It isn't quite as easy to handle a super-charged speedboat at full throttle in a rising gale as you'd think. I did fine for some way but the situation began to deteriorate rapidly just after I'd taken her in a racing-turn round a water-logged rowboat lurking just beneath the surface. From that point, Thunder-bird started rolling as well as pitching, barely answering to the rudder.

"What are you doing now, you fool?" -- Victoria's hands were over her eyes, the wind billowing in her dress. -- "Sope! Watch out, you fool! I'm going to have you locked up, I swear I am. Where's Luigi? Where are you taking me?"

"I'm not taking you anywhere, it's this bloody boat. Anyway, no sign of the photographer yet so be happy. He either got away or he's in trouble too."

"I don't give a damn about your stupid photographer! Where is Luigi? That's all I want to know. Where is he, I can't see him!"

The wind dropped briefly. -- "Luigi's back there somewhere. Don't worry, he'll be ok. Rats swim like they had flippers. That's why they're at home in sewage pipes. But I suppose you wouldn't know about sewage, would you? -- You did say you couldn't swim, didn't you?"

"You scum! I know what you're after, money! Go on, admit it!"

"Scum yourself! I'm not interested in your bloody money. All I'm trying to do is save your aristocratic neck. Come on, I asked you a question. Is it true you can't swim?"

"I cannot swim, no, and it's none of your business."

"But it may be any minute. Don't worry though, Luigi's not the only rat in your life. I'm brilliant in water myself and, whatever happens, I won't abandon you. I really do mean that. If you really can't swim, how did you manage back there? Come on, I want to know."

"You know, I don't think you saw a cameraman at all. You were spying on us, weren't you, pervert?"

"Ok, have it your own way. There was no one watching you, just me and I saw fuck all. Now it's your turn to lie."

"How about doing something constructive, like stopping that engine? Pull out some wires or something!" -- The wind was going full blast again.

"And let go the tiller? Can't you see, I'm having a battle to steer? She keeps trying to go to port."

"Oh come here!" -- She battled over the pitching, rolling seat and snatched the tiller -- "I'll take over. You just get on and pull something out."

The difficulty about vandalising a marine engine, as I soon discovered, is getting through the water-proofing. When, after breaking a few nails and opening up several more cuts, I did manage to get to the wiring, I seized a handful and pulled -- heave! Sparks, a bang and the shock made my heart bounce. I tried a second time, more cautiously. The motor was in the middle of a high pitched shriek when everything stopped -- everything, that is, except our dash down stream. That barely slowed -- "Don't applaud too loudly, woman! I've only performed a minor miracle. -- Hang on, why is this rope so tight?" -- What was left of the mooring rope was over the port side and so tense it looked like we'd hooked a shark at least. I looked over the side. We were indeed towing something but not a fish. It was a man. I couldn't make him out clearly in the turbulence but it had to be either the reporter or precious Luigi hanging on for dear life. I looked round to check. Victoria had noticed nothing. She was too busy battling with the tiller. I untied the rope and watched it streak away astern.

"What on earth's happening now? The boat's steering worse than ever! Help me, I can't do anything with it!" -- Victoria was swinging on the tiller to no effect.

Another huge obstacle about thirty yards from our bow and that was it. Thunder-bird mounted the tree trunk then slid back, turning turtle.

"Josie!"

I surfaced next to the boat and managed to grab on. Victoria was thrashing about only a few feet away, hair fanning out behind her in a bridal train -- "Grab onto me!" I shouted and, with the luck of the panic-stricken, she caught hold of my legs. "Well done, Victoria! Hang on! You're going to be alright. She won't sink. There must be a pocket of air trapped under her. Just hang on to me and you'll be fine."

"Oh God, please let this stop!" she kept moaning into the wind and rush of water. "My arms are being torn out! For Christ's sake, God, help me! I can't hang on much longer!"

A few minutes more of that and it would have been over for both of us but we suddenly ran into white water and there, up ahead, the shoulder of a fall churning over the abyss in a roaring curtain. We were carried to the edge and shot out into the void.

"Luigi!"

Parting company with the boat, we went into free fall through the thunder of the falls. Then the light went out as we plunged into the churning depths. For an age, it was like being in a diving-tower, descending into the darkness, gurgling and echoing, then I shot up to the light and broke surface. Victoria was only a few yards off, gasping for air, her hands beating the water. I swam across and, grabbing her by the shoulders, started for the bank. About a hundred yards of struggle, me swimming on my back with her on top of me, fighting the water, fighting me, fighting to the death for air.

"Stop struggling, woman! Relax! You'll drown us both! I can't keep going like this! Stop it, I say! Lie still, damn you!"

At last I felt my heels touch bottom but as I began to get a foothold, she went limp. I managed to keep her face out of the water. I dragged her unconscious onto the bank.

--- * * * * * ---

Behind some bushes a few yards from the water, deep, sweet grass and birds singing. -- "What happened? Why am I here? Where's Luigi?"

"We had an accident in the boat and ended up in the river. I brought you here. You're ok, took in too much water and passed out but nothing serious. How do you feel?"

"Where's Luigi? Something bad happened! God, I'm feeling so sick!"

"Just try to stay calm, My Lady. I'm going to see if I can find out what happened to Luigi for you. You rest here. I'll be back in a couple of minutes. That's right, shut those lovely eyes of yours. What you need right now is sleep."

There was plenty of activity on the river, rowboats, the police, everyone wanting to know what had happened. I kept out of sight. Thunder-bird was floating bottom-up in mid stream but there was no sign of Luigi or the cameraman -- Perhaps they'll think she broke her moorings and went over empty, I thought, watching a police launch take her in tow. -- Nothing in the water to show -- Hang on, what's that though? --- Caught up under the bank, a black leather case with a shoulder strap. I climbed down and fished it out. It was a camera, good enough for a professional. I carried it behind some bushes and investigated -- Beautiful camera, very powerful! This must be worth a pile. Well, now it's mine. I'll see if I can use the lens to see exactly what's what out there.

I trained the telescopic lens on the police launch. It was all very interesting, watching how they fixed up the tow and got under way but there was nothing to get excited about except, perhaps, the man in charge, a captain with a fine, hooked nose. I pressed the trigger and heard the shutter go but presumably there wouldn't be any pictures. -- Time to go back to Sleeping Beauty, I thought. We don't want some tramp or other undesirable stumbling across her lying there behind the bushes.

I turn round to leave and there he is, watching me. -- "Where do you think you're going?" -- A police officer!

"Me, lieutenant? I'm just taking a walk. And you?"

"I've been watching you for quite a while. What were you doing with that camera?"

"Nothing special, just looking for a good shot for my paper. You know the sort of thing, fatal accidents, interesting women, anything to liven up the so-called news. That's why I'm a bit damp as a matter of fact. I fell into the river."

"Did you now? -- So you're a professional photographer! Which paper are you on?"

"Did I say I work for a paper? If I did, I wasn't being quite precise. I'm not employed by anyone in particular."

"You mean you're a free-lance?"

"You've got it. I'm a self-employed photographer specialising in disaster and gossip. I do a lot of work for the ministry as a matter of fact. -- Well, I must be getting along. Thanks for the chat."

"Work for the ministry, do you? Then, you'll have a pass."

Christ! Why did I have to say that? -- "It's not on me, I'm afraid. You know how it is, rush out to be first on the scene and find you've left half your stuff behind. It's always happening, especially to me."

The lieutenant made no attempt whatever to hide his smirk. -- "For a professional journalist, you're pretty wet behind the ears, lad. Ok, let's have that camera!"

"But why?"

"Why? Because as any professional photographer knows, it's forbidden to take photographs of police operations without prior permission, that's why. Under a state of emergency, a man can lose more than his licence over a thing like that."

"State of emergency? What are you talking about?"

"It was declared a good two hours ago."

"Jesus! Here, take the thing! It's got nothing in it except, maybe, a shot of a couple of animals copulating and, of course, lots of water. I would like it back by the way."

"And the pass?"

"Well, I'll take another look but I'm sure it's not on me." -- I made a pretence of checking, fumbled around in my pocket and produced a few wet but still good banknotes. -- "See? That's all the paper I've got on me. Not really what you're interested in, is it?"

My part in our little pantomime was over. The lieutenant took the money, grinning as he made his closing speech -- "Ok, you can go this time. Just make sure you fix it up with me, Lieutenant Armstrong, first another time."

"And the camera? -- No? How about a receipt then?"

"You'd have to give me your details, name, address, call-number, the lot."

"Ok, you keep the thing."

I returned by a circular route just in case and got back to where I'd left Victoria. She wasn't there.

Chapter 4

"Don't panic," I told myself. "Think a moment before you go dashing off. Someone's got her or she's wandered off on her own. Either way, judging by the way those leaves are dripping, someone was here not many minutes ago. Chances are it's her and she's heading for the road. Come on, it's not far."

Once on the road, it was a toss-up which way to go. I headed for what looked like a shopping mall. Saw a good many good-looking girls on the way, including several blondes, but there was no sign of her. A good hour's wandering around later and still nothing. I retraced my steps, came back again and suddenly that was it. I felt in my bones I'd seen the last of Lady Victoria Hunter-Jones of Bingham Hall. She'd been kidnapped or she'd run off for good. Whichever it was, it was my fault. I should have stayed with the woman.

For a good while, I sat on someone's doorstep talking it over with myself. – "Where the hell do I go from here? Only a few hours since we met and I've failed already! Surely she wouldn't have gone off without a word-- "Thanks!" or "Good luck!" or more likely "Now, don't you dare try following me, Sope!" – Something at least. She must have been kidnapped. They've taken her for sex. Christ Almighty! Maybe it's not that bad though. With luck, it's only money they're after. A girl like her would fetch a princess's ransom, more in a slave market. Jesus! I'd never be able to get my hands on that sort of cash even if they did get in touch. What if they send bits through the post?"

I tried to stop my legs shaking, rubbing them, standing up, kicking out. Nothing worked. Panic's like that. It's the mind that's out of control, not the muscles. -- "Maybe it isn't so bad after all. She could have got up and walked off all on her own. Could be she's wandering around suffering from shock what with nearly drowning and losing precious Luigi, not to mention the bombing. Then, there was that cameraman business. -- Failed there too, didn't you, Sope?

Nothing for it," I decided, "I have to ring the police right now, no more mucking about, stuff my mouth with paper and start talking. -- "There's something you people should know. It's urgent, very, very urgent. -- Who am I? What's that got to do with it? -- Oh alright, if you absolutely must know, I'm Umm, I'm just another Joe Soap.". -- It's no go. I mustn't be a coward as well. I'll simply have to find a station, walk in and tell them face to face what's happened. That will be me finished.

But what if she simply wanted to be rid of me, grabbed her chance and ran off? I'd be in a cell and all for nothing. It's quite likely when you think about it. After all, what am I -- or what are they trying to turn me into? A nobody, a grey man with no past and no sodding future. No-one at the top 's going to risk a scandal over scum like me, not to mention I'm in deep trouble anyway. Christ!

Of course, could be she wasn't snatched and didn't run away either. Perhaps she wanted to give me a fright that's all. You never know, she could be watching me at this minute, watching from a distance and laughing. On the other hand, she could be watching me and praying. One thing's for sure, if she doesn't pitch up very soon, I've no option but to inform the police. Give it an hour then that's it."

I turned into Teens, a bar strictly for the young and unhouse-trained – thick smoke, heavy metal slugging it out with hormone-babble and coffee machines -- but that was ok. It was what I needed. Who can possibly endure peace and quiet when they're waiting to be told whether they've got cancer or just indigestion? I took the table by the window so I could watch the street. The clock on the wall said 11. – "Wait till noon then start walking. High noon!"

One small espresso down, two, the third just arrived when a physical looking girl with bottle-red hair came through the door. -- "Hi there! Mind if I join you?"

"If you reckon I'm up to it. What's yours?"

"A large Bloody Mary, thanks. You waiting for somebody or are you on your own?"

She was plump, baby blue eyes and pretty dimples. Not my style but then maybe, I thought, she'd been sent by the kidnappers or else the police. -- "I'm just killing time."

"Great! Let's kill it together. I do love your smile. Pity you don't use it more. -- Cheers! -- What happened to the forehead? Get into a fight or what?"

"All in a day's work. We journalists have to be prepared to mix it now and then."

"A journalist? Great! Funny I haven't noticed you! Do tell me, which channel are you on?"

"I don't do television if I can help it."

"Oh, so you're not on the telly. Too bad! What do you do for a living then?"

"I work for a press agency. I'm a society correspondent. That's how I got wounded as a matter of fact. The competition beat me up while I was taking pictures. Nice lads! It ended up with me and my new camera in the river, can you believe?"

"Well, I'll believe you. But I have to say, that looks like a burn to me. Still, I suppose it would explain why your sandals are thick with mud! I thought you might be a cockle—picker or whatever. So, you're a professional journalist. Fascinating! You must tell me more. What were you photographing, the terrorist atrocity?"

"Which one?"

"Don't tell me you don't know what happened in The Phoenix Arcade a few hours ago. Some religious nut blew himself up on the pool deck and a whole lot of shoppers got killed. I don't understand it. You're a journalist, you should know all about it! That's why we've got the state of emergency, for God's sake! It's been all over the telly and everyone's talking about it. They're appealing for a young guy who ran around saving people to come forward but he's disappeared. If you ask me, he was one of the terrorists. Probably at the bottom of the river with his throat cut by now. In a way, you can't help admiring these fanatics, can you? Must take a special kind of courage to blow yourself to pieces."

"A special kind of insanity, I'd say. Anyway, no, it was nothing to do with the arcade bombing. Apart from your missing hero, are they looking for anyone else? Or maybe they're not saying."

"A blonde apparently, some lady or other. One of the shopkeepers told the police she ran off with wonder boy. They say the palace is practically in melt-down over it. -- What were you doing then, down by the river when you got into the fight ?"

"I was taking shots of a little mishap, that's all. A posh boat went over the falls and they don't know whether anyone went with it."

"This gets weirder and weirder! That's been on the box too! They're saying now it was the two kids for certain. Incredible that you should be a journalist working on the case and not make such an obvious connection! Are you any good at what you do?"

"Depends what you ask me to do."

She laughed, leaning forward so I could see what was on offer. -- "Tell me, how come you heard about the boat in the first place?"

"Sorry. We never disclose our sources. -- How about talking about you now. Tell me, what's a girl like you doing out on her own?"

"Oh that's easy, nobody wants me. Real men don't seem to find me sexy and I'm not interested in girls so I have to amuse myself a lot of the time. You got a smoke by the way?"

"Sorry, I came off it way back."

"Good for you! Still, it doesn't matter, they sell the stuff here. The girl behind the bar's waiting for you to go up. She knows what I need at this time of the day."

It was strong stuff by the smell of it and very expensive. -- "And what's on your programme for the rest of the hour ... I mean day?" I asked.

"Filling in the void mostly. How about another Bloody Mary? You won't kick up a fuss if I slip out of my shoes, will you? It's like an oven in here." -- She kicked her shoes off like she was sliding into bed and stretched her legs out beneath the table. I felt the soft caress of her foot on mine. She was really good at what she did and could she drink! Time for another.

"How do you find it, ok? An extra shot of vodka, more tomato, Worcester sauce maybe? You're alright for the other, I guess."

She didn't go for another joint but fairly jumped at my offer of less tomato and more vodka, twice as much. I had a large single malt, no water of course. And why not? It really was hot in there and I might as well make use of the cash before the hangman took it off me. -- "I'm having another. How's yours?"

The clock coming up to ten to and, what with the alcohol, the fumes and racket, I was slightly pissed. In the heat, the redhead was undoing her shirt front when I glanced out the window and our eyes met. Victoria glaring in at me!

"Hey! You'll have the table over! Where are you off to now? Hey! That was my fucking foot! What about the bill? I'm not ..."

--- * * * * * ---

"I do not wish to know, Mr Sope. You're perfectly entitled to spend your time as you see fit." -- On the other side of the road, beyond the traffic, a massive building set far back, on its steps, half a dozen soldiers with rifles. Victoria was looking at them.

"But, My Lady, can't you just hear me out? I thought you could be in trouble so I decided to wait there till 12 o'clock and, if you didn't turn up, go for help. I was going to report you missing."

"Judging by your breath, you wouldn't have been capable of reporting anything after another round with that tart. Well, it doesn't matter because you won't have to bother now, will you? They can see with their own eyes I've survived in spite of you all."

"In that case, why go to them at all? I'm not interested."

"Because Luigi's missing, that's why."

"But…"

"Look, I know why you don't want me to go to the police. You don't want me to tell them what happened because you've already given them your own version. Don't bother to deny it. I saw you down there by the river talking to a policeman."

Gee! And I thought she was half—dead! -- "You've got that all wrong, My Lady. I was only trying to find out what's going on. I wouldn't dream of letting them know we had anything to do with it."

"I wonder. Anyway, I've got to report Luigi missing if nothing else. I've been along the bank right up to the falls and there's no sign of him, only your police friends and they refused to look in my direction. What you do 's your affair. I'm going to talk to the authorities. They must mount a proper search."

"Talking about searches, you do know they're looking for us, don't you?"

"Looking for us!" -- She went pale. -- "Where did you hear that?"

"In the café, it came over the radio. Apparently it's all over the television as well."

"Television!" -- It looked like her eyes were going to fall out. -- "Oh God, no! You mean I'm all over the news! Television! What are they saying about me?"

"They're putting out some story about us running away together."

"Tell me I'm dreaming! Me running off with you!"

"Grotesque, isn't it? They obviously have film of us in the arcade plus it seems they know we were in the boat when it went over, don't ask me how."

"And Venus Island, what are they saying about that? They haven't been showing a film, have they?"

"Not as far as I know, no. But they're definitely trying to implicate us in the bombing."

"But there's no film! Thank…"

"I didn't say that. I said not as far as I know."

"Well, if there was, you'd know, wouldn't you? What are they saying about me and the bombing? I didn't have anything to do with that, nothing at all. They must know that. You say they filmed everything. How could they possibly say I was involved?"

"I didn't have anything to do with it either but that won't make any difference. That's the line they're taking and it doesn't matter if it's wrong. As ever, they want to be seen to be on top of the situation and they're desperate to make some arrests."

After that, you'd have thought I'd won the argument but not a bit of it. Maybe because she was what she was, a true aristocrat, or, more likely, because she was plain dumb, Victoria stood up straight, shoulders back, her face set. -- "That settles it! We'll definitely have to go and get this sorted out. You'll have to tell them about the bombing and how I had nothing to do with it. You can also tell them about Luigi and I'll insist they mount a full scale search immediately."

"After what I've told you? You're asking me to as good as put myself under arrest?"

"Don't be ridiculous! All you've got to do is tell the truth. Another thing, we must tell everybody this eloping story is absolutely, I don't know, infantile. Also, I'm expecting you to back me up when it comes to getting on with the search. After all, you were the last person to see Luigi alive. Now, let's go and get it over with!"

There wasn't a lot of traffic at that time of day but even so dashing across the road after her could easily have been my end. As it was, I only just managed to leap clear of a vintage Bentley speeding towards the river, its hood down and bonnet gleaming. The man behind the wheel, straw hat, sunglasses and tweed jacket, simply didn't see me. He had eyes only for Venus in flight. -- "Lucky I'm not just a fading memory," I said as I caught her up. "That idiot in the Bentley couldn't peel his eyes off you."

"A Bentley? Oh my God! What colour was it?"

"It was a vintage, green with a leather strap across the bonnet. It had a fancy number plate, LBW1. Must have cost a pile, that."

"Bertie! Christ, do you realise what this means? It means they've heard about it already. I knew it couldn't be long but so soon! Well, that confirms it. Come on!"

"Just one last thing, My Lady. You do realise that, if we walk into police headquarters, we won't come out again."

"I will but you certainly won't if they have to take you there in chains. I've nothing to hide and if Lord Bertrand's getting involved, that's it. They won't dare do anything now."

"Look here, before we go up those steps, I think you need to understand something. Friends in high places or not, this business isn't going to be as easy to clear up as you seem to think. This regime needs a war. It always comes to that in the end. Dictators under threat try to cover up their mal-administration, lies, corruption, their general incompetence, by identifying a common threat. This regime needs an enemy and who better than a group of religious fanatics? That's why they've been waging war on The Phoenix and his sect, goading them into revolt. This morning's outrage was a God—send. It's given them the excuse to declare a state of emergency. Of course, there'll be a lot of resistance at first, demonstrations, strikes, civil disobedience of every sort. The masses need to be convinced that the threat is real. So they'll put on trial as many so—called collaborators as possible and the more prominent they are, the better. That's the way it works with regimes under threat. The first to get the chop are the so-called celebrities. I promise you, My Lady, this mob will grab at any pretext to pin a charge of treason on you."

"Treason! Don't be ridiculous! They wouldn't dare! You're paranoid, that's what you are, with all this stuff about war and God knows what. Anyway, I'm safe. I'd never heard of this wretched Phoenix man before I met you."

Before she'd met me? She didn't hear about him from me. She read it in the paper. – "It'll be useless you protesting innocence, My Lady. Wait till they start asking questions about the relic."

"What are you jabbering about now? Relic? What relic?"

"The Christ Phial. The bomber gave it to me to look after. It contains the blood of the risen Christ."

She smiled contemptuously. -- "You mean that little bottle I saw you hang round your neck in the jeweller's? That contains the blood of Christ?"

"That's what the followers of The Phoenix believe, yes, and that's why the regime is desperate to get their hands on it."

"Well, they're welcome to it as far as I'm concerned. God, how gullible can you get! It's just one of those glass tubes perfume companies use for samples. The blood of Christ! At the very most, it'll have a few drops of scent in it, coloured water more likely. No—one's going to give up their life for a thing like that."

"That's what you think. Genuine or not, the Christ Phial's a revered relic and relics are the banners of the faith. If the government can prove I'm its keeper, that'll be the end for both of us."

"Why both of us? I'm not anything to do with it."

"It's as I told you. As far as the authorities are concerned, you and I are hand—in—glove."

"But any fool can see that's not true. Give the thing to me. I'm going to hand it over myself then, they'll know where I stand in all this."

"You still don't understand, do you? Anyway, the answer's no. I'm not going to hand the Christ Phial over to anybody and that includes you. I'm … I'm not that wicked – or stupid. I'll find somewhere to hide it then I'll come with you."

"Hide it! What's the point of that? You say they have film. A thousand to one, they know you've got it already. We must hand it over."

"I'll tell them I lost it."

"But they're not that stupid, surely! They'll know you haven't lost it. It will be obvious you've hidden it. Lying will only make things ten times worse."

"Oh have it your own way. I got you into this, I suppose, so I'll have to hang with you. Here!" -- I unbuttoned my shirt.

"Sope!"

We both stared, united in disbelief. Where the flash of silver had been, the naked truth. I had been robbed. -- "I can't believe it! It's gone, bloody gone! I'd failed anyway"

"This gets worse and worse! You should have handed it over straightaway and that would have been an end of it. Are you absolutely positive it hasn't slipped down somewhere?"

"Slipped, woman, of course the bloody thing hasn't slipped!" -- I explored. No sign. The Christ Phial had gone. -- "I have to ask you this, Lady Victoria. You say you saw me with it. You didn't…"

"Steal it? You know, I almost wish I had. No, of course I didn't steal your beastly relic you must have lost it in the river, when we went over the falls. Did you have it when we got back to the bank?"

"I never looked but back to the bank's where I'm going, fast."

"And I'd better come with you!"

--- * * * * * ---

We turn and run back across the road, dodging the traffic, down the avenue and, swinging round the corner, head for the spot where we had landed. Nothing. The police have gone, only the slap and gurgle of the drowsing river against the bank, the shimmering reflection of leaves, the cold scent of clear water.

"Let's try along the bank, Josef. If it didn't go straight to the bottom, it could be caught up somewhere. Come on."

We trot upstream towards the falls, Victoria in the lead. Nothing to see but people enjoying themselves -- innocently -- boats, bulrushes lifting up out of the water in islands of green, their heads bowing and bouncing under the weight of river birds. We reach the foot of the falls, towering into the blue sky, a roll of plunging spray on the heights of a giant's shoulder. We separate to search between the rocks, stepping out as far as we can on the backs of foaming boulders but no, nothing -- or is that something over there? I slide and stumble across to a pool sheltered by the overhang. The water is very still and blood red. -- "So it was you! Good God, man, even your rag wouldn't print a picture of the way you look now." -- Hell, I bet that was his camera I handed over!

"No, Victoria, it's nothing. Don't let's waste any more time. We've seen all there is here."

We return to the bank and, like a pair of hounds, jog back, looking in reed-beds, searching through tangles of tree-roots, staring into the darkness of otter-holes below the bank. The relic has gone for good.

"It's no use," Victoria said at last, stopping and burying her face in her hands. "We won't find the phial now. If you dropped it in the river, it's at the bottom or else miles down stream. They're never going to believe this. We'd better walk all the way back to that cafe of yours. If by the remotest chance you lost it on the road, we could still find it."

Chapter 5

"Do you mind waiting for a second, Victoria? You never know, the relic could be on the floor or even waiting for me behind the bar. Anyway, I owe them some money. I'll be right back."

An astonishing change had come over Victoria as she stood, looking in through the glass doors. It was as if she'd reverted to her true self. -- "I'm not staying out here on my own! I'm coming too. I might as well. I won't get a chance like this every day and I've been dying to find out what really goes on in places like this. It looks like a dive, a genuine dive!"

"But it's not safe! You get all sorts in a place like this."

There was a distinct pause in the chatter as Victoria marched in ahead of me and sat down at my old table. I looked around the room. Thank God, the red head had gone. I went up to the bar. -- "Sorry I left in such a hurry. I didn't want to bring up on your floor, that's not nice. How much do I owe you? -- That's fine! And the red head? -- You don't say! Went running after me, did she? -- Don't worry, I'll settle with her some time." [Quite a bit of cash passing across] "While I think of it, has something been handed in for me? It's a keepsake, only a little flask. -- No? Oh well, too bad! -- Mine? I'll have one large coffee, black as pitch and twice as strong. -- I doubt she will but I'll ask anyway."

"Victoria, it's not there, I'm afraid. Oh well, too bad! At least I won't have to tell any lies. You said you don't touch alcohol. How about a coffee? Oh no, I remember, you don't like that either. Never mind, there's always fruit juice or your usual carrot if that's what you'd prefer."

"Carrot juice? You must be joking. While I'm here, I'm going to get the most out of it. I may never have the chance again. Let's see now," -- She studied the drinks' menu -- "What did bottle-head have?"

"Quite a few Bloody Mary's as far as I remember."

"Ah yes, here it is -- vodka and tomato with -- Um, I wonder what Mary, would have thought of that. Later perhaps. I say, this sounds rather exciting, Screwdriver! Just look what it's got in it! Alright, that's for me. Bring me a screwdriver and make it a large one."

"I wonder if you shouldn't try a small one first."

"You are not my nanny, Sope! Make that a triple if you please."

We sat in the uproar and clouds of smoke for a good time hardly exchanging a word while Victoria sampled the pleasures of the common man and found them increasingly to her taste. She got through two triple screwdrivers and a Bloody Mary and thought about trying grass but, after some persuasion, agreed to postpone that adventure till later. As for me, I stuck to black, black coffee till my stomach rebelled and tried sending it back. Nothing to do after that but sit and think.

"I still can't work it out," I said as much to myself as to her. "How did I get involved in all this? Why should The Phoenix, whoever he may be, place such a responsibility on my shoulders? How did he come to know about me at all, I'd like to know."

"Don't be so silly, darling!" -- Victoria's voice wobbled gracefully. -- "The Phoenix doesn't know you from Adam. I expect he told the suicide to grab any old Joe Soap and there you were, waiting on the shelf as it were."

"Ha, ha, very amusing, I'm sure! How about explaining this, then, seeing you're feeling so clear headed? The bomber said he remembered me, called me Joe. Or was it Josef, I don't quite remember. Come to think of it, he wasn't the only one. Remember the car when we were on our way to the river? That guy called me by my name as well."

"But he was from the police or so you said. The bomber's different. I bet he didn't know you from a bar of soap. He just took a chance. I say, do you realise what I just said? I said "He didn't know you from a bar of soap!" [Tipsy giggle] "The truth is, there are millions of Joe Soaps, millions and millions of you! You're in super abundant supply, darling. Buy one, get half a dozen free."

"I don't think we should continue like this, Lady Victoria. What I'm saying is, it only makes sense to find out if a man's sympathetic to your cause before putting trust in him. He did say something about remembering me from way back – whatever that may mean – but people can change. In one life, you may be a revolutionary but in the next, you're a dyed in the wool conservative. I wonder why he didn't bother to check."

"But that's exactly my point, darling. The Joe Soaps of life don't need to be convinced, they just need to feel wanted. They're like suits off the peg, waiting to be put on. I'm afraid to say that you are what we call cannon fodder. Yours is not to reason why. Yours is to do and dry."

"You mean "do and die". Anyway, I don't think you should have another. It brings a side out I'd rather not see. In vino veritas as they say."

"Oh, you are so clever! -- You know, I quite like this place and I shall have another. Let's see now, what shall it be?"

"Hello there! If it isn't Victoria Hunter-Jones!" -- A six and a half footer loomed suddenly out of the smoke, stepped behind Victoria's chair and put his hands over her eyes. -- "Guess who!"

"Bertie, darling, of all people! What on earth are you doing in a hole like this?" -- It was the Bentley driver. He squeezed himself into the chair next to her and stretched an arm across the back of her seat -- "What do you think I'm doing in Teens, you naughty thing? I'm under orders to collect you and take you back where you belong. Good lord! The fright you've given everyone!"

"Have I really? That's marvellous! Serve them bloody well right! Bertie, this is Mr Josef Sope, spelled S o p e. -- Tell me, did he send you himself?"

Her friend let out what is called a guffaw. -- "I say! Is that really his name, Sope?-- Good afternoon, Sope. -- You know very well who sent me, old girl. Now, be good and start getting your wits together. It's time for sack-cloth and ashes."

"Oh no it's not, not till I've had one more screwdriver at least. I'm really going to enjoy myself now. -- Mr Bar of soap, I'm going to get screwed so bring me a driver and a stiff brandy for Lord Bertie."

The same again a few minutes later but with the best Polish vodka for Lord Bertrand, neat. -- "You know, Bertie," Victoria drawled, "I've been frightfully remiss. I've neglected to, to introduce you to Mr Sope. He's awfully clever, you know. He talks Latin. Latin! Can you believe it, Latin! Amo, amas, amat."

"It's alright, you introduced us a while back, old thing."

"Oh, did I really? But what did he say and -- and did you understand it, that's the thing! He talks a lot, does comrade Sope. I can't understand all the time but it's killingly funny, specially when he gets stuck into politics. He sounds for all the world like a party-political broadcast!

-- Come on, Sope, give his lordship one of your terrorist speeches, the one about going to war. -- Now you listen to this, Bertie. You'll pack in laughing!"

Josef Sope had had enough. I went to the bar, settled up and, grabbing a jumbo-size ice-bucket, made my way back. The two of them were flirting away totally unaware of the coming peasant's revolt. I stood behind his lordship and, just as he was about to whisper in her ear, turned the ice out onto his head then rammed the bucket down over his eyes. It was a deep bucket and a very tight fit. It would cost blood to get off. -- "Come along, Lady Victoria! You're coming with me."

Without too much fuss, I managed to manhandle Victoria out onto the street. To me, the change of air was wonderfully refreshing but it's effect on her was a disaster. She staggered a few paces, babbled something about big noses and Greek pirates, clung onto the wall, vomited then collapsed unconscious into my arms. Nothing for it but to carry her off like a bride across the threshold.

--- * * * * * ---

A park some distance from Teens. I found a bench in the shade. Victoria didn't look her best, sleeping on her back with her mouth wide open so I covered her face with a newspaper. I would have liked to stay there till she came to but people, men especially, were curious and by the time I'd had to shoo off an idiot from the Salvation Army and stare out two mounted policemen as they trotted by, I knew we had to move on.

I was carrying her down a quiet path between banks of rhododendrons, hoping to find somewhere secluded where I could put her down, when a fresh difficulty arose -- old Adam was waking up. Victoria felt so light and pliant in my arms, her head cradled against my shoulder! There was nothing I could do about it. -- "Down, beast, down! Not now for pity's sake! Don't I stand out enough as it is? Any minute, a keeper or worse is going to turn the corner and, before you can say Jack the Ripper, I'll be up for kidnap and rape on top of theft, fraud, treason and whatever else they have in store for me." -- It's no good, I told myself. I must find somewhere to put her down. Why the hell can't the silly bitch start coming round? -- "Hey, you, wake up! We can't go on like this. Wake up, woman! Do you hear, wake up and walk for the love of Christ!" -- I lowered her onto the grass and, kneeling beside her, tried pinching both nostrils between thumb and forefinger. It didn't work.

I was about to pick her up and set off again when an old chap with a goatee beard came over. -- "What on earth were you doing just then?"

"What do you think I was doing? Trying to bring her round, of course."

"Well, that's a very peculiar way of going about it. What happened?"

"Nothing happened. She's suffering the effects of…something she's taken, that's all. She'll be ok in a minute or two. Nice of you to ask anyway. Enjoy your walk."

"She looks far from ok to me. Why have you got her on her back like that? Turn her onto her side in case she vomits. -- Gently, man, gently! She's not a bag of potatoes. -- That's more like it." -- He got down onto his knees beside her. -- "Lovely creature! You know, I could swear I've seen her picture in the paper. How on earth did she get like this? What did you give her?"

"Give her? What are you suggesting? I haven't given her anything."

"Haven't you then? Well, it certainly looks like drugs to me and I should know, I have a good deal of experience in these things."

"Look here! I have not drugged the young lady and I'm more than capable of dealing with the situation. Now, kindly push off and leave me to it."

Victoria began to moan. The old man bent over her again. -- "What's the matter, my pet, feeling sorry for ourselves, are we?" [More moaning] "Tell me, has she been in this state for long?"

"It has nothing to do with you but the answer is no. Now, just clear off! She's coming round and when she does, she's going to feel embarrassed enough without having to cope with strangers. As soon as she's over it, I'll tell her how concerned you were."

"Thank you but she's going to need a lot more than an old man's concern. Come on, own up, what did you put in her drink and how long ago was it? I need to know."

"Listen to me! You'd better watch it, I'm on a very, very short fuse. This young lady is not a junkie and I'm not a rapist. She's had too much to drink, that's all, and it's my official duty to look after her. Thank you for the advice about turning her on her side. Now, bugger off."

He sniffed her breath. -- "She certainly has been drinking a good deal but I suspect that's not the whole story. If it's your duty to look after her, how come you allowed her to get like this? She's been drugged. I'm sure of it."

"If you don't fuck off, I'll…"

He was feeling Victoria's pulse now. -- "The more you carry on like that, the more I'm convinced you've something to hide. This young woman needs proper attention and I'm going to take a closer look at her whether you like it or not." -- He went to unbutton her dress.

"Oh no you don't!" -- I seized his wrist. -- "If you lay a finger on her, I'll beat you to death! Fuck off and mind your own business!"

"You don't seem to understand. This is very much my business. I'm professionally obliged to render assistance in an emergency. Let go, you're hurting my wrist!"

I released my grip. -- "Are you really telling me you're a qualified doctor?"

"You've got eyes in your head. Make use of them." -- He raised her eyelids. -- "Well, at least everything seems to be in order there. How about making yourself useful? Run along and get the ambulance people while I see what I can do for her in situ."

"You've got a hope! I'm not leaving her side for one single second. I'm going to stand here and watch every little move you make, Mr Doctor."

"You know, you're not helping her, behaving like this. You're not qualified to supervise me but you are capable of getting assistance. This young lady should be admitted for observation and it's urgent. We must have a stretcher."

"But don't you have a mobile? -- No? I thought doctors always carried a phone. Then you'll have to go for help yourself."

"And what sense would that make? I know what I'm doing. You obviously do not. I'm old and likely to take some time to bring help. You're young and presumably fit. You'd be back in less than half the time. Run along! I'll look after her. Don't worry."

"Look, if you insist she needs to be hospitalised, we'll take her. I'll do the carrying."

How long would it take us?"

"It's a good mile and a half to the first-aid centre. I can't see us getting there in under three quarters of an hour, not with you carrying her. Frankly, if you're as innocent as you make out, I can't see why you're being so uncooperative. I wonder if you really want her to recover. -- Alright, alright, there's no need for violence! I'll go but I'll have to report you. You will, in any case, be held responsible if anything happens to her while I'm gone. Don't let her turn on her back and make sure she can breathe freely. It's vital the airways are kept open."

I watched him hurry away. -- Nothing wrong with your legs, old man. Well, don't get back too quickly or you'll get what you deserve, not what you're after. -- I took Victoria up in my arms yet again. -- "Sorry, little lady, we'll have to find somewhere else to hide and let's pray it doesn't take too bloody long."

For once, my prayers were answered. A couple of hundred yards further on, I found a narrow path running at right angles away into the trees. I carried Victoria down and there it was, a shed used to keep tools and what not. The bolt had been slid across but there was no padlock. Inside, barely any light, only a cobweb glow from a small square of green glass at the back, and the air smelling of grass and machinery. I lowered her onto a pile of sacks by the far wall and pushed the door to.

Ten minutes, fifteen, twenty, sitting on the floor beside her, I was growing frantic. Quite apart from anything else, how much longer could I keep old Adam chained up? After all, what harm could it possibly do just to take a look? She wouldn't be any the wiser. Would I get such a wonderful opportunity ever again? Not a chance! I strained my ears. Nothing except for Victoria's deep, childlike breathing and the peaceful disturbances of woodland life, brush of leaves on the roof, whistle of birds. -- "Come along, you gorgeous bitch, wake up! Come on, wake up! You can't expect me to hold back much longer." -- I put my hand on her forehead, it was warm but not unduly so. I found the pulse in her wrist -- a bit fluttery maybe but so's mine. Perhaps it's normal. -- Hang on, I nearly forgot! What about the breathing? -- Sounds alright. Nothing tight around the throat but what about here? -- Oh Christ, I can't help it! "Wake up, woman, wake up before it's too late for both of us!"

I was suddenly aware of being watched. No sound except our breathing, nothing to see then a shadow passing over the tiny window. I crept out, closed the door behind me and slid the bolt across. There was no sign that we had company. I checked round and round the hut, examined the bushes for broken leaves, the grass for prints, nothing at all.

Probably some animal, I thought, a squirrel quite likely. Just the same, I'll watch out here a bit. -- I crouched down behind some bushes and, as I did so, felt an irresistible urge to crap. Just got going when -- "Bloody hell! No!" -- A gardener, pushing a motor-mower down the path. -- A final and mighty effort followed by leaves, leaves and more leaves, grabbed by the fistful.

I broke cover just as he drew level. -- "Hi there! Just the man I've been looking for! Did you know a whole lot of goats are loose in the wood back there? They're busy stripping the trees, leaves, bark, the lot."

"Goats again! I can't believe it. Where?"

"A few thousand yards in that direction. They're having a whale of a time. Look, see that big oak? That way. You can't miss them. -- Don't worry about that, I'll put it in the shed for you."

I watched him run off into the trees then ran back to the hut. The bolt had been drawn back.

Fling myself at the door. It is not closed, just to. I tumble inside, momentarily confused in the semi-dark. Over in the corner, the old man with the beard, crouching beside her on the sacks. I go for his white face as he looks up, miss, punch into thin air then the floor comes up to meet me. I feel him half trip over my legs leaping out the door.

"Victoria! I'll be right back!" -- I make for the open door, the old man is nowhere, only the motor-mower waiting to be brought in. For an instant, I want to go after him but see sense. Back into the hut. She's propped up on one elbow, staring. -- "Victoria, are you alright? What happened? Is everything ok?"

"I don't know. You tell me. What is this place?"

I knelt beside her, tried to take her hand but she snatched it away. Her breath smelled awful. -- "There's nothing to worry about, Victoria. You were unwell, that's all. I brought you here so you could rest a minute. What do you think? Shall we make tracks? We'd better not hang around too much longer."

"What do you mean, unwell? And who was that next to me? Was it you, kneeling there? Someone was touching me down there in the dark."

"I don't know who it was but, honestly, it wasn't me. I had to leave you for a second and when I got back, he was next to you. Did he do anything? Did he ... For God's sake answer me, Victoria! What did he do? I'm going to kill the sod!"

She sat upright, put her head in her hands and groaned. -- "Now I remember! It's all coming back. You persuaded me to go into that dreadful place. You said I would be in trouble then you brought over a glass full of something and I stupidly drank the stuff -- Ughh!" -- She looked me straight in the eyes. -- "Just what did you put in that drink, Sope? Come on, tell me. I have to know. What did you put in my glass? God, my head!"

"Victoria! I didn't persuade you to go anywhere. It was you who insisted on going into Teens. I did my best to stop you. And I didn't put anything in your drink. I..."

"Silence! You drugged me, you despicable little goat! You put something in my drink so you could take advantage of me! Well, Mr Sope, I just woke up in time, didn't I? You were there, where you are now, and you were trying to undress me. Don't bother to deny it. I saw you. -- And you were so scared, weren't you, when I caught you? You tried to run. You're a pig and a coward and I don't want you near me ever again. Do you understand? Never, never again!"

"And after all I've done for you! Where would you be now if it wasn't for me? I even saved you from drowning, for Christ's sake. Anyway, I'll tell you this much -- you carry on the way you are right now and you'll regret it."

"Oh, will I? And what will you do, beat me up while I'm not looking?"

"I'll tell you what I'll do, My Lady. I'll tell you the truth about yourself.

"Huh! Talk like that doesn't mean a thing. It's all come back now. I remember you sitting there and filling my glass with some poison called screwdriver. You get me drunk and the next thing, I wake up on a pile of sacks in a shed! Well, little goat, you've picked on the wrong woman this time. I'm going to see you're castrated. Get out of my way."

"So you can call in at police headquarters I suppose. Off you go then. After all, we don't want to keep the BBC waiting, or Sky Television."

--- * * * * * ---

The path Victoria took came to an ornamental bridge arching a stream, its banks deep in wild flowers. She marched over without looking to right or left while I took up the rear. On the other side, the banks of flowers gave way to immaculate lawns umpired by low bushes, trimmed and topiaried into stiff sculptures as if they belonged in the grounds of a French chateau. For one brief instant, I felt completely at home. -- "I want us to have a talk about what happened, Lady Victoria. You're making a great mistake and doing me an injustice. I never dragged you into Teens or plied you with drinks or -- No, Mademoiselle, you listen to me for a moment! It was you who insisted on going in there. I said it wasn't suitable. It was the same with the drink. I advised you to go steady on the screwdrivers but you told me to mind my own business. As if that wasn't enough, when your friend, Bertie, barged in, you had me running around fetching and carrying for the pair of you as if I were your footman. You drank so much, Lady Victoria, you threw up in the street and passed out. I tell you, I had one hell of a job to…"

She turned round and stared at me, her eyes wide in horror. -- "Lord Bertrand! Are you actually telling me Lord Bertrand of Wells was there too, that he saw what happened? He saw me getting drunk and … and everything? Lord Bertrand saw that?"

"Surely you remember! He joined you at our table and the pair of you sat there having a fine old time at my expense. I don't begrudge paying for the drinks but I do object to being made fun of. Oh, and by the way, I didn't have anything."

For a moment, it looked like she was going to cry, standing there, shoulders hunched and her hands clasped. -- "Oh God! Why is this happening to me? Why me, on top of all I've been through? I can't believe it! Lord Bertrand of all people! How did he react? What did he say? Do you remember? Did I really drink so much? And afterwards out in the street, it couldn't have been that awful, surely! You mean I was sick? I literally passed out in front of all the people? Please, tell me it isn't true!"

"Sorry, I didn't mean to upset you. It wasn't that bad. It was just one of those things. You were enjoying yourself, drowning your troubles. I suppose you could say you were having a right royal time. It's expected of your sort. Look at Prince George something or other. He got like that often and often and the ordinary man in the street couldn't have cared less. It's what you expect. You behaved very well on the whole. Certainly, there was nothing outrageous. It's true, you did say a few nasty things about me and there was a lot of laughing but I'm sure it was all in good fun. Why don't we just forgive and forget?"

"Well, I'm not sure I can go that far but at least I know now, I didn't do anything too shocking. The one thing I cannot afford is publicity, the wrong sort of publicity, that is. I take it there was the usual mob of reporters and cameramen milling about all over the place."

"Not as far as I know, no. Don't count on it though. I couldn't see or hear everything that went on. I was too busy running round getting drinks and so on. I couldn't possibly keep an eye on you and Lord Bertie all the time. There certainly weren't any reporters in the street or afterwards. There is one thing though. I am very much pissed off at being accused of spiking your drink. I wouldn't dream of such a thing. Nor did I try to rape you. Quite the opposite. I risked life and limb protecting you. Something I shall continue to do for as long as I survive."

"As long as you remember that it's for me to choose my own bodyguards. -- You still haven't told me about Lord Bertrand. I suppose he was outside with me when … when I became unwell."

"You and I left Teens without his lordship. He had to stay behind for some reason."

"But for heaven's sake, why? He's such a perfect gentleman and always so attentive, always. He must have been absolutely furious!"

"I wouldn't know about that. Why should I? As you informed me, I'm just Joe Sope, cannon--fodder. I can't be expected to interpret the finer points of courtly behaviour."

"Did I really say that? Sope, you're not good for me. The next time I fall into a river, you'd better let me drown."

--- * * * * * ---

The park loo was a rustic affair sheltering behind thick hedges, ladies on the right, gentlemen on the left. I followed Victoria at a respectful distance and hovered on the other side of the leafy screen for her to reappear. A minute passed by, two, getting on for three. What was she up to in there, taking a shower? My bladder was starting to press its own claims. -- Oh do speed up, you little Madame, I thought. -- On second thoughts, take your time, I must pop in myself.

I started for the stand-ups, got into the echoing gloom and saw my mistake. -- She can't be much longer. Better not risk it. [The uproar of a nearby flush] Nothing for it, I'll have to manage outside where I can see what's going on. Oh well, prepare for death, ye banks and bushes, here cometh acid rain.

I found the perfect spot, out of sight of passers by yet with a view of the shadowy door of the ladies', unzipped and began emptying. Looking round, the way one does, I suddenly noticed them, a camera-crew lurking behind some bushes about twenty yards off. Not thinking what I was doing, I tore round to the ladies' and stuck my head in at the door. -- "Stay where you are, the press are waiting!"

Victoria's voice echoing from behind a distant door --"Christ, not you again! Where are they?"

"Hiding in some bushes about twenty yards off. They'll have a perfect view as you come out."

"How low can you get! A woman can't even go to the toilet without those rats spying on her! Go and get rid of them!"

"What do you want me to say?"

"Get their identities and say you'll be putting in a complaint to The Press Council."

"And if they want a story out of me?"

"Go ahead and give them one. Tell them you're a gentleman in disguise."

I turned to go and it happened. A heavy-weight woman in tweeds turned the corner and just about walked into me. -- "And what, may I ask, do you think you're doing in the ladies toilet?"

"It's alright, Madame, I was just looking for something."

She stood at a safe distance and, opening her umbrella, held it in front of her like a shield. -- "Looking for what exactly?"

"Umm … Some—one reported a burst pipe." -- I was suddenly conscious of a draft. [Zip]

"Checking for a burst pipe in the women's toilet with your fly wide open! You're not a plumber. Where are your tools? Come on, show me your identification."

I went through the familiar routine of patting my pockets. -- "Umm … I'm afraid I'll have to go and get it. It's the wife, you see, she put out clean things for me this morning. Can you hang on a minute?"

"Oh no! I've met your sort before, too often. I'll come with you."

We'd gone a few yards when the madam spotted a chap doing some weeding. She produced a whistle and gave a blast. – "Brown, come here! Get a move on, man! I haven't got all day."

A man in a boiler suit came pounding up. It was the gardener I'd sent on a wild goat chase. He saluted. -- "Ma'am?"

"Recognise this one, Brown? He claims he's on the staff!"

The look on his face! -- "Blimey! You, is it? -- I've met this one before, Ma'am. He's not one of us. Up to no good. He sent me off on a wild goose chase only a short time back."

From the corner of my eye, I picked up a flash of blonde hair behind the bushes and heard a groan.

"We can go into that later, Brown. First things first. This is urgent. Looks like I've cornered yet another rapist." -- She waved her shield in my direction. -- "You know what to do."

"Ma'am?"

"Arrest him, man! Go on, citizen's arrest."

Brown advanced on me a trifle warily. -- "Now, don't you give me any more trouble, Mr. You're under arrest."

"I didn't intend to give trouble to anyone. The truth is," [Back-step, once, twice] "I went to the wrong side, that's all."

"Then, why did you say you're on the staff? There are too many of your sort about these days, Mr. You come along with me and let's have no more arguing!"

"Mr Brown, you lay a finger on me and you'll get more than argument, that I promise you."

"Don't dither, Brown!" The madam interrupted. "Take hold of him. I have my rounds to finish." -- She folded her umbrella as if my trial was over.

"I warn you, Brown, don't come any closer! I said no…" -- I took the first blow above my right temple. My vision went funny and it sounded like someone had let off a soda-fountain in my head.

Wrestling the umbrella out of the Madam's grasp, I stood my ground and for a few moments, the fight was pretty even, me parrying the gardener's fists as he did his best to tenderize my face. Suddenly, however, things got really serious. The point of the umbrella glanced off the bridge of Brown's nose and entered his right eye. With a fearful shriek, the poor sod collapsed onto his knees and stayed there wailing with his hands over his eyes. [Blast, blast, blast after whistle blast]

"Hell! I'm sorry, brother! Believe me, I wouldn't have done that for the world! Really I would not. It wasn't my fault. You should have left me alone." -- Kneeling beside him, I prised the fingers free and took a look. The eye was a globe of blood. -- "God! I'm so sorry, brother! I'd give anything not to have done that, really I would. If we ever meet again, you can pluck out one of mine."

I rounded on the madam. -- "Here, woman, take your blasted umbrella! And, for everybody's sake, don't creep around without a professional bodyguard in future. If you'd had a trained man with you, nobody would have got hurt except me." -- She just stared, eyes wide with indignation.

--- * * * * * * ---

Apart from journalists lying in wait behind bushes, the area had been pretty well deserted up to that point, the odd bird singing but otherwise nothing. With all the whistle blowing and what-not, however, that was about to change. I was on my way round to explain what had happened to Victoria when they arrived, a pack of young men, much the worse for wear and hungry for Hell. -- "Oh, do look, chaps!" -- He had cut glass English and Napoleon's nose. -- -"Auntie's caught another one! That's three of the blighters this week. Well done there, aunty! -- Good grief! What have you done to Brown, you nasty little beast? -- I see, you've nothing to say. -- Ok, aunty, you give Brown an arm to the first aid and leave this to us. We're about to spill blood. Don't worry, security are on their way. They can clean up the remains."

So many of them! I appealed to the madam for fair play but she looked down her nose and walked off, Brown clutching onto her arm, sobbing.

The pack of drunks gather round me in a circle. -- "You know," one of them says, "I'm sure I recognise this joker. He's that Joe Sope character who got Victoria stoned in Teens and skinned poor, old Bertie's nose with an ice-bucket. Nasty bit of work!"

"Is that right?" -- The one with the nose fixes me with an alcoholic glare. "Well, we'll bloody soon stone you, Sope, and skin you as well. We're going to put you down, old lad!"

"Bags I stuff his head down the loo!"

"Granted, Albert, old man! First though, a bit of sport. What do you say, chaps, the blanket treatment? Come on, let's be having you, who's for tossing the baby till he cries to die?"

"It's no go, Claude, we don't have a blanket with us."

"You know what he reminds me of?" someone says. "To me, standing there like that, he looks and smells for all the world like a baby bear. Yuk! No wonder good old Victoria brought up all those screwdrivers!"

"I say, chaps, he's absolutely right! And what does one do with a bear? Bait the bugger, that's what. Come on, everyone, grab hold."

So many of them! In seconds, they have me down on the grass, holding me there and laughing. -- "Turn him over! -- Over you go, Bear Sope! Heave ho, heave ho and over you go!" -- They pull off my trousers, tie my hands behind my back. -- "I say! Doesn't his bum feel soft, just like a girl's!"

Several of them haul me to my feet. They try for a while to make me dance, prodding me with sticks and hitting me across the buttocks, but I refuse. -- "How about setting fire to his shirt? That'll get him going!"

"Anyone got a cigarette? -- Thanks, old man. -- I'm going to give you a smoke, Sope, ok?" -- Even my experience of torture has not hardened me against that concentrated heat. It has me dancing in the air. Jump, run a few steps, hop back, jump again, fall over twice.

Napoleon steps into the ring, holds up a hand. -- "You there, Percy, let's have that belt off you. Right, tie it round Bear Sope's ankle. -- That's the ticket! -- Ok, get him dancing again and, when I say heave, bloody well heave!"

Under the sticks and cigarettes, I start up again, shuffling and hopping about. -- "Heave!" -- I fall flat on my face. Hands tied, all I can do is roll over, struggle to get up again. [Raucous laughter] After a while, they haul me back onto my feet. Another round, another fall, more howling, another and yet another. I try to lie there but they won't let me. I begin to cry.

Suddenly, hoofs pounding the turf. The laughing stops. The two mounted policemen I'd seen earlier come galloping up, long truncheons drawn like sabres, horses snorting. The journalists break cover and fly off in terror. This is a new sport. The revellers career after them, jeers and laughter, horsemen in pursuit.

--- * * * * * ---

"I'm so sorry, Josie! I'm so terribly, terribly sorry!" -- Victoria was kneeling beside me on the grass and crying as she freed my hands. -- "I just don't know what to say! I'm so ashamed! Oh, Josie, how could we have sunk so low! I feel so disgusted and let down! They were like wild beast! And in my name!"

Chapter 6

"Josef, I'd like us to go somewhere private. There are a few things I need to talk to you about." -- We had been walking East for a good half hour in silence.

"You mean what happened? Don't worry, I'm alright."

"Glad to hear it. You're not looking too bad, considering. No, it's nothing to do with those thugs. I'm going to talk to somebody about them. It's not that. There are some personal issues we need to sort out."

"Sounds ominous!"

"It doesn't have to be so long as you're sensible."

We came to the grand basilica, a magnificent building set in spreading grounds, all honey-stone walls and copper domes pierced by slender towers. Who's to say, it's perfection might even justify the loss of the thousands who died in its building.

"Heavens! Just look at all that beautiful work, Victoria!"

"I am looking and, frankly, I'm wondering who needs it, not God in his Heaven, that's certain."

"But God has no need of beautiful music or painting or prayer or sacrifice either. He doesn't need anything we humans have to offer, including love. We are the ones who yearn for all things bright and beautiful and that's why, if dreams were reality, I would never wake up."

She flushed but with embarrassment rather than anger. -- "Let's not go into all that now. Come on, this looks like a place even I could be private in for a few minutes. Let's go in."

The gates into the grounds of the basilica were at least twenty feet tall and made entirely of oak. Folded back against high walls, they were more impressive than any I've seen, before or since. There is something truly noble about time-blackened oak — its weight, its iron-hard surface, its stubbornness beneath the axe. That's how a man's will needs to be, especially if he's an outsider. Perhaps in the end, I wouldn't be the only one who would come to regret. --"Aren't they huge," I said, "Impregnable, built for a palace! The masses could never break through gates like those."

Her head tilted back, Victoria was staring at the topmost beams, their razor spikes stiff-fingering the sky. -- "And the miserable people inside couldn't break out either."

--- * * * * * ---

To an ignorant eye, what a romantic couple we must have made as we wandered through the grounds, up narrow paths and down broad ones, over lawns, by flower-beds, in and out of elegant shrubberies and, finally, across a hump-bridge into a walled garden, full of ornamental trees and the scent of flowers. There was a fountain there with a leaping fish at its centre and, about ten yards back, a yew, its branches stirring in the soft breeze.

"Josef, look!"

"You mean the fountain? It's an ancient, Chinese motif. The fish is supposed to be trying to leap from the waters of life into Paradise."

"I wasn't meaning that, no. I meant the tree. It's just like the one you fell from on Venus Island, remember?"

"I remember all too well but I'll get over it. What about that bench, shall we have our heart-to-heart there in the shade?"

She wasn't a bit enthusiastic but she did allow me to sit next to her in the deep cool, not too close though. There was a tangible awkwardness as if an invisible wall had risen up between us. It felt like we were mistress and servant met for a mutually embarrassing talk in which I, as the inferior party, must wait respectfully for the firing to begin. She thought for a while then opened up, surprisingly by resting her hand on my arm. -- "Josef, there are certain issues between us which need to be settled once and for all. The first one is more important to me than you can possibly imagine and it's this – what really did happen to Luigi?"

"So that's it! I might have known. Well of course, I can't possibly say exactly what happened but I'm sure he's ok. The last I saw of him, he was swimming very strongly towards the bank. I'm tempted to say strongly as a rat"

"Now why did you have to say that? You give me good news in one breath then poison it with the next! I'm not interested in what you think of Luigi. All I wanted to know was if you had any grounds for believing he wasn't drowned."

75

"If he hadn't made it, we'd have found his body at the foot of the falls or, if we didn't, the police would have. We didn't find him and there's been nothing as far as I know from the police. While we're on the subject of Luigi, there's something I want to say. In my opinion, he was up to no good from the second he set eyes on you. That trip to Venus Island, it was obviously a trap. That photographer wasn't perched up there filming wild life. He was after pictures of you. The whole thing was a set-up, set up by Luigi."

"That's just not true! I know Luigi and you don't. He's a gentleman. He wouldn't get involved in that sort of thing. I wish I could be as sure about you. This cameraman of yours, how do I know you didn't climb the tree to see what you could see?"

"I wouldn't lie to you, My Lady, never. The photographer was real enough and he was waiting for you. I saw him up in the tree and afterwards, creeping around by the rock."

"So you say." -- She gripped my hand involuntarily, shuddering at some vivid possibility. -- "But maybe you're making that up as well and even if you're not, it doesn't mean that Luigi had anything to do with it. I'm always being pursued by photographers and they'll stop at nothing. Just look at those creatures you spotted outside the toilets'! No, if there was some—one, it had nothing to do with Luigi. He wouldn't get involved with the press anyway. He may look like a playboy and he does like to put on an act but, when it comes to publicity, he's a shy man. And what an honest, honourable man he is too, the perfect gentleman!"

"How well you've got to know him already!"

"Much better than you anyway. In my experience, Luigi is one of the finest and truest people one could hope to meet and I've met a great many. If only I could be as sure about you! I'm not hopelessly naïve, you know. In fact, I know better than most what lengths some men will go to when they're … when they're … mad with jealousy."

"Look Victoria, I didn't want to go into this but I'd better tell you. I found a body back there under the falls. It was the photographer. The good news is, he won't be taking any more sneak pictures of you or anyone else."

"So there won't be anything in the papers! Thank God, thank God for that! Oh Josie!" -- She hugged me, sobbing with relief. I should have warned her about the camera I'd handed over but she was so happy, I couldn't. Instead, I kissed her full on the mouth. It may only have lasted milliseconds but, for me, that kiss was worth a lifetime. Not for Lady Victoria of Bingham Hall though. She tore herself away and for a moment it looked like she was going to slap my face but she thought better of it. -- "Don't you dare touch me ever again, Sope! Who do you think you are? Just because I show a bit of gratitude doesn't mean you can treat me like a call girl!"

"Me! All I did …"

"Silence! I am not one of your bar women and I won't be treated like one. And while we're on that subject…"

"I do believe it's going to rain."

"And while we're on that subject, there's something you simply have to face up to. The only relationship that can ever exist between us is one of friendship. I do not love you and never shall. Love is not a game. Love is a serious matter and not to be confused with gratitude nor with common kindness. How ever often I sympathise with you, how ever grateful I may be to you, I cannot love you. It's not that you're not good enough for me. Not at all. Love has absolutely nothing to do with class. It has nothing to do with your politics either even though I'm sure you'll end up badly, very badly. It's not because you're unattractive. In some ways, you are. It's not because you're so pompous. That goes with being a revolutionary. Revolutionaries are always pompous. That's why they're hardly ever invited out to dinner. The reason I do not and cannot love you is very simple. As a man, you just don't appeal."

"So that's all it is! As a man, I just don't appeal. Well, well, maybe there is hope for me after all."

"When it comes to finding a partner, there's always hope, always. The thing is, you mustn't despair. One day, you'll find some—one. You've so much to offer! If only…"

"If only what, My Lady? -- Please do go on, we peasants are not on the whole sensitive. We tend to be like the clogs we wear. There's no need to be squeamish about how you nail down our souls."

"For God's sake, stop trying to be so damn clever! It makes you ridiculous and puts people off. You'd do better to make use of sign language, talk with your hands, anything but this phoney repartee of yours. What I was going to say is, you should get rid of that huge chip on your shoulder."

"Alright, I'll talk with my hands. How's this?" – I put my hand in her lap.

"Sope! Take your grubby paws off me!"

"Grubby paws?" -- I curled my fingers over her firm thigh. -- "Do I take it we've run out of soap, My Lady?"

"Sope, for the last time, I'm ordering you, take your hand away!"

"Ordering me? I think we're forgetting something, My Lady. You only have power if I feel like obeying. At this moment, I don't feel that way. In fact," -- I put my free arm round her and pulled her close. -- "I feel like making love!"

Victoria writhed about, hitting out at me but it was no good. When it came to strength, I was much her superior. -- "I'll scream!" she yelled. "I will! I'll scream!"

"Scream away!" -- I started getting her into position. -- "Don't worry, I'll soon have you screaming for more! You just be a good girl and stop fighting! You're about to become a member of the Sope family." -- We struggled for a second or two then, suddenly, she fell back, giving her head a tremendous crack on the bench. I was panic--stricken -- "Oh my God! What have I done! I'm sorry, Lady Victoria! What have I done? I'm so sorry! Please, I didn't mean it! I wasn't going to do anything, it was just a game, one of those things! For pity's sake, say something! Please!"

She lay motionless on the bench, her head on one side and her eyes shut.

--- * * * * * ---

Victoria still inert on the bench, obviously badly, badly hurt. I knelt by the fountain, trying to fill my cupped hands with cool water. It wasn't going to work.

"If only I had a glass or something! If only I hadn't …" -- I looked over my shoulder to check and my stomach shrank. A violent wind sprang up from the North, swept through the garden, tossing the flowers, tugging

at the leaves of the yew, bending the fountain spray back and forth. --
"Victoria! Where are you? What happened! Victoria!"

--- * * * * * ---

Paradise is not the place for torrential rain. Each crystal drop should
fall refreshingly there, splashing mercy and forgiveness, love and
happiness all around. It was not so with that garden. One brilliant flash,
crash of thunder and the place was deluged, water emptying out of
the sky, stripping the leaves from the trees, massacring the blossoms,
swamping the fountain in a lake of mud. In seconds, the scent of flowers
had gone and the air was stained with the smell of torn foliage, the birds
silent and the ears deafened with the bombard of rain.

I went over to the empty bench. She was sheltering on the other side
of the tree. -- "Victoria! What a relief! Oh, my love, I was terrified!
What happened?"

She refused to look at me, wouldn't say a word, just stood, staring
out at the storm. -- "I've learnt my lesson, My Lady. There's no need
to stand there. Come over and sit down till it's finished. I won't come
anywhere near you, I promise. I'll never lay hands on you again, never!
All I ever wanted was to take care of you, serve you, to make amends. It
wasn't my fault, you know. Some demon, a fit of madness, did that, not
me. Please, come over. You don't have to say anything. If you would
only sit here, I'd know it was still worth going on!"

I went to approach her but she backed away with a shudder and so
the pair of us endured the flood, never closer than ten feet, devastated
by what I had done and deafened by the press of roaring water till, with
the abruptness of a tropical storm, the deluge stopped. The sun blazed
once more and all around, birds began to sing while torrents shrank and
gurgled into silence.

Lady Victoria stalked off without once looking back and, at that
instant, the great bell of the basilica began to toll. It was a grand tenor
and must have weighed at least half a ton. There was no need to ask for
whom it tolled.

Chapter 7

Heading for the sea, Lady Victoria way out in front and, all around, the tolling sky booming bad, bad news. The tide of fortune had turned against me and, slithering down the slope onto the white sand, I knew the very most I could hope for now would be the chance to sacrifice myself for her and even that would go unnoticed. Like it or not, she was a different order of being, a queen good as, while I was a criminal, unfit to be her slave – or so the world would say.

On the left, the open sea, white horses racing for the beach, a commotion of gulls feasting in the wake of a fishing-smack. On our right, a mountain-range, sand-dunes, the coast road running away to the horizon with the silhouette of a huge suspension bridge, its support towers etched against the sky. We'd covered half a mile or so in complete silence when she suddenly stopped, staring down the beach. About two hundred yards ahead, the pack of revellers sitting in a circle round a hamper. Napoleon was haranguing his troops, a champagne bottle in one hand. Without so much as a glance at me, she turned away from the sea and headed for the coast road.

--- * * * * * ---

A street market, hotchpotch of country fair and car-boot sale "Where are we going, my lady?"

Lady Victoria had to slow down a little because of the crowds but kept going straight, ignoring everybody and everything until she came to a refreshment stall. Behind it, an old woman serving and -- what a shock! -- "Good God, Victoria! If I didn't know better, I'd swear you've brought me straight to our old friend, the arcade jeweller. -- What do you think, could it be her? Surely not, not unless she's been in some appalling accident. What courage to carry on the struggle with all those cuts and the collarbone like that!"

It was, indeed, the jeweller but Victoria acted like they'd never met. -- "I'll have a glass of blood orange." -- Without so much as glancing in my direction, she walked off with her drink and stood among the crowd -- a Ming vase surrounded by a rabble of beer bottles.

"I'll have the same as the young lady, please. And while we're about it, I must pay you for that bracelet I picked up, the one out of moonstones. -- What on earth happened? You been in a helicopter crash or what?" -- With her mouth the way it was, the poor creature couldn't speak. -- "I suppose it's all to do with that devilry in the arcade. What happened when we split up? Did they catch up with you? -- What's this?" -- She passed me a message on a scrap of paper. "The master is dead. Guard the phial. I was weak. I failed you all. You'll be next."

"God bless you, mother!"

I went over and more or less joined Victoria. -- "What did you think of that?" [A hissing straw] "The poor woman's been tortured. It's that cursed relic I lost. He said they'd stop at nothing." [Hiss, hiss] "Well, all I can say is, they who punish others had best themselves be guiltless." [Rattle and hiss, vacuuming up the last drops of blood]

--- * * * * * ---

Forewarned one may be but how well forearmed depends on how much time there is. As it turned out, the jeweller's note didn't give me enough. I'd hardly got through half my drink when Victoria suddenly spoke -- "There's only one way to get rid of you, Sope!" -- She'd spotted a patrol car drawn up some twenty yards off. She ran across and rapped on the window. -- "Good afternoon, I'm Victoria Hunter-Jones. May I get in for a moment? There's something I need to talk to you about in private."

The captain I'd seen earlier on the river smiled up at her. -- "By all means, My Lady! I'm Captain Wolf by the way. Here, let me help you." -- He climbed out, ushered her into the back and slammed the door.

"Hang on! Hey, wait for me!"

"Miracles will never cease! Two pigeons in one shot! What can the police do for you of all people, Mr Sope?"

"So, you know who I am!"

"Who doesn't? We've been looking for you."

"And just as well you found me, captain. I can't afford to be left out now. I'm ... I have a personal stake in what happens next."

"You can say that again!" -- He turned and smiled at Victoria who was sitting back and glaring at me. -- "Sorry but it looks like you're to have company, My Lady. Not to worry, we can speak privately afterwards in my office. -- Right, Master Sope, in you go." [slam]

"But why do we have to go to your office?" – Inside the car, Victoria's voice was shrill. "I only wanted to discuss one or two things with you. It won't take a moment. There's no need for us to go anywhere at all. I certainly don't want to be driven away in a police car!"

"There's no need to upset yourself, My Lady. It's just routine. I can't take statements or whatever sitting here in the car. These things have to be done properly, you see, according to the book. With any luck, it won't take long, a couple of hours or so. We'll lay on a limousine to bring you straight back. Don't worry, nobody will notice and that includes the media."

We pulled away from the kerb in a magnificent surge of engine power and, sitting back, I began sizing up the enemy. Quite the movie star, Wolf was, with those grey eyes, hawkish nose and narrow mouth -- the sort of face you'd love to photograph or punch. I opted for polite enquiry. -- "and where is your office, captain, at police HQ, round the corner from Teens?"

"No such luck. I'm in the camp. It's not all that far, about ten miles as the crow flies, further on wheels of course."

"And is there really no way you can fit in with Lady Victoria? It seems a bit over the top to insist on taking her miles and miles to a police camp when you don't have any idea what's on her mind. Why don't you ask her here and now?"

"That's not on, Sope. Rules are rules and they have to be followed to the letter. I'd have thought you'd know that. Anyway, as it happens, I have a pretty good idea of what's troubling her ladyship already. The subject's now closed."

"Captain Wolf," Victoria said with sudden resolution, "I'm sorry but we'll have to arrange another time for the meeting. I never dreamt it would take more than a few minutes and I have another engagement. I'll get out here if you don't mind."

"We've done over a mile already. Be a bit of a walk, wouldn't it? Tell me about this engagement of yours. Who's it with, what time and where exactly?"

"That is not your affair. Be so good as to stop the car."

"I can't do that, My Lady, but if you care to give me the number," -- he produced a mobile, -- "I'll ring through your apologies."

"Sorry, it's … it's not permitted."

"So you see, we both have rules to follow! Tell me, is this meeting at the palace by any chance? I'm sure we could pass by and leave a message at the gate."

"I'm not in a position to give you any further information,Captain. Kindly stop the car and allow me to get out. I shall contact you again later."

He gave her a long, straight look. -- "I thought I'd made that clear. The driver will stop the car when we reach our destination and not before. However, I don't want to be unreasonable. After all, this other engagement of yours could just possibly be genuine. Ok, to speed things up, I'm prepared to make an exception and bend the rules a little. We'll try and get the formalities out of the way here and now. -- I take it you have some means of identification."

Victoria's face maintained its haughty expression but her voice let her down. -- "You know perfectly well who I am, Captain."

"Show me someone who doesn't! After all, you've had so much exposure of late."

"Exposure! What on earth do you mean?"

"You mean nobody's told you? What a pity! You've become a screen idol, My Lady. I'll have to make sure you see the footage for yourself. You'll be astonished how well it's come out in spite of the water. Anyway, famous or not, I'm still obliged to ask for formal proof of identity. It's something to do with possible court action. I'm sorry about that but, as I say, rules are rules and must be observed."

"Court action! What do you mean?"

"I'm afraid I'm not in a position to discuss legal problems at this stage."

Victoria's haughty look had vanished. -- "But I don't understand! This has nothing to do with the courts! I'm not getting mixed up with that!"

"Now then, now then! No need to get excited. It's nothing unusual. We may have to call you as a witness. Don't worry, we can talk about that later."

"And this film I'm supposed to be in, I don't know what you're talking about. What film?"

"If you don't know that, you should. Now, that proof of identity if you please."

For a moment, Victoria's voice deserted her entirely. -- "I see … Well, I … I was presented with a card at the, the umm, the central bank. Is that what you want?"

"May I take a look? -- Thank you. My, my! this really is something to remember. Positively regal, wouldn't you say? Thank you very much. I'll see you get it back, never fear"

"I'd like it back now, if it's all the same to you." -- Her normal assertiveness was beginning to resurface. -- "Didn't you hear what I said, Captain Wolf? Give me back that card."

"Assuming everything's in order," he said without smiling, "you'll get it back, don't worry."

"I think you should demand to see a lawyer," I said.

Wolf smiled as if I'd said something quite charming. -- "I'm afraid you'd find that difficult, My Lady. Sope of all people should know there are no lawyers left. No work for them, you see. That's one small step forward, is it not? We have our critics of course, Master Sope here for example, who claim we are running a police state and, in a sense, they're right. The pity is it won't last. What with foreign interference in our affairs, the so—called United Nations and what not, and now these suicide bombings, we've had to declare what is called a state of emergency, not to be confused with martial law of course. Once normal conditions are restored, I fear the legal vultures will return to feed and justice will again be the province of the wealthy. Never mind, for the present, I, Captain Francis Wolf, am the law."

"But even so, I surely have rights!"

"Ask Sope, My Lady. Nobody has rights under a state of emergency. Some do have privileges, of course, but as we all know, privilege can be taken away as well as bestowed. -- Come now! There's no need to look so shocked, I'm only giving you the facts. You can trust me to be absolutely impartial."

"Trust is like loyalty," I said. "It has to be earned."

"Once again, the voice of the common man! You know, I thought you'd gone to sleep, Sope. Anyway, I'm glad to hear you say that because it's exactly what we in the military think! When an organisation, inside the system or outside it, puts its trust in somebody, that somebody must have earned it in some way or other." -- Eyes narrow, predatory beak advanced, he reminded me at that moment of a hawk sizing up a sparrow. -- "Sometimes, of course," he added menacingly, "trust turns out to be misplaced as does loyalty."

The suicide bomber's words -- "The master puts his trust in you as must we all." -- came back to me. If only I didn't have to watch Victoria sitting there, her little fists in her lap! If only I didn't know what went on day after terrible day! -- I felt sick inside but, outwardly at least, I stayed arctic. -- "I haven't the faintest idea what you're driving at, Wolf."

"The same old Sope! Ok, since I've obviously distressed her ladyship, I suppose I'd better go through the formalities with you as well. Where is it?"

"I don't have a card if that's what you mean. Sorry." -- My tongue could have been made of leather.

"No need to feel embarrassed, we know all about your credit difficulties. Bare your left forearm!"

"There's nothing to see. Here, look for yourself." -- I showed him the place where they would have burnt my number had I not walked out of the lowly cattle shed.

He grimaced. -- "Oh well, not to worry. It doesn't change anything. We'll just have to make sure it is done this time, on the forehead perhaps. That's if there's room of course. Here, let me have a look!"

"I'll do no such thing!"

Wolf grabbed me by the hair and pulled me towards him. -- "Well, well! So the jeweller wasn't exaggerating! You're not just a number after all! You'll come to regret that, sonny."

"What's that supposed to mean?"

"Poor sod! You'll find that out soon enough. The point is, whatever your status may or may not be, I can't see you surviving yourself let alone saving anyone else -- unless we can come to an arrangement of course."

"Everything has its price. Go on, try me!"

"Wise boy, Sope! I don't know whether or not you realise it but you've made it onto the big screen as well. Everything that went on in the arcade, clear as day. I'm sure that tells you what's required, doesn't it?"

"It's that damned relic, I gather. Well, unfortunately, I don't have it any more. I lost the thing."

"Come now, Sope, I know you can lie better than that! Lost the relic? That's what those fools told you to say. I'm surprised at you, especially now!"

"But it happens to be true."

"Perhaps you'd care to be explicit then. Where did you lose the Christ Phial?"

"If I knew that, Wolf, I'd tell you. I don't approve of blowing innocent women and children up, much though that may surprise you." –This was the right line to take, I was sure of that, but Wolf wasn't impressed, obviously.

"I'm not impressed, Sope, not in the least. As if that scar wasn't enough, I've read your file, remember. You do realise, I take it, that we have a good many other things to iron out between us quite apart from your role in The Phoenix atrocity. Take the governor, for instance, he's not at all happy and neither is the central bank or the river authority and so it goes on and on. -- Look here, I don't want to be hard on you or Lady Victoria so why not be cooperative? All you have to do is hand over the Christ Phial or take me to where it's hidden and you can go free, the pair of you, with no further difficulties. What do you say, Sope? I would even be willing to talk to His Excellency about … Well, you know what I'm saying."

"Now, that could be interesting! The difficulty is, one can't get blood out of a stone because stones have none to give. If I knew where I lost the relic, I'd take you straight there."

"As you like. We'll come back to it later. Meantime, think about my offer. Think about it -- and by the way, I can see how your mind's working and I agree, it would be a good idea for her sake if not your own."

Captain Wolf turned back and pressed a button on the dashboard. -- "Captain Wolf."

"Receiving you, Captain."

"I should be in camp in around twenty minutes. Arrange for an escort." -- Shoulders hunched like vulture's wings, beak face tilted towards his chest, Captain Wolf settled back to doze.

.

Chapter 8

We turned left onto the coast road above the beach. Victoria's friends, so—called, were still there but playing cricket now. On my side, the dunes and the distant mountains, on Victoria's, long waves of surf rolling onto the white sand.

"Wonderful car!" I said to the driver, feeling the need to distract his attention as I struggled to stuff most of what money I still had deep down behind my seat. From what had been said so far, I would have enough against me without being charged with being a mercenary. Why was Wolf so surprised to see my scar?

"Depends on what you're used to," the driver said. "To me, it's nothing special."

"Oh really! What's our speed?" [All but a couple of bills gone]

"120 mph."

I tried to distract my thoughts by concentrating on an image of the pistons beating up and down so fast they appeared not to be moving but that only made things worse. It wasn't just Victoria, my own future or that cursed relic. I was battling against an urge to give the dozing Wolf a karate-chop. If only I could break his spine! Things would certainly change and probably for the better. On the other hand, what if I made a mess of it? If only I had a knife! -- "What on earth made you join this outfit, driver? Were you drunk or couldn't you get in anywhere else?"

"I signed up for the kicks, simple as that."

"Well, all I can say is, driving at this speed should ensure you get plenty of those."

Swinging right, we headed away from the sea and onto a side road, twisting in and out of the sand dunes at white knuckle speed. It was a miracle we didn't have a string of accidents, including wiping out an old woman on a bike. Picturesque in floppy sunhat and apron, she was cycling towards us as we hurtled around one hairpin, only missing her by an onion skin. As it was, she wobbled onto the hard shoulder and came off, the heavy bike on top of her.

"Stop! Stop! You've hit her!" -- Victoria and I looked back, united in alarm. The old woman clambered to her feet and shook a bleeding fist but to no effect, the driver had no interest in history.

The road climbed steeply up into the foothills but we went on as fast as ever, gliding softly down the gears. There were trees now, mostly conifers, but it was impossible to take them in. -- "This scenery must be a knock out," I said to the driver. "Couldn't you slow down so we could catch a glimpse?" -- If I had a knife or even a screwdriver, I thought, I could stab Wolf in the ear.

"What's up, going too fast for you?" -- The driver looked round with a grin.

"No, no! I love having my vital organs in my mouth."

Streak through a fir plantation, the branches overhead briefly cutting out the light. The momentary change must have released something in Victoria's nervous system. She kicked me in the ankle and hissed at me to shut up.

After the forest, the road flattened out onto a wide plain with the mountains arching the Western horizon, buttressing the sky with their steep sides and rock-bald heads. Higher still, I counted at least eight great birds circling. -- "What are those birds, driver, eagles?"

"They're vultures," Wolf said, coming cat-like out of his doze.

"Ah yes, I can see their heads hanging down -- and I can guess what they're looking for."

"I'm sure you can. It's coming up to feeding time. Know what's on the menu?"

"What?"

He chuckled. -- "It's nothing to get excited about, just hospital waste. There's a big body dump over there."

We swung off onto a single track and I was relieved there wasn't another cyclist in the way. -- "Lucky for you we didn't meet another cyclist."

"What cyclist?" The captain yawned, not bothering to look round.

"You didn't notice but we just missed killing an old woman further back."

"You suggesting we're driving too fast?"

"This isn't driving, Wolf! It's flying!"

Cheeking the driver had been bad enough but, when it came to Captain Wolf, that was too much for Victoria. She kicked me hard and rammed her elbow into my lower abdomen, only just missing my genitalia. --

"Keep quiet! You and your stupid chatter! You're only talking yourself into more trouble."

"That's impossible," Wolf said.

--- * * * * * ---

Inside its security wire, the atmosphere in the camp was pretty much typical of a police state in terminal decline, surface calm covering mounting panic -- whitewashed buildings drowsing in the sun, neat lawns, neurotic flowerbeds, elderly prisoners in the kitchen gardens, a group of men running round the parade ground, armed guards looking on through cigarette smoke, women and children breaking rocks. We purred majestically by, drew up in the shade of some eucalyptus trees and waited while a good-looking cop with the face of a boxer ran over to swing the captain's door open. -- "Escort, sir!"

"Hang on for the sergeant's report and take charge of these two till I'm ready, O'Toole. Just don't let them out of your sight, not for one second, ok?"

"Wait a minute!" Victoria was struggling with the door. -- "I understood we were going to talk in private! What is going on around here?"

"Later, later! I'm in a bit of a rush."

O'Toole frowned in through my side window -- Victoria was already out, hands on hips, staring in fury at the captain's retreating back. -- "Do get a move on, ducky! What's keeping you?"

"I'm waiting for you to open the door, O'Toole."

The door is wrenched open and, the next I know, I'm being dragged out and literally tossed onto the ground, ending up with a nosebleed. I tried staunching the flow but my handkerchief, already stiff thanks to Napoleon's efforts, was useless. Clearly, some sort of retaliation was called for. Wolf had disappeared into administration but the driver was still with us, apparently too busy with his report to notice anything. -- "Sergeant, I want to file a complaint against this man!"

He carried on writing. -- "Complaint about what? Too fast for you, is he?"

"Police brutality! Just take a look at my face!"

"So, you've given him a bloody nose, K-O. What happened?" -- He went back to his paperwork.

"It wasn't my fault, sarge. He was refusing to obey orders. At least that's what I thought it was but …"

"So, Sope, you refused to obey orders given to you by a police officer, did you? That's really bad, that is. That's a flogging offence in this camp, a heavy flogging, and I'll see you get one. -- Now, K-O, just move the pair of them away from here. I'm trying to concentrate. We don't want Frankie coming back and busting his voice-box yet again."

We moved off in the direction of the administration block, Victoria shaking with anger -- Or was it fear? -- and me still trying to staunch the flow of blood. -- "Prisoners, prisoners, halt!"

"You know, K-O, you need to smarten up a bit. We're not prisoners, not yet anyway."

K-O's iron fingers clamped onto my shoulder. -- "We're all prisoners round here, Ducky, so you'll have to make the best of it. Sorry about that flogging charge. If I get the chance, I'll see if I can't get you off. Here, use this." -- He gave me his handkerchief – nice scent!

The sergeant came over waving a sheet of paper. -- "Right, this is for Frankie. I've added the bit about refusal to obey orders."

"Oh that! Let's forget about it, sarge. He'll have more than enough to cope with, poor little sod! I'm willing."

"That's your trouble, you always are. -- By the way," -- he winked at me. -- "Thanks for you know what!"

--- * * * * * ---

"The Captain's going to be tied up some time, K-O," the duty clerk said. "You're wanted urgently over at Z-block. Better take the kids down to the holding-room. Don't worry, I'll see you're covered. Take your time, no need to rush. I'll let you know the moment Frankie's free."

There were three of them who came to take over from O'Toole. – "Why are they out of uniform?" I asked myself. "And why three? They look like special branch."

The men obviously were specials. They smelled like specials and had that stiffly casual look which specials always have. I didn't like it and neither did O'Toole.

"Listen, you lot," he said, "If anything happens to either of these two, you'll have me to deal with." -- He turned to go. -- "I'll be right back, duckie. Try to keep out of trouble while I'm gone and make sure you hold your tongue!"

I'd had dealings with specials before, often and often, and knew what to expect with K-O out of the way. -- "But you can't go, O'Toole! The captain told you to stay with us!" – He shrugged his powerful shoulders and left.

"Ok, let's get on with it," the one in charge said, jamming the door shut with one of the two chairs. "Our corporal friend won't be back for a good while. I suggest you two take the bunk and relax, lie down if you feel like it, I don't mind. Go ahead and make yourselves at home."

I instinctively went to throw myself on the straw mattress, remembered I wasn't yet in my cell and perched on the end instead. Victoria didn't move.

"No need to be alarmed, My Lady," their leader said. -- He could have been a house agent, the way he oozed confidence and synthetic bonhomie. -- "Unlike the infamous Captain and his bunch, we're not in the business of causing grief and suffering. On the contrary, we have only one goal and that is to be helpful. That's why, at some risk to ourselves, we arranged for O'Toole to be called and kept away. Do go ahead, sit next to your friend. He looks lost, poor man."

"I prefer to take the chair, thank you."

"Then, the chair it shall be. -- Get up off that chair, Buz! Her ladyship needs it."

Buz was so obviously a special! He had staggered into the room, loaded down with cameras, leads, a dictaphone and something in a canvas case which could have been an assault rifle or just a fancy tripod. -- "Sorry but I must take the weight off my corns for five minutes! I've been on my feet since last night and, frankly, I'm buggered. -- Hope you don't mind, Miss."

"Umm … no, of course not. It isn't "Miss" by the way."

Mr Bonhomie puffed out his cheeks. -- "Let's get it right, Buz! She's "My Lady" to you from now on, ok? -- Sorry about that, My Lady. You really don't mind standing?"

"I believe that's more or less what I said."

"And what you say goes of course, My Lady, but unless you propose to stand for the next couple of hours, I fear you'll have to dethrone poor, old Buz or settle for the bunk after all."

"Two hours! Doing what, for God's sake?"

"We'll be laying the groundwork for your release. It's a tall order I know but, with luck, we'll just have enough time. Everything creeps along at a snail's pace in this camp. They're all so demoralised, you see, demoralised, unmotivated and bored. Apart from Frankie, Major Stubs and most of the interrogators, psychopaths all of them, nobody gives a damn any more. They know it's only a question of time before the sky falls in and it's too late to change sides so they're just going through the motions. They'd desert tomorrow if they weren't terrified to go outside the camp."

"You should know, you're one of them," I said from the bunk.

"Not I, sir! I'm no friend of the police, quite the reverse in fact." -- His smile was friendly but not so the pale eyes. -- "Allow me to introduce myself. I'm Jack Ready, lawyer. This young lad is Bob, a reporter friend of mine, and that hunk of depression on the chair is Buz, cameraman and sound-engineer extraordinary."

Victoria gasped. -- "A reporter! And another photographer! That's all I need! What on earth are people like that doing here?"

"Like me, My Lady, they're here to place their full expertise at your service. They're a couple of fine lads and brilliant at their jobs as you'll discover should we decide to go public."

"Go public! What are you talking about? I'm here t…"

Ready was gazing through the barred window as if into the future. -- "It may well come to that, I think. In my experience, it's always a good idea in high profile cases to let the man on the clapham omnibus know exactly what the opposition's up to and I'd have thought it would be especially advantageous here. The public will be outraged to learn how you've been detained without charge, interrogated, physically assaulted and Heaven knows what else. There'll be enormous pressure on Wolf to release you, enormous, and public pressure is something he cannot handle. He'll cave in. He always does. So now you know why I've brought these lads along, to see your case gets the highest profile possible, to blow the news black out wide open and to Hell with the lot of them!"

"But the last thing I wanted was more publicity!"

"And, if you still feel that way when we're through, My Lady, that's how it's going to be. You need have no qualms whatever on that score. The last word must always rest with the client."

"But I don't understand. I wasn't aware of being anybody's client. How did you become involved? You say you're a lawyer but this is a police state. There are no lawyers here. The captain told me that himself."

"Lesson number one, My Lady, never believe a thing Captain Wolf tells you. Of course there are lawyers here. As they say, turn over a sod and you'll find a lawyer. We're like the poor, always with you." -- His two friends grinned mechanically. -- "Now, are you sure you won't make yourself comfortable on the bunk? Come along, why not take a perch and tell me what the problems are in detail. Once I've got the facts, I can begin cutting through the legal barbed wire and get you out of this Hell hole."

"If I may say something, Victoria," -- The lawyer and his friends looked at me reproachfully. -- "I would have nothing to do with them. They're police in plain clothes, I'm certain of it. It's a trap, say nothing."

"Oh dear!" -- Lawyer Ready put on a great show of good humour. -- "I'm not doing too well today, am I? What on earth makes you think we're police, young man?" -- He made a sign to Bob. -- "Hope you won't take it amiss if we sit down for this one, My Lady." -- He and the young reporter settled down on the floor and gazed up at me, leaving Victoria standing in the middle of the room.

"It's clear as day," I said. "You engineered the corporal's departure so you have influence, a lot of it. Even more to the point, you look like cops, you behave like cops and you smell of government-issue soap."

"Lesson number two, when a dictatorship is in its death-throes, money can buy pretty near anything except good looks and decent soap. Personal interest takes over from loyalty and everything, but everything, is up for grabs, including as much government-issue as a man's skin can take." [titters] "But you still don't look happy, standing there, My Lady. You won't join us on the floor, I take it."

"Certainly not!"

"But we can't go on like this! Can't I prevail on you to sit down? Please, I beg you, either turf poor, old Buz off his perch or…"

"Oh, if you insist! -- Kindly move across to the other end, Mr Sope. I prefer having the light behind me."

"And so you should, My Lady," the lawyer drooled. "It sets you off, brings out those lights in your hair. Make a super picture! -- Come along, Buz, while she's got that royal gaze in her eyes." [Click, click]

I wanted to go across and smash the camera but Victoria took over. -- "Very well, Mr Ready, I'm prepared to accept your offer. I had intended to contact a lawyer in any case. As for the media, provided it's clearly understood that I retain the sole right to say exactly what is to go out and what may not, I believe they could be of some use to me. -- There's no need to look like that, Mr Sope. I know exactly what I'm doing, thank you. -- Very well, where do you wish to begin?"

Lawyer Ready beamed up at her. -- "I suggest we start with the basics, My Lady. Would you object if I took a look at your card, simply to check that I've got the background right?"

"I'm afraid to say that's impossible. I don't have it at this moment. The captain took it."

"He did! And did he give you a receipt?"

"No, he did not."

Ready buried his face in his hands. -- "Wow! Make sure you get that down, Bob! -- My Lady! What on earth possessed you to hand over your bank card to Wolf of all people? Did he threaten you or was it just that intimidating look of his?"

"It was neither! I would never bow to threats, never! As for his looks, appearances do not impress me in the least. He said, as you did just now, that he needed to see it. I handed it over, quite unsuspecting, and, of course, he refused to give it back."

"Refused! -- Lesson number three, always remember, your personal documentation is just that, strictly personal. If an official asks to see it, let him do so but don't hand it over unless and until he furnishes you with a proper receipt. I'm afraid we'll have to spend a good deal to get that back but get it back we must. In the meantime, allow me to summarise what little we have on you." -- He took a notepad from his pocket. -- "You are Lady Victoria Hunter-Jones of Bingham Hall,

Surrey, England. You have double gold status and unlimited credit. The details of your travel arrangements are classified information."

"To be absolutely correct, my name is Victoria, Mary, Elizabeth Hunter-Jones."

"Ah! Thank you for that, My Lady. Got that, Bob?"

"More to the point," I said, "how do you know all that if it's so private?" [A furious look from her ladyship]

"I'm not sure it's your place to contribute at this point and in that manner, Mr Sope." -- Ready looked indignant. -- "However, if Lady Victoria will permit me to reply, it's the same old story, money."

"Then, if you were willing to pay good money," I said, "You presumably have confidence in your sources. Why all this messing around now?"

"What say you, My Lady? I can answer him if you wish."

"You may carry on." — Victoria was acting more regal by the minute.

"Much obliged, My Lady. -- Let's not be naïve, Mr Sope. I'd have thought it was obvious that where there's political upheaval bordering on chaos, there are likely to be as many selling false information as the truth. I prefer to check and double check everything."

I opened my mouth to ask the obvious question but -- "It won't do," Buz Suddenly announced from the chair. "I must have them close up, next to each other. You won't drum up much sympathy if they look like they can't stand to be in the same room."

"He's right, you know! Would you mind, Lady Victoria? Just for one shot. Move up closer. -- Happy with that, Buz?"

"Better but not sitting like that! It would be a whole lot more convincing if they had their arms round each other. Babes in the wood, that's the line we should take."

"I've had a brainwave," Bob informed us from the floor. "What's his credit rating?"

Everyone, including Victoria, looked at me. I took a deep breath. -- "Officially, I'm not credit worthy. On paper at least, I have no status, courtesy of the governor, who's frightened of me and my politics as are the police, of course."

"Fantastic! That's it!" -- Bob's face was flushed with excitement. --

"The angle must be -- terrorist and aristocratic bride under detention! What do you say, Mr Ready? A dead cert if you ask me."

"Yup! That sounds really good!" -- The lawyer was smiling more broadly than ever. -- "How about 'freedom fighter' for 'terrorist'? -- Don't take the bride bit too seriously, My Lady. It's only a first rough. What counts right now is the general idea. Ok, if you don't mind, cuddle up, just for one second." -- Victoria embraced me stiffly. -- "Rest your hand on her thigh, please. -- That's lovely! Ok, one small kiss. -- Not a peck! Give it a little passion! -- Hold it there!" [A flash, another one] Buz sat back, looking more or less happy, the on-light flashing on the dictaphone.

"Spectacular, Lady Victoria!" Ready gushed. "Absolutely spectacular! You have such talent! I've never seen such acting! You'll see the pictures first, of course, but I don't mind putting my head on a block, you'll go crazy over them as will your public. Now for the piece de resistance, the heaviest gun in our armoury. What is your message to be? Remember, this is for the common man so keep it very, very simple, words of one syllable and right from the heart."

"I wish all of you to know," -- Victoria was sitting bolt upright, an earnest look on her face, the look of a wronged princess. -- "That I remain quite well in spite of everything and that I have not the smallest intention of failing either you or my family or myself. No matter what hurdles I may have to surmount, I am determined to see that this unfortunate affair, by which I mean my unlawful detention, is brought to a swift and honourable conclusion. I am, needless to say, completely innocent of any crime and have done absolutely nothing which could in any way be regarded as prejudicial to the security of the state or reflecting badly on myself or my family. My only fault, if fault it be, is that I am determined to be my true self, not a mere bauble of tradition and privilege, a fairy on the Christmas tree of state. I am, naturally, most distressed to have to inform you and the whole world that my treatment here has been disgraceful. For reasons which I do not wish to divulge at this time, I have become the victim of a cruel plot to blacken my name and deprive me of my birthright. Nevertheless, I remain resolute yet without the least desire for revenge. I love everybody, absolutely everybody, even those who have brought me to this dreadful place!" --

The speech went on for a good three minutes like that and would have continued for much longer if lawyer Ready hadn't spoken up.

"First class, Lady Victoria! We'll supply the conclusion etc later and bring it to you for final editing. I promise you, once that speech hits the streets, perhaps the odd pirate TV broadcast, plus the internet of course, you'll be for ever queen of all hearts. -- Right, you two, we must be off. There's a great deal to be done and quickly too."

"Wait a moment! What about legal advice? I thought you were going to tell me what to do next."

"And so I am, My Lady, just as soon as I've had time to study the legal snares and snags Wolf has set around you. It won't take long. I'll be in touch in an hour or so at latest. It is a great honour to me personally to be entrusted with this case and I will not fail you, of that you may be absolutely certain." -- With that, the three of them were packed up and out of the door before you could say special branch.

"Satisfied, My Lady, or should I say Your Majesty?"

"I don't find that at all amusing, Mr Sope. As for my handling of the situation, I do have some misgivings, of course, but on the whole, I am satisfied -- no, completely satisfied."

"You do realise what you've done, don't you? There's obviously some sort of war going on between Wolf's department and the branch and you've almost certainly involved us in it. I told you not to say anything but, of course, you must know better. Well, you've poured petrol on the fire the captain's busy getting ready for us. If I'm right and those three were from special branch, they'll pass everything over to The Minister with copies to Wolf simply to make him look politically inept. At the same time, they'll leak it all to the media so that Wolf will have everything on his desk within hours but too late for a cover-up. Meanwhile, our position is worse than ever now."

"Nonsense!" -- She tossed back her head and went to the door. -- "Mr Ready's no policeman and neither are the others. What I've achieved is to obtain the help of a good lawyer and ensure I get justice by appealing directly to the people. Whatever you may be, I am an innocent victim caught up in all this and I'm not going to let my enemies get away with it! I'm going to find that monster, Wolf, take back my card then leave this frightful place for ever!"

"Watch out for the guillotine!"

--- * * * * * ---

"Are you awake, Josie?" -- Victoria was sitting beside me on the bunk.

"What the hell happened to my head? It feels like it isn't attached to anything."

"They kicked you when you were on the ground." -- The blind was down and in the dim light, she looked terribly fragile, her face white, hair all over the place and little hands trembling. -- "I've got something for you to drink."

It was a flask of strong whisky, very strong and very long. -- "Wow! Thanks! At least my heart's beating again. What happened to you, what's wrong with your voice?"

"Nothing, it's nothing."

"Nothing? You're not sitting where I am. What on earth's been going on?"

"One of them punched me in the mouth when I tried to bite. That's why my voice sounds like this. My mouth's been bleeding and … and there's a swelling under my nose. See?"

"Who the hell did that? Come on, tell me!"

"I was on my way down the passage when two men came up behind and … and tried to …"

"And tried to what? Go on!"

"You ran up to help me but they threw you down and kicked you in the head. I thought you must be dead!"

I propped myself up on one elbow, pulled her face closer and kissed her on the forehead. -- "Don't worry, don't worry! I wouldn't die and leave you behind! What happened afterwards? Did they…? -- No? Thank God for that at least! Did you see who they were, that so-called lawyer and one of his pals?"

"Not them, no. I'd never seen them before. One of them had carrot red hair. That's something I'll never forget!"

"Were they in uniform?"

"They were wearing boiler suits."

"And what about O'Toole, where was he?"

She put her arm round my shoulders. -- "He's been called away. He's been sitting beside you for at least an hour. He keeps saying sorry and trying to get you to drink his whisky."

"He'll be drinking blood when I catch up with him! What happened to the animals who attacked you?"

"I don't know. O'Toole pulled them off me. The one who kicked you, the red head, ran off. The other one was carried away on a stretcher. -- They were going to use me, Josie! I'm a normal young woman and they were going to do that to me!" -- she broke down, sobbing behind her hands, tears running through the fingers. -- "I feel so, so defiled!"

"It's not you who's defiled, Victoria. You're pure as driven snow. Those swine are the corrupted ones and we'll have them screaming like the pigs they are, honest to God we will."

A few minutes later, Victoria still fighting to get the better of her tears, me feeling like I had a head full of gravel, the lock turned and O'Toole came in. He stood by the door a moment, enormous and child-like, staring across at me. -- "So, you're back with us, ducky! I thank the good lord above! Take your time but, when you're ready, we have to pay the Captain a visit. Don't mind me, tell him exactly what happened, how I left you , everything. I don't care what becomes of me any more." -- He came closer, lowering his voice. -- "The doctor's going to see you but don't worry, he's not one of them."

--- * * * * * ---

Captain Wolf and another man were seated at the long desk, behind them, a view of the weedless garden. -- "Well, well! The Queen of Hearts with her humble knave in train!" -- Wolf's greeting wasn't at all in harmony with his expression. He had a newspaper in front of him and his teeth were bared in a savage grimace. -- "I gather from this rag that I have exceeded my authority, made The Minister a laughing-stock and, as if that weren't enough, that the Queen of Hearts is outraged. Well, so am I! The difference is, I have the means to do something about it." -- He folded the paper and rammed it into his jacket pocket. -- "Come, doctor, let's get on! We'll go through to the other room. Everything you'll need is there."

The two men stood a moment behind the desk, the doctor whispering audibly. -- "But why the devil can't I see them alone? If you feel you can't trust me, you have no business calling on my services. This is not ethical and I do not like it!"

Wolf didn't answer him. -- "Right, O'Toole, stay with the boy -- and I mean stay this time, do you hear? -- You can come along with us, young woman!"

Victoria emerged about ten minutes later. She looked flushed and angry, outraged. -- "I'm going to do something about that man if it's the last thing I ever do! Anyway, it's your turn now. Wolf said you're to go in. At least, you needn't worry about the doctor. He's very kind and professional. I have a feeling I've met him before somewhere."

Kind, he may or may not have been but professional, the doctor certainly was. While the captain perched on a stool in the corner, he had me strip off, minutely examined every part of my anatomy, took my blood pressure, listened to my heart, cleaned up my face, stuck plasters on, everything. He even asked about my mental state, entering the responses on a personality profile. When he was through at last, I left them together.

"You're right about the doctor, Victoria, but what a nasty bit of work friend Wolf is! God grant we don't have to see too much more of him! -- What's his status, O'Toole? He doesn't act like a mere captain."

"I don't know but it's supposed to be something to do with the old man himself."

"The old man?"

"The minister of police. I've never set eyes on him and I hope and pray I never do."

When they came back about five minutes later, the doctor said nothing, just went up to Victoria, bowed, kissed her hand and left looking like he had murder on his mind. Wolf, on the other hand, looked grim and business-like, taking his place behind the desk as if he were about to chair a meeting. -- "Right, we'll deal with the minor problem first. Lady Victoria, let's hear your version of what went on outside the holding-room. Keep it short and to the point. Time, like so much else at the moment, is not on your side."

"I was walking down the passage when two men in boiler suits attacked me from behind. They were going to rape me and when Mr Sope tried to stop them, they kicked him in the head. Thankfully, the corporal came back in time and dealt with them."

"And the famous speech to the nation, you gave that before you were assaulted?"

"I was interviewed by Mr Ready, the lawyer, yes. He and his colleagues seemed very anxious to see that my situation was made known to the general public." She paused. -- "But I now see it might have been better for me to wait until I'd talked to you."

"You're one hundred percent correct there but before we get onto that, where were you going when you were assaulted? Not to bake tarts, I presume"

What a marvellous woman! Victoria responded with such frigidity, her face set in that awesome, haughty expression I knew so well. -- "As a matter of fact, Captain Wolf, I was coming to find you and collect my bank card. You took it from me, if you remember, without so much as asking if I wanted a receipt!"

"Is that so? How awkward for you! -- And where were you while all this was going on, O'Toole? I told you not to let them out of your sight!"

"There was a message I was wanted urgently in Z-block, sir. When I got over there, nobody knew anything about it so I ran back here. That's when I found a couple of men attacking these two and sorted them out."

"Well, you didn't make much of a job of that either, did you? One got away and still hasn't been found and the other's dead so we've no-one to interrogate. Whose signature was on the message?"

"It was a verbal, sir. I didn't think to ask who'd issued it."

"What a bloody fool you are, O'Toole! You've nothing to contribute to this department because you're genetically stupid. You should know that I'm the senior officer around here and no-one else's orders take precedence over mine, The Minister excepted."

"I'm sorry, sir."

"You'll be a lot sorrier yet, O'Toole. Ignoring orders is among the most serious offences in the book. It amounts to mutiny. Know what that means?"

"I do know, sir, yes."

"Then you know what the punishment will be."

"Yes sir. Permission to report to cells, sir?"

"First things first. Tell me, what's all this about Sope refusing to do as he's told?"

"Oh that! That was all a misunderstanding, sir. Sope didn't refuse, he just didn't hear what I said. I got angry and threw him out of the car and when the sergeant asked me what had happened, sir, I … I got it wrong. I'd like the charge dropped, sir."

"Would you indeed? The request is refused. -- Sope, you will be flogged for disobedience probably later on this evening."

"But, sir, he didn't …"

"Don't you but me O'Toole! The sentence will be carried out in a few hours time and you'll be detailed to watch."

"As you say, sir."

"But not as I say," I interrupted, that old, familiar glow beginning to re-assert itself, thanks in large measure to Victoria's example. "In view of what the corporal has said, you have no option but to drop the charge."

"When I want your opinion, I shall ask for it!"

"I'll give it when I feel it's called for whether you ask or not. You can't stop me."

"In Cromwell's army," Wolf told me with a smile, "It was standard practice to burn a hole through the tongue with a red—hot poker."

"Then I couldn't tell you anything at all."

Wolf's handsome face broke into a grin. -- "Nimble little sod, aren't you, Sope? Even so, not nimble enough. The punishment will be carried out … unless, of course, we reach a settlement first. Before we come to that, though," -- he addressed himself once more to Victoria. -- "This interview of yours, why did you give it?"

"I thought that people should know how I'm being treated, of course."

"And it was Ready who set it up for you, the press statement and everything?"

"Yes. I was against it at first but Mr Ready convinced me otherwise."

"Well, it may interest you to know that your friend, Ready, is in reality not a lawyer but the head of special branch or, as I prefer to call it, the dirty tricks division. Captain Ready has used you, as he does everyone else, for his own ends. He has no interest in you whatever or in Sope. His sole interest in all this is to embarrass me and my department and that," -- he thumped on the desk. -- "With Your Majesty's royal assistance, he has bloody well done! Well, I am not amused and, more to the point, neither is The Minister."

"It's not necessary to shout at me, Wolf! And please do stop your mocking! I'm not responsible for every word Mr Ready says to the papers and I certainly never had any intention of embarrassing you or your department! If you remember, I sought you out voluntarily in the first place. I wanted to speak to you about a young man who was involved with Mr Sope and myself in the speedboat affair and who might, as I thought at the time, have been drowned. I took that to be my duty as a citizen. But what happens? I'm unlawfully detained, my card is confiscated and I'm generally treated as if I were a criminal! I'm sorry if your minister friend is upset but that's your fault and maybe Mr Ready's. It has nothing to do with me. Now, please may I have my bank card and someone to drive me back to town? If you do what I ask, I undertake to overlook what has been going on here and publicly to disassociate myself from the article. Furthermore, I undertake to give no more interviews to the media or allow others to do so in my name. -- And you can have that in writing if you wish."

Wolf leaned back in his chair and sighed as if it was a labour of Hercules, this dealing with women. -- "Most generous of you, Miss, but I'm afraid your undertakings come too late, far too late to help you or my department. The damage has been done. What on earth possessed you, presumably an intelligent woman, to pour out this," -- he yanked the paper out of his pocket. -- "This impertinent clap-trap here in this of all rags? The friend of the people, for God's sake! You know, I don't think you have the remotest idea of what's involved both for you and my department. The headline is -- "Freedom fighter and aristocrat bride in detention!". In what follows, the down-trodden masses are informed that you, Lady Victoria, Mary, Elizabeth Hunter-Jones of Bingham Hall, popularly known as the Queen of Hearts, have been detained along with your freedom fighter husband, Josef Sope, in a spectacular foul-up by the security police under the command of Captain F. Wolf. Apparently, while in custody, you've been interrogated for many hours, deprived of food and water, severely beaten and sexually assaulted. -- There's a full page of that, that stuff, Miss Hunter-Jones, one whole page of it!"

"But as I told you, I'm not responsible for every word Mr Ready put in his article. I didn't set out to embarrass you. That was his doing and the motive seems to be that you and he are at war with each other. It's nothing to do with me, nothing. I'm a completely innocent woman who you seem to be determined to humiliate and ... and ruin!" -- her voice broke.

"And you may be a lot closer to ruin than you think, my girl! I've had calls from just about everyone who's anyone in this set up including the governor. I've been asked for an explanation from the palace and even been summoned to a meeting with The Minister! The minister! What do you have to say to that? -- No, don't bother! I can see by your face what's going through your mind and I have to say, I'm not surprised or in the least bit sympathetic."

Her expression had changed completely at the reference to the palace. -- "God! Why is all this happening to me? What am I to do?"

"That, young lady, is as plain as you are! Show what a model citizen or, if you prefer, citizeness, you really are. Cooperate with me in every possible even every impossible way. Now, there's something for you to get that trusting head of yours around!" -- Wolf ripped out a handkerchief, blew his roman nose vigorously then leaned back in his chair. -- "Ok, Sope, while her ladyship tries to fathom the mysteries of the English language, let's turn back to you. I'm going to be absolutely open with you. There are a lot of people, especially Ready, who are using this bloody Christ Phial nonsense as an excuse to stick knives into my back and I'm determined to get it sorted out and quick. You can help me do that and, if you do, as I said in the car, you and she can go free with immediate effect. I can also tell you that, having spoken to several people, I am now in a position to assist you in sorting out your personal affairs."

"If only I could take you to the phial, Wolf, I most certainly would but I cannot. As I've said again and again, I have no idea where the bloody thing's gone. Surely, you can see that I really am telling the truth!"

"What sort of pervert are you, Sope? Are you actually trying to get yourself re--admitted?"

"Of course not."

"And her?"

"Oh to hell with it and you as well! What would you have me do, take you to some place or other at random and tell you to start digging? What would that solve for either of us, for God's sake?"

"So, I've been right all along! You didn't lose the relic, you buried it!"

"Oh come on! That was just an example. I could have used hundreds of others."

"Such as what?"

"Oh, I don't know…"

"There you are, you see! You said "start digging" because that's what I'd have to do. You're nervous, Sope, who wouldn't be in your situation? I ask you a question and you come up immediately with a slick answer which just happens to contain one very specific phrase, "start digging". Maybe I didn't make it clear that as well as the film, we have a record of every word the bomber said to you, including the bit about burying the phial and claiming you'd lost it."

"Then you'll also know that I did my best to stop him blowing himself and everyone else to kingdom come. I didn't want to be part of all this. I didn't ask to be landed with the damned relic and I did not bury the thing, Ok?"

"You did say something about atrocities, yes, but that was because you couldn't be sure who was listening. I think you just lost your nerve, couldn't go through with it. It's not unusual. Anyway, let's just talk about it for a moment. You say you didn't want to become involved but, listening to the recordings, it's perfectly obvious that you are a member of The Phoenix mob and have been for a long time. When did you become involved with them, in prison?"

"That's ridiculous! How on earth could I join anybody or anything from where I was?"

"Quite easily. In fact, more revolutionaries come out of prison than ever went in, if the truth were known."

"I am not a member of The Phoenix's sect and never was as far as I know. I hadn't even heard of the master until..."

Wolf's self-satisfaction seemed to grow with every word I uttered. -- "The master? What a title! And what a man he must be! You'd never heard of him yet you were prepared to carry out his orders, orders not issued directly but passed on by a total stranger, a mere teenager drugged out of his mind! Do you seriously expect anybody to believe a story like that?"

"Why not? I wouldn't be the first person in the history of man to react that way. It's not my fault, it's the fault of this regime and people like you who keep it going. You lot brand me as a nobody, a mindless number, and that's the way I turn out. Someone with the stamp of authority says come, follow me, and I do just that. I'm a simple, trusting soul looking for a place in the scheme of things, pure cannon-fodder and that's how you all want me to be so where's the mystery?"

Wolf burst out laughing. -- "That's what she called you in Teens, wasn't it? How does it feel to be a suit off the peg waiting to be put on? Quite made my day, that did! The problem is, like most ready-made clothes, the description doesn't fit. Sope, I've read through your file from page one. I've discussed you at length with the prison staff, with the governor, with The Minister's secretary himself. There's absolutely nothing I don't know about you and your devious personality. Would you like me to remind you, tell you and your lady here of what you once were, what you did way, way back and what you've become?"

"Go right ahead!"

Hawkish eyes staring at me, calculating. I stared back, hungry to know every detail and to Hell with what Victoria or anyone else might think. In the end unfortunately, he thought better of it. -- "We'll be talking again very soon, I've no doubt. -- Right, Miss Hunter-Jones, since Sope is only interested in himself, you seem to be our best hope. After all, you're not a simple, trusting soul wandering about looking for someone to tell you what to do. As we all know, you're your own woman, clear-sighted, independent-minded, a slave to no-one. It's not preordained that you follow this goat to the slaughter. Who knows, you may even be able to save him as well as yourself. Indeed, depending on the quality as it were of your cooperation, I might even be prepared to give you access to a file I have on Luigi Rotti and destroy the one on you. Well?"

Victoria looked at me eagerly. -- "For my sake, Josef, tell the truth. Did you bury the phial?"

"Oh alright, yes I did."

I thought Wolf was going to throw himself across the desk. -- "At last! Where, where did you bury it?"

"Up my arse."

--- * * * * * ---

It was a small cell with no window and no furniture apart from a wooden bunk. Victoria and I had been taken and locked in there while Wolf went off to answer a summons from on high. We didn't speak at all at first and I wanted it to stay that way but suddenly -- "You know, it's no good, Josef! I can't carry on like this. You must tell them what they want to know, it's the only way."

"Keep quiet! It's very dangerous to speak in these places."

"I don't care! I said in the beginning, you must tell the police exactly what happened but you refused. You told me you'd lost the phial so we went looking for it but that was all a charade, wasn't it? You said, yourself, that you had to bury the phial and that's what you did. I saw you with my own eyes poking about in the bushes when I was on my way to look for Luigi. For pity's sake, tell Wolf the truth and get us out of here!"

"So that's what you were up to, spying on me! Well, you'll soon wish you hadn't! As it happens, I wasn't hiding the Christ phial. I was trying to destroy a camera, the one the photographer used on you."

--- * * * * * ---

Wolf was on the phone when O'Toole took us back to his office. -- "That you, doctor? What's the answer? -- You don't need a training in psychiatry to know that. Of course he's complicated, which of us is not? -- Well, time's something we don't have. This isn't a big deal, you know. I only need a couple of lines for The Minister. Nobody else is going to read it. -- Oh him! He's a left-over from another age, burnt out. The liver condition's driving him over the edge and he's lost all interest in human affairs. --Yes, he'll get a copy of course he will. As the official opposition's representative on the liaison committee, he gets all the papers but he never reads them. We take care to see that the old fool blunders about in a permanent snowstorm of paper. -- As a matter of fact, I do have some, yes. -- No, not just that. This is absolutely fresh evidence, straight out of the horse's mouth – or should I say the mare's? -- That's none of your business. I'm satisfied and that's all that matters. -- You won't? Are you sure? -- Then it can rest on your conscience and to Hell with it! I'll simply call on the traditional technology. -- Of course! She's doubly important now. -- No, don't bother to think it over, I've reached my decision. And, while I think of it, be available at a moment's notice!"

We waited in complete silence and mounting suspense while the captain covered three pages in scrawl, put them into an envelope, closed and sealed the flap. -- "Alright, O'Toole, take them and this over to Major Stubbs's office in E-block. If, as is all too likely, Stubbs is confused or unhappy, say I'll come across and sort everything out as soon as I get back from the river. -- Use handcuffs on these two and, for your own sake, do not let them out of your sight for one, I repeat, one instant. Understood?"

"You're burning the wrong boats, Wolf," I informed the captain.

Chapter 9

Chained together at the wrist, we walked in front of K-O out into the sunlight, across the crunching gravel and into a building about two hundred yards to the North. A drab, breeze block construction, E-block's only claim on the eye, the criss-crosses of sticky paper on the windowpanes, Hitler's kisses to prevent flying glass. I looked back. Just pulling up in front of the administration block, the vintage Bentley with the huge figure of Lord Bertrand behind the wheel.

--- * * * * ---

The brass plate on the door to the major's office had "Stubbs" in fancy lettering and, pinned under it, a notette with a border of pink roses bore the message -- "Operating. All consultations to be rescheduled."

"Bloody hell! Now what do I do?" -- K-O's alarm echoed around the scrubbed passages. "Frankie isn't going to like this! He wants the major to see you immediately."

What a reaction! -- "I don't see why that should worry you. It's nothing whatever to do with you. It's his problem." -- K-O's whisky had been of the very best but its anaesthetising effects had worn off and what with having my head kicked, I had a king-size headache.

"His problem? That's what you think! Oh hell, this on top of everything else!"

"But I can't see why you're making such a thing out of it. It's obvious enough. We'll either have to hang around and wait or you'll have to report back for further orders. You could always let us go free of course. Be easy enough. If you've got a knife, I don't mind cutting you up a bit to make it look good."

"I've got it!" he said. "I'll ring up and ask when Stubbs will be back. She may only be five minutes. I'll have to find a phone, that's the thing."

"What's the matter with you, man?" Victoria shrieked. "We must leave! I can't take any more! Hurry up and get these chains off me! Come on, hurry up! I want to go!"

K-O's huge, boxer's face was sagging with anxiety. "If only I could help you, Miss, I would but it's no use. We wouldn't even make the door. Please don't cry! You'll have to take what's coming like the rest of us. All we can do is pray."

Around echoing passages, past a leaky loo and finally halting beside an ancient telephone mounted on the wall. K-O unhooked the receiver and spun the dial with all the enthusiasm of a blind man trying to defuse a bomb. "Corporal O'Toole here. Put me through to Stubbs's secretary and make it quick!"

"Hello there, sweetheart!" -- The owner of the voice had evidently had his nose amputated. -- "We haven't had a peep out of you since you killed friend Skalk from special branch. That wasn't a bright idea, you know. You're on the wrong side as it is. Frankie Wolf's good as lost the war already."

"Get me Stubbs's secretary, it's urgent! I've got a big problem."

"No can do. The secretary's left, said she would and so she has. -- What's that noise?"

"I don't know. Someone crying in one of the offices. Anyway, let's get back to my problems, shall we?"

"I wonder if you really know what your problems are, sweetheart. If you want my advice, you'll clear out of here while the going's good. The branch has put out a contract already and there won't be any meat left on your face if you hang around."

"I can look after myself." -- In spite of his words, the blood had drained out of K-O's face and his great hands were shaking.

"Being cut up by the branch isn't something even you could handle, K-O. I can tell you that from personal experience. Anyway, you can't say I didn't warn you. Ok, if it isn't your profile you're worried about, what is it?"

"I have to get a couple of prisoners to Major Stubbs but her door says she's operating."

"Is that where the crying's coming from, Stubbs's office?"

"She's not there. I told you, she's operating."

"Could be she's left her baby-minder on. She's always doing it, full blast."

"Bugger Stubbs! What am I supposed to do about these prisoners?"

"I'd have thought it was simple enough. All you've got to do is ring

Fancy Frankie and ask for further orders."

"Not likely! I know what they'll be and I don't want to hear them. When will Stubbs be back from theatre? Don't you have any idea at all?"

"Hang on, I'll have a look." [Sound of papers being pushed around] "Sorry to keep you, sweetheart. It looks like the old bag went down at midnight. She's got her hooks into some top terrorist. Poor bastard! What time she'll be back depends on how long he holds out but it can't go on much longer, surely. My guess is, she won't be more than a couple of hours at the outside."

K-O whistled incredulously. "Two hours! I haven't got half an hour, man! You'd better put me through to Wolf."

Victoria had lapsed into what appeared to be mute despair so we waited with only the leaky loo as background. The news of our arrival had obviously spread and every now and then cops went past, pretending to be running errands or whatever. They invariably took a very long look at Victoria and one or two took photos with their fancy mobiles. At last the operator came on again. "Sorry, K-O, Frankie's not answering, neither is his secretary. What do you want to do, try again in fifteen minutes?"

"I don't know what to do. You'd better put me through to Stubbs, I suppose."

"What! Disturb Stubbs in theatre, you must be joking! Who do you think I am, the bloody minister? Not bleedin' likely! Who are these prisoners anyway?"

"Mind your own business!"

"And after all I've tried to do for you! Don't worry though, it's all over the building anyway. They're saying down here you've got those two kids Skalk and young Zeb were trying to screw. She's a queen or something. Is that right? Lovely joint if you can get your skewer in by the look of it, a royal roast. We've been watching the film down here and I can tell you this, she's a right nymph, that one, goes like a rabbit. Wait till Stubbs gets hold of her!" [gasp from Victoria and the blood thudding in my ears] "How long before they've finished with her, I wonder. Wouldn't mind being a fly on that wall, I can tell you. Tell you what, how about bringing them down here till Stubbs gets back? We'd make it worth your while, cash or whatever. We could even get you out of the camp. How's that for an offer? You'd be clear of the branch! Well?"

O'Toole's handsome, knock about face had changed. It was thunderous. He tossed back the receiver, missing the hook so that it swung impotently from its chord. "Alright, you two, we're going straight back to Stubbs's office. If the cow doesn't pitch up, too bloody bad. They're not getting you down there and that's final!"

--- * * * * * ---

I was prepared for Major Stubbs being a woman but I wasn't remotely ready for what hit my eyes when we walked into her office. I'd been expecting someone of years, quite likely wearing a moustache. Not a bit of it. The young blonde who sat behind the desk, puffing on a Turkish cigarette, was a real lens-smasher. She had everything, beautiful features, the body of a super model and wearing the cutest gold-rimmed specs. If there was any blemish at all, it was in her pixy ears and her eyebrows, cat-arched and setting her expression in a permanent interrogation mark.

"So what are you three after?" -- She blew scented smoke in our faces. "Be quick. I'll be needed in theatre again in fifteen minutes."

On the principle that a good way to save one's hide is to tan someone else's, I spoke up before K-O could get started. "Captain Wolf sent us, Major. He said he was sending you his instructions."

Behind their flashing lenses, the major's green eyes darkened and, jaw jutting, she leaned toward me. "Said that, did he? Damned nerve! Let me have his instructions, huh! I've had nothing but crap from Wolf since I got this posting. Thinks he's the cat's testicles and every woman in the camp's after him. Well, he's got it coming to him, he has." -- She turned to K-O. "Where are these so-called instructions, Corporal?"

The boxer did his best to delay matters. "I think maybe we should wait till the captain arrives, Major. He said you might have problems with them."

"He did, did he? It's O'Toole, isn't it, the one who killed off a special earlier. I tell you this much, O'Toole, you'll be on a meat-hook by sundown if some people get their way. I stress "if". Anyway, while you're still with us, you might as well get this straight -- in my department, other-ranks do not tell their superiors what they should and should not do. Is that clear?"

"Sorry …umm …" [blushes] "Umm…"

"Oh do stop making a fool of yourself, man! You're sorry "Sir". Ok, hand over Wolf's instructions. I suppose I'd better see if I can work out what he's up to this time. I tell you this though, if you've brought these two for questioning, you can take them straight back again. The equipment's booked solid till further notice. With the state of emergency and everything, we're up to our fannies in suspects right now." -- She turned to Victoria and me. "I do hope you'll overlook the general mayhem around here, you two. The fact is, the current chain of command in this camp isn't fit for a lavatory never mind a decent police state. It's chaos around here, I tell you, unimaginable chaos! And my work-load! -- Well, O'Toole, I'm waiting."

K-O drew the papers out of his pocket and offered them up.

"May I say something, sir?" I said. "I don't know what's in those papers but what I do know is, the captain wants to pass us on to you because he doesn't know what else to do with us. As I'm sure you're aware, he's made one hell of a foul-up and now he's got The Minister on his back. He's absolutely desperate, told us as much himself."

Major Stubbs turned her cattish gaze on me. "Foul-up? What foul-up?"

"He's in hot water over our detention, specially Lady Victoria here. It's splashed all over the Friend of the People. Apparently, his phone hasn't stopped ringing since the paper hit the streets, calls from all over, the palace, even The Minister himself. He's in one hell of a panic about it."

"You don't say! And it's all come out in The Minister's favourite reading, has it?" -- She picked up her phone. "Get Captain Ready. -- That you, Jack? Tinkers here. Have you been through the banned papers yet? -- Well, apparently, Frankie Wolf's in big trouble. It's all over the Friend. I presume you've got your copy. What's it all about?"

Major Stubbs held the phone so close it was impossible to hear what friend Ready said but, from her reactions, his account of his own story gave her no end of pleasure. She whistled, clicked her tongue, snorted and at one point, threw back her head and guffawed. When at last the erstwhile lawyer had finished, she smiled at Victoria and me. "So, you are the lady and the tramp all the fuss was about earlier. I thought so. What a pity I had to miss the show!"

"I wouldn't have called it a show, major," I said.

Frosty seconds of silence from across the desk. "Would you like to explain that remark? I don't quite see what you're driving at."

"I was referring to the way our so—called custodians of the law behaved, sir."

"Tell me, Sope, are you really a terrorist or just a fool?"

"Neither as it happens. I'm of above average intelligence and I've never been involved in terrorism. Quite apart from anything else, I don't believe in killing and maiming innocent people in order to punish the wicked."

"You know, I'm disappointed in you, Sope. You have a reputation for being quick witted but if your performance so far is anything to go by, I'd say you're not even half witted."

The major turned to Victoria. "Now you, Queenie, you're something else again! Come on, no need to look so miserable! I think you've done a wonderful job. No wonder Wolf's got it in for you. He'll never survive that marvellous article. Well done! – O'Toole, take that chain off her. The Queen of Hearts deserves better than that, being chained up to a prize goat. She's really, really special!"

Major Stubbs tore open the envelope. "Before I forget, tell me, O'Toole, why didn't you want me to see this report?" -- She leaned back in her officer's swivel-chair, springs creaking somewhere deep behind her knees, and waited.

"It's ok," I said, go ahead. Tell the major what happened with me. Not what Wolf says, what really happened."

"It's like this, sir. There was a small incident involving me and the boy and the captain's over—reacting. Truly, it was nothing."

"Tell me more." [more creaking accompanied by clicks and zinging sounds]

"As I say, sir, there was nothing to it, a bit of playing about between the boy and me, that's all. It was the captain's driver who insisted on reporting it."

"So? You still haven't told me what happened."

"You see, sir, it was like this. When I asked the boy to get out of the car, he couldn't hear on account of the window being up. When I opened the door, he fell out and got a nosebleed. Simple as that. Captain Wolf's having him flogged for disobeying orders. You know what he is, sir."

Stubbs swung harmoniously into an upright, let's-get-on-with-it position and spread Wolf's document before her. "I know what both of you are, O'Toole. Now, let's see what we have here."

We waited in silence as she studied the report, drawing on a fresh cigarette, blood-red nails drumming a tattoo on the desk. When the last pixel of information had been extracted, she yawned and pushed the document away. "Quite disgraceful the way these men throw reports together! Your Majesty should just read through this half-educated babble. And, needless to say, not one word about your super article. Speaks volumes, doesn't it? Anyway, as far as I can make out, he would like me to embark on a course of treatment, what and for how long to depend on how far you're willing to help in tracing a missing relic. Missing relic, a bottle of blood! What damned nonsense all this religion is! I could let him have a bathful of blood anytime. Never mind, as I tell the staff, without religion, most of the jobs in Technical Services would dry up overnight. Faith fuels the furnaces, I always say. -- Well, O'Toole, as I told you, I'm unbelievably over-stretched right now. I simply cannot take on another client today and that's all there is to it. Wolf's problems will have to wait."

"Then what must I do, sir?" O'Toole asked.

I was thunder-struck. What sort of imbecile was this man? What must we do? For Christ's sake! Turn about and march straight out of course. It was too late to do anything about it though, K-O had burnt the bridge as well as the boats.

Stubbs tilted back again and, rocking softly, studied the ceiling. A sunbeam streaming through the window planted a kiss from Hitler on an anatomist's chart of the human nervous system. The beam's depths were crowded with hosts of particles engaged in a soundless gavotte. I sneezed, scattering them, but they quickly crowded together again.

"You have a weak chest, Sope? If so, I need to be told about it."

"My chest is fine right now. It's probably something to do with being kicked in the head."

"And how is the head? It looks like there's a good deal of swelling. Did you lose many teeth?"

"A few broken, that's all."

"As long as the wisdoms are still in. You've had a lot of therapy I see. How did it work, make you feel good?"

"Good? I'm not a masochist, major."

"But you are very hardened, I understand. Tell me, those cigarette burns on your hands, they're very fresh. How did you come by them?"

"To tell the truth, I don't remember. Probably something to do with my getting drunk. There was a fight. That much I do know."

Stubbs turned to Victoria. "Now, what about you, Your Majesty? I see from Captain Wolf's report you had a medical. Was that a thorough examination or just a check up?"

"I'm not prepared to discuss it."

"I see. What about a psychological test? Do you still love everybody in the world, absolutely everybody?"

"I refuse to answer."

"No need to be so snooty! I only ask because if you do love everybody, you must love me. That's a nice thought, you know -- that someone like you could love someone like me. I don't get that every day!"

Victoria's face had its haughty expression again. "All I can say is, if you're hoping to get information out of me, you're wasting your time. I don't know where the phial is and I don't wish to know. All I want is to have my card back and to be allowed to leave."

The major smiled and jotted something down on her pad. "Well, at least we've made a good start. We know now where the weak link is." -- She creaked upright in a sudden burst of good humour. "Right, O'Toole, I'd have to study the medical records but, presuming there aren't too many surprises, I suppose you could bring them back the day after tomorrow. There may, just may, be some machinery free by then. I'm not promising, mind. Unless, of course," -- surveying Victoria and me with her cat-gaze -- "unless we can get it all settled and out of the way here and now. Why don't we do just that? Ok, where is this wretched relic of yours, Mr Sope, or should I say your master's?"

"I don't have a master and as for the Christ phial, I have no idea where the thing is. If I did, I'd take Wolf straight to it, don't worry."

She made another note. "So, Mr Everyman's following orders as always. What about Her Majesty? I understand you actually saw him burying the phial."

"I repeat, I know nothing. Release me immediately!"

"My! I do like this, bargaining with a real lady -- And so good-looking! I tell you what, how about us settling this on our own, just you and me, and to hell with the men including Fancy Frankie and his circus. What do you say?"

Victoria looked at her warily. "What are you proposing exactly?"

"Let's call it a sisterly get-together. I'm sure Your Majesty knows perfectly well what I have in mind."

"I do not! Just be good enough to order my release this minute! I have appointments to keep."

"So Captain Wolf says in his report. Anyway, I probably will let you go if you're cooperative. -- O'Toole, chain Sope to the desk"

"Come on, Ducky, don't fight me! I have to do as the major tells me." -- I was too taken up with Victoria to even think of fighting. I just allowed K—O to chain me to a leg of the Major's desk.

We waited in silence while Stubbs sent off an e-mail from her laptop. When it had gone, she looked at Victoria. "So that's that. Ok, Your Highness, get those clothes off!"

"She knows nothing, major! She just got it wrong about me and the bushes, that's all. It'll all be on the recording. All you have to do is check it out."

"Keep out of this, boy! -- Did you hear me, sister? Get undressed! Don't be put off by these two, they're just men."

"Please!" -- Victoria looked terrified. -- "I don't know anything about the Christ phial and I don't want to." -- Looking at me chained up -- "Sope told the captain he had it for a time but lost it. I don't know any more than that, really I don't. Please, please let me go! We're both women. Please!"

"Come here, you little Madam! You will learn to do as you're told!" -- Victoria inched reluctantly forward. -- "Come on, come on, I want you here, right next to me! It won't hurt, don't be so stupid! You heard what I said, come here! -- Alright, have it your own way." -- She caught hold of Victoria's arm, yanked her close and deliberately dropped the remains of the burning cigarette into her dress. Victoria screamed and jerked back, fighting to get the dress over her head. Stubbs watched, an evil smile on her face. "How very clumsy of me! We'd better make sure it hasn't done any damage. Don't want you burnt as well, do we? – She subjected Victoria to the ultimate humiliation. "Well, I must say, you do appeal, Queenie, you appeal to me very much indeed!"

I tried frantically to break free, yanking on the chain, a wild strength flowing through me. "Stay where you are, O'Toole! And you just leave her alone! Let her go! I'll break every bone in your back!"

"Quickly, O'Toole, he'll have the desk over! Stop him!"

I didn't see what happened. A stupendous blow over my heart like I'd been hit with a chunk of concrete then nothing. When I came to, I was on my back. Victoria was dressed and cowering in a corner. Stubbs was sitting forward, mocking her. "Too bad, Your Highness, but it looks like we'll have to resort to machinery for you as well. -- Where will the captain be at this moment, O'Toole?"

"I don't know, sir, but he's probably back in his office by now sorting things out. -- Oh, look! The boy's come round at last! Thank God for that!"

"So he has! I just hope his heart will last out now. Go on, take the chain off."

I got to my feet and stood shakily in front of Victoria. Stubbs dialled a number, the receiver once more pressed against one pixy ear. -- "Major Stubbs here. -- No, captain, I have not. -- Of course I did. Did you find anything? -- She's not much use to you then, is she? -- Yes but you need much more than that, a couple of words! -- Trouble? From whom, may I ask? -- Oh him! Tell him he can go and -- The what? -- Nonsense! Sope's not worried. In fact, I'm sure he's looking forward to it. -- When we've got through the backlog in the machinery, which includes your special client, I should remind you. -- No, he's not shown any signs at all as yet. -- The day after tomorrow at soonest. -- Bad luck! You should be more careful. I gather you only sent them to me because you're on the carpet over that article in the Friend. -- No, I haven't read it. I don't need to, it's already passed into legend. -- Look here, if it's that urgent, you'll have to clear up your own mess. -- Of course I know why I'm here. The mystery is why you're there. -- I see. Well, as I say, it will have to wait. -- Don't mention it. -- In that case, you should make sure you go about things properly, i.e. with courtesy and due respect. -- There will, will there? Am I supposed to go into labour just because -- No! -- Who? -- Oh alright, but the best I could do would be a preliminary run in, thirty minutes each maximum. -- Very basic, psychological preparation and maybe electrodes -- You don't say! I'll pass on your views on that. He's got chapters on both in his handbook. -- You haven't read it! -- I think you'd better not go to bed tonight. -- No, all the bags are occupied. I can't guarantee success. -- It will have to do or you will have to go without, one or the other. I can't say any more. -- No, as I keep telling you, I'm tied up. -- Ok, but get down there within the hour. I've a couple of things to attend to then I must get on with my own work. -- You may tell your big friend whatever you like. -- Thanks for nothing!" -- She banged down the receiver and shook her curls, making the motes drift and swirl in the sunbeam's eye. "Alright, O'Toole, escort the pair of them over to Z-block and if the Knave of Hearts gives you any more trouble, do not hit him in the groin. Got that? Not between his legs!"

We were just about through the door when it happened. Starting as a distant whimper and building into a wail, an unearthly moan filled the room, so loud it made the windows shiver. Victoria and I stood there, frozen till the noise abruptly vanished. Major Stubbs grinned proudly. "Sorry about that. A very important client, in for major surgery. He's coming round at last. Simple idea, these baby-minders, but oh so handy!"

"But what on earth are you doing to him?" -- Victoria's voice scratched like dry bamboo.

"You just let your imagination run free, my fine lady. See what you can come up with for when we're alone together."

The sound started up again, rapidly swelling into the eerie groan, rattling the room. -- "Josef! Help me, Joe!"

Major Stubbs leapt to her feet. -- "Excuse me, you two, I must fly! This sounds really promising! You and your captain will have to wait a bit longer." -- The telephone rang. She threw herself across the desk. -- "Stubbs. Hurry up!"

"The captain told me to check that you've left for Z-block, Major." -- It didn't bother her this time that we could hear every word.

"Christ! What's the matter with the man? I've only just finished talking
to him!"

"I gather it's a priority, sir."

"And you may tell your precious captain, at this minute, I've got
higher priorities on my plate than saving his bacon. I shall meet him in
Z-block as soon as I conveniently can and not one second before. You
may also say I shall have news for him which he would prefer not to
hear."

We went from the office, boomed our way through E-block and out
into the brilliant sunshine, urgent calls from the major's special client
floating after us.

Chapter 10

The very name "Z-block" has a dismal ring, one which perfectly suited the three-story building which glared down at us from sunless windows as we crossed the river by the iron bridge.

"I bet they don't get too many suicides jumping off this bridge," I said, looking down at the water only a foot or so below, its depths thick with excrement, the remains of creatures long dead, plastic bags, all the rubbish of life parading silently among caps of evil-looking foam to God alone knows where. "If that's the Styx down there, then the Styx stinks." -- nobody laughed.

We moved slowly down the cinder track, Victoria shuffling beside me, massaging her breasts and whimpering, K-O bringing up the rear. Past a clump of trees and up the concrete steps, round the barrel-door and emerge in the reception area of the hospital. There was a riot going on -- a dozen or so orderlies battling to control a mob of patients, most of them still in chains. -- "Make for the desk!" K-O shouted, propelling us through the tumult of white coats, ankle chain and handcuff, arm lock, flying fists, snarl and yelling chaos.

"Name?" -- The woman behind the desk could have been good-looking but for the hole in her skull. The hole was covered by a flap of skin and, as she bent over her work, you could see it pulsing like an enormous eardrum.

K-O came to attention. "Party for Major Stubbs!"

"I asked for your name, corporal, not your description."

"Corporal O'Toole and party."

From somewhere behind the desk, a camera flashed, once, twice, three times. The clerk called up a file on her computer. -- "Ok, take them to the truth room and wait." -- she dropped a set of handcuffs onto the desk. -- "And by the way, you're supposed to have them secure at all times, remember? I don't know what's the matter with you lot, don't you want to get a pension?"

K-O gathered up the cuffs, dithered a moment then linked us together again, wrist to wrist. "Which way, Miss?" -- She waved towards a distant door and we re-entered the pandemonium, K-O behind, driving his two sheep to the slaughter.

"What's happening, Josie?" Victoria whined. "I don't know what's going on! What's this truth room?"

"There's nothing to worry about. It's supposed to be a joke."

"I'm so frightened! Are they going to torture me?"

"No, no! They'll just keep us waiting. It's standard procedure, not too good for the nerves but that's all. You'll be fine as long as you don't take it too seriously. I always put my mind out of gear as much as I can, try not to work out what they're up to, just relax and let it all wash over you – like sunbathing on the beach and listening to the rollers coming in. The thing is not to let it get at you. That's exactly what they want. You won't be on your own, remember. I'll be with you and I've had a lot of experience. We'll be ok as long as you keep calm and do exactly as I tell you."

"But what about when that woman comes? I don't know what to do! I couldn't … couldn't … Oh God! Why me? I don't know where you hid the phial! I only wanted to tell them about Luigi!"

"That's just the problem. Back there in that cell, remember? You actually said you saw me hiding the thing. That place was bugged. They always are. Anyway, now Wolf's convinced we're both in on it."

"Then, why wouldn't you tell him where it is?"

--- * * * * * ---

The swing doors thudded to behind us and we were in the room of truth, dimly lit, windowless and apparently deserted. It was sickeningly familiar and as always my palms and the soles of my feet began to sweat the moment I breathed in the stench of torture, especially the hot wire. Apart from a giant TV screen, machinery and cupboards round the walls, the only furniture was a semicircle of chairs round the truth couch, its straps and buckles trailing.

"One thing we can be glad about," I whispered to Victoria as we sat down to wait, "and that is there's no future for Wolf in all this. He's as much on the rack as we are, worse probably. Special Branch is going to roll right over him while Stubbs and her outfit push from behind. Remember how that creature behind the desk sneered at K-O over the handcuffs? Like his friend, the one with the missing nose, she knows Wolf's finished and isn't scared to say so. He's like a dying dog, that one, the smallest cat can call him names. It isn't just him though, this whole set-up's like a rotten tree. It's riddled with rivalry and self-interest. The only thing keeping it from collapsing altogether is fear and fear can always be exploited. Stubbs said faith fuels the furnaces. What I think she should have said is, "fear fuels the furnaces.". It fuels hatred too, of course."

I was just talking of course, trying to take her mind off the horrifying reality of our position, but it was breath wasted. She'd become like a rabbit staring into the hunter's light, not reacting to any other stimulus at all. I doubt she even registered my voice. Obviously, if I was to break the spell and get her just half functional, I'd have to think of something really spectacular. -- "Guess who I saw as we were going in to see Stubbs. Lord Bertrand!"

"Bertie!" -- her shout of joy rang around the room.

"For Christ's sake, woman, remember where you are! Whisper and try not to move your lips! -- I saw him pulling up in front of admin."

"But why on earth didn't you tell me! Are you sure it was him?"

"Look, Victoria, speak in a whisper or not at all! These walls really do have ears. -- It was Wells. Your friend, Wells, in that Bentley of his. Just as we were going in, I saw him pulling up in front of Wolf's office."

Victoria didn't give a damn. Her face was radiant and her voice likewise. "Then there is hope for me after all! Bertie can do anything! Oh, Josie, I'm going to be released after all! He'll soon have everything sorted out and they'll be forced to let me go. They'll realise they don't have any choice once they know who he is and who he works for. I'm surprised it's not all over already. Perhaps Wolf wasn't in his office and they've had to go and look for him. He wasn't there when the switchboard rang through, remember?"

"But he was when Stubbs rang."

"That must be it, Wolf hasn't come back yet so Bertie's having to wait." -- Now she was too buoyed up. This could be even worse. -- "That's the answer, he's been kept waiting," she said, clapping her hands. "Well, he won't like that, not Bertie. He's so impatient – and so lovable! He's like a little boy. If he doesn't get his own way immediately, he gets terribly cross. He never could stand waiting, not even for me! You'll see, he'll be here any minute!"

"So will a few other people if you don't quieten down. We'd better change the subject. Tell you what, while we're waiting, let's be kids again. Let's pretend we're at the movies. After all, that's all this is really, a dream. In a few minutes, you'll wake up safe and sound in a great mansion and you won't even remember you were here, let alone that Joe Sope was next to you."

"It wasn't a dream, Josie, but who cares! We're leaving and you're coming with us! -- Oh, do come on Bertie! Why on earth is the man taking so long? Come on Bertie!"

"I expect he's having problems with Wolf. Not to worry, he'll come soon enough."

"Soon! Soon isn't good enough, I need him now, now! Come on, hurry up! -- The fool! What on earth's he up to? If he doesn't get a move on, it'll be too late and I'll never get out of this awful place, never! Where are you, Bertie, for God's sake, where are you? Come on!"

Oh God, I thought, this is getting worse and worse. She'll be hysterical, the way she's going on, and what do I do then? Leave her behind? -- I took her arm and whispered softly -- "If you don't calm down, Victoria, I'm going to hit you, ok? Keep quiet! Wells will be here in a minute or two but to be on the safe side, I'm going to see to O'Toole. Ok?"

"I won't have you doing anything stupid, not now! What about Bertie? He'll be here in a minute, you just said so. Don't you dare do anything! You'll only make things worse. You always do! Keep quiet! Quiet, quiet, quiet, quiet, qui." [A sharp slap across the face from me]

I turned to K-O who seemed all this time to have been on another planet. "Look, K-O! Look at her! She's just about over the edge. Look at the poor creature! I can't do anything with her. If you want me or her to have a chance, you must take these bloody cuffs off me."

The boxer buried his face in his hands. "God, I'm sorry for what happened back there, ducky, I really, really am! Stubbs gave the order and my fist just swung out like I was a bloody puppet. It didn't belong to me, honest to God it did not. I haven't been responsible for half of what I do since I got mixed up with this mob. They've turned me into a fucking robot, they have. It wasn't always like that. Believe me. I used to be a good boxer. Everyone said I was the best, a real gentleman, scientific and clean. I never once fouled or deliberately injured a man, never. You wouldn't credit it but I even got to be a sidesman in our local church. Now look at me! I've become a machine. Order me to put a bullet through your head and I'd probably do it. Well, I've had enough! All I want now is to break down and stop working for good. There's no hope left for me now. I've missed my last chance. You hate me, I know you do and you always will."

"Hate you? You must be blind! I don't hate you, quite the opposite. None of this was your fault and, if I survive this, we're going to go around together, permanently. Just hurry and get me out of these cuffs before it's too late. Come on, if you really love me!"

"There's something I must tell you first. Back there in Stubbs's office, I didn't lay a finger on the young lady, I swear to God I did not. Ask her yourself."

"I don't have to, K-O. Just take off these cuffs while there's still a chance for the three of us! -- -- There's a good robot! You've become very special to me, my dear, and we're going to look after each other."

I turned back to Victoria. Her elation hadn't lasted long and she was now in the silent, shaking phase, only her teeth chattering delicately. "There, there, my love! Don't worry, Sope is going to look after you. You can rely on your knave. He's been through what felt like a thousand years of this sort of thing and knows every trick in the book." -- I whispered right in her ear. -- "I'm sorry I hit you, it just had to be done. Anyway, things are beginning to happen, we won't be here much longer."

Victoria's hysteria gave way to a moment of frantic calm. "Josie, where's Bertie? Where's he got to? He should be here by now! I'm terribly frightened! Why did you say they may have taken him as well? What made you say that?"

"But I didn't say that! All I said was, he could be having problems with Wolf. Don't worry, he'll sort it out alright. It's his job. Even if he doesn't, we'll be able to make it on our own now anyway. Try to relax. Exist in the minute and don't let yourself think of the next. Breathe in, count one and breathe out again. In, out, two. In, out, three. Concentrate just on the breath going in and out of your body till you reach ten. Then stop counting and concentrate on what's going on in your mind. If a stray thought comes, start the counting again. It's alright, the air isn't sweet in here but they haven't put anything in it, not yet. Now, I'm going to check if K-O knows what's likely to be next on the programme. We'll move from there."

"What's next on the programme, K-O? What do you reckon they'll start with? Certainly not that stun gun over there on the cupboard."

To my surprise, that business about myself and K-O hadn't all been play acting. As I looked at him, I felt deeply maternal. He looked an absolute wreck, sitting there, shoulders bowed, huge hands clasped in his groin, his battered face a nightmare of anxiety. "Blessed if I know what they'll do," he mumbled unconvincingly, eyes fixed on the floor. "But whatever it is, we'll cope, the two of us, because we'll be together right up to the end. All we have to do is be faithful. I love you, Joe!" -- He planted a hot, wet kiss on my hand.

"I love you too, K-O!" -- I patted his knee then turned back to Victoria. "Not surprisingly, K-O is on our side. Everything's going to be ok."

Victoria had given up on the relaxing exercise. "Where's Bertie? I thought you said he was on his way!"

"It doesn't matter! We're fixed up now!"

"So, you made it up! You didn't see him at all! God, I can't stand it! God! I can't stand it! What's the couch for? You do know what that woman says she's going to do to me?"

"Forget about Stubbs!"

Forget about Stubbs? My imagination was running amuck. And I was appalled at my reaction. The thought of Victoria's rape made me shiver but not just with fear.

For God's sake, I thought, what sort of monster are you, Sope? -- "You must have faith, Victoria," I heard myself saying. "If not in Lord Bertrand, then in me and, if not in me, then in God. He won't let you come to harm. Every hair on your head is numbered, every single one, and that's a wonderful fact to think about."

"Oh Josie, I'm sorry!"

"You have every reason to be sorry, seeing what a mess I've made of it."

"You didn't bring this on me. I brought it on myself. Why, why, why on earth was I so naive? Why did I refuse special treatment? Why are they doing this to me? What did I do to harm them, what?"

"You've done nothing at all! It's just that you got mixed up with me and didn't have the experience to do as I told you. There's nothing extraordinary in that. We all try to go our own way and almost always end up regretting it."

"But that woman!"

"Forget about her! That's part of the price you'll have to pay for being so special, I'm afraid, the cross of the icon. You'll be forbidden fruit and your humiliation will become part of the universal sex-fantasy. People will love and lust after you simultaneously and, above all, they'll long to pluck you down from the top of the tree."

She began sobbing again but with the quiet intensity of total despair. Evidently, the flame of hope which news of Lord Bertrand had ignited was gone for good. "I should never have played the fool in the first place! More than anything else, I should not have encouraged you, Josie. It was just a game, a stupid, conceited game and look where it's got me! It's all my fault. Without me, you wouldn't have gone to The Phoenix arcade in the first place. I've brought so much misery on everybody! I'm cursed, Josie, cursed!"

I drew her closer. What a pitiful, young witch! Even in that place, the pressure of her body made my manhood rise up, blossoming in a bulge of love. "If you're cursed, my lady, then being cursed along with you would be the most wonderful blessing a man could know! I thank God for your little game! It has brought me the only true happiness I shall ever know. As for all this, don't despair. Lord Bertrand could turn up yet and if he doesn't, I'll get you out of here. In the end, good always triumphs over evil. You'll be happy again very soon. Talking of which," -- I brought the moonstones out of my pocket. -- "You'd make me happier than you could know if only you'd accept these. While there's time, please, please say you will."

She put up no resistance and in the gloom, I fumbled the bracelet over her wrist. "There you are, Lady Victoria, free to leave but not to forget. I pray with all my heart I'll be there to see you married one day." -- Burying her face in my lap, she broke down utterly, clinging to my knees and wailing like an infant new-born. Sad but not surprising perhaps that even the best of us should enter life in tears!

128

--- * * * * * --

The three of us had been there in the gloom for easily half an hour, silent -- apart from Victoria's intermittent bouts of weeping -- when the giant screen burst into eye-blazing life and the walls reverberated with mega sound. The scene was the car-park of a huge shopping centre and the ear-splitter, the wail of a police siren back grounding away into the trundle of hundreds of shopping trolleys.

[A sharp, sexless voice-over] "We interrupt our scheduled programmes to bring you live coverage of the inevitable outcome of The Phoenix-terrorism trials. Thanks to the vigilance of The Minister and the untiring efforts of the security forces, the self-styled Phoenix and those of his followers who have survived interrogation, are about to undergo their ultimate humiliation in one of the citie's most popular down-town car parks, one of the many provided by the government to accommodate the ever growing needs of our modern and technologically advanced society. His Excellency, The Minister, trusts that this live broadcast will serve to remind all would-be citizens of the world of the folly of nonconformity and resistance to established and, therefore, just authority. He trusts also that, following the arrest of two further anarchists in the last few hours, this disgraceful chapter in our history will be for ever closed."

For several seconds, the camera panning the scene, hundreds of people pushing their trolleys across the concrete desert towards their distant cars. Then home in on a roped off area alongside a public lavatory. A bearded man waiting, black robes fluttering in the breeze, a naked scimitar cradled in his arms.

Looks like this is going to take some watching, I said to myself and, caressing her hair, pressed Victoria's head down, shielding her ears and eyes as best I could.

A siren blast, the single note bringing the trollies to a halt. Close up of the sword's point, slow slide down the curved blade, voluptuously up, swing left. A dozen men and women, chained together, tracksuit bottoms, herded towards the toilets.

"This I do not like," I whispered to K-O sitting far forward on his chair his boxer's face aghast.

The victims are shepherded to the sacrifice, forced to their knees, raw backs exposed to the blade. -- I wrap Victoria's head in my arms. -- For seconds, the only disturbance, flutter of robes, feeding pigeons, a distant dog, one baby voice. The siren wails and the decapitations begin, methodically, one after another. Always the same technique –blade point stab into the base of the spine, the back arching in agony and head thrown back, screaming throat exposed to the blackening sky. Flash of steel, a soggy, chopping sound, the rainbow of blood. [A commotion beside me] Profile of a severed head raised by the hair, blood dripping from the stump of neck. A universal silence then clamour of car-horns. The face swings round and fills the screen.

"Good God! That's my face!" -- I cannot turn away from the sight of my own face grafted onto the severed head. The eyes are half closed and, as I stare, the mouth falls open, the tongue dribbles blood. "Hi there, Josef! Long time, no see!"

"And no bloody see again! That's it! I've had enough!" -- But it is not enough. A gigantic picture in the sky above the car park, Victoria and Luigi making love. Throb of heavy metal, rhythmical blowing of horns, the severed head smacking its lips.

"Do something, K-O!" -- No response from K-O. He is kneeling on the floor, praying. I leap up, grab the stun gun from the cupboard and ram its point into the base of his skull. Press down on the button, a bright flash and crackle of angry volts. "Sweet dreams, robot! If we ever meet again, it's your turn!" I took the cuffs and chained him unconscious to the couch.

"Victoria, don't just stand there! We couldn't take a robot with us. There'll be enough to do avoiding security. I'll have to leave the stun gun, worse luck, it's too bulky. -- Hang on, though, better take a quick look through his pockets." -- I fumbled around for an instant before finding the knife. "Look at this, a jack-knife! Marvellous steel! Come!"

Seconds later, we were peeping like children up to no good round the door into reception. "The gods really are with us, Victoria!" The hall was deserted except for the clerk and she was deep in paper work.

"Josef! I can't move! I can't move! My legs, they're not working!"

"You'll never move again if we don't get out of here! Keep still, breathe deep and just focus on our escape. Don't worry, she won't see me, her sight won't last that long."

"You're not leaving me!"

"It'll only be for a second. Stay here, just inside the door and, when I call, come flying!"

"I'm coming too!"

"Do as you're told for once, woman! Stay here! A million to one, she has control of the door. If she's startled, she'll clamp the locks on. There's no need to panic, she won't see a thing."

I drop onto my stomach and slither out into the huge reception-hall, making my way softly over the deserted floor toward the desk. I can see the pulsing skin on her bald crown as she bends over her work and move towards it.

Just as well that's not an eye! It's fixed right on me. -- Bloody awkward, carrying a knife like this!

I can hear the scraping of my chest as I snake my way over the floor. I put the knife between my teeth. Suddenly, the wall of the desk is towering above me. Moment of truth. I turn onto my back, grip the knife hard in my left hand and, springing up, plunge the blade down through the pulsating skin. An instant of silence, the beginnings of a gasp then the woman is gone.

"Come, Victoria!" [stampede for the door]

"Hell! The bloody locks are on! Wait!"

There are rows of buttons beneath the desk, some under a film of blood. -- "Buttons, buttons everywhere but which to punch? -- -- Not red, of course not! Whoops!" [a series of camera flashes] "If in doubt, try it out." [a distant alarm] "What's this, green? Green's for go. Right!" -- A friendly buzz from somewhere and we are on our way, round the barrel-door into the bright, clean air, down the steps three at a time and off.

Chapter 11

The alarm sirens came wailing after us as we ran towards the stinking river. Victoria was covering the ground at a tremendous speed.

"God, woman! I'll never keep this up." -- I managed to stay on her heels for the first hundred yards but, as hope took over from panic, she settled into a flowing rhythm which took her way out in front, blonde hair streaming in the wind. What an athlete! The rate she was going, she'd be out the gates and free in no time, assuming she could dodge the sentries. She flew across the iron bridge and I followed to a point where the path made a steep turn to the left. I was taking a short cut across the grass, hoping to catch up, when a wire snagged my ankle and sent me flying. There was a loud report a few yards to my right and, sprawled on the ground, I swear I felt the bullet as it whistled over. I waited a moment for the second shot and when it didn't come, scrambled to my feet. -- Too late. Three of them were just about on top of me. Nothing for it. I gave myself up.

"Well, well, look who we've got here!" -- The warrant officer grabbed me by the shirt. "Welcome back to law and order!" -- He turned to a redhead. "OK, Zeb, we'll deal with the rat. You go after the rabbit and mind you bring her back in working order. -- Alright, Sope, this is for ruining a lady's hair-do." [a punch on the mouth] "And this is for breathing our air." [iron fist in the stomach] "Speak up! What happened to him?"

"Who, who are you talking about?" -- it was all I could do to answer him.

"I'm talking about your boyfriend, Sope. Come on, what happened to K-O, otherwise known as Slaughterman O'Toole?"

"I can't tell you."

"Don't want to, you mean." [another punch on the mouth]

"Ok, ok! He's in Z-block, the truth room."

"And what's he doing there?"

"I don't know. -- For Christ's sake, stop hitting me, man! I do not know what O'Toole's doing or who's with him. He had an accident with a stun gun. He could be dead for all I know or care."

"K-O had an accident with a stun gun! What sort of monkey do you think I am? Come on, out with it, what have you done with O'Toole?" -- After about five seconds of it, the bugger left off trying to shake my eyes out and produced a set of handcuffs. "Alright, have it your own way! Stick out your hands, it's begging time!"

"Up your mother!"

He took the feet out from under me and I hit the ground with just time to slap my hands over my eyes and genitals before the beating started again. I couldn't take it, nobody could have, and they had me screaming out for mercy when the roar of a vintage exhaust burst in on us.

"Stop that, you two! Stop kicking the man, do you hear?" -- Lord Bertrand's snooty face was looking down at us from the open Bentley.

I some how got myself into a sitting position. "Am I glad to see you! God! Feels like my ribs are broken."

"What happened to Lady Victoria?"

"Don't ask me. The last I saw, one of this mob, name of Zeb, was closing on her fast. He's probably on top of her by now. Forget about me and go after them! It's that way."

He wavered for a moment before taking charge of himself and the situation. "Right, you two, get over to Z-block. The riot's started up again and Captain Ready wants you there urgently. I'm taking over here."

"Don't hang around, man!" I said. "Go, go! You could still be in time."

"Keep quiet, Sope, you've done enough damage already! -- Why are you men hanging around? I told you to report back to Z-block. Get going! I'm in charge here."

"That's what you think!" the warrant-officer retorted. "We caught the boy and we'll take him back with us."

His lordship flourished a sheet of paper. "Here, man, read this, if you can read. See what that says? "The prisoners, Hunter-Jones and Sope, are to be handed over immediately to Lord Bertrand of Wells." That's me. And there's Captain Ready's signature countersigned by Captain Wolf. Got it? Now do as you're told and be quick about it!" -- In the end, they did go off but not until they had a signed receipt.

"Right, Sope, now that's over, hop into the back. -- Come on, man!"

"What about Lady Victoria? You do know some specials tried to rape her earlier? Well, I think friend Zeb was one of them."

"I don't need you to tell me what happened, Sope. Get in, we're going back to Z-block."

"Z-block! Then, you're on your own, Mister. I've got other plans, like going to look for …"

Having a couple of hundred pounds of upper-class meat fling itself at you, scoop you up and drop you into the back of a sports car is pretty traumatic, especially coming on top of a beating. I impacted with the hump of the crankshaft and [thump, thump] before I could sit up, his lordship was back behind the wheel. "I owe you one, Sope, remember? Well, watch out because it's still to come. You just stay down there out of sight."

"But you've got it wrong, Mister. I'm not going anywhere near Z-block and I'm certainly not going to abandon her ladyship either."

He looked down at me over the seat. "Look here, Sope, in some ways, I have to admire you. You're like a good many of your class, a plucky fellow and sometimes well-intentioned. However, you're certainly no genius. Nobody's abandoning Lady Victoria. We're going back to Z-block to wait for her."

"And the special? He's tried to rape her once already, for Christ's sake!"

Lord Bertrand suddenly looked fatigued. "Damn you, man! There are times when it is necessary to choose between evils. If I go chasing after them, the chances of getting to her in time are probably zero. It could end up with her head getting kicked in or worse. On the other hand, if I'm waiting back at Z-block, I may be able to save her from worse." -- I didn't argue. The time of reckoning between Josef Sope and Lord Bertrand of Wells had not yet come. Beside, he was probably right.

We skirted the torture hospital, bumped across the grass and pulled in under the trees. It was quiet now and, out of sight of the building, things seemed quite normal until I looked around. About twenty yards off, the naked body of the clerk was hanging from a branch, my knife still in the skull. She had been split open at the crutch and the entrails dangled in a cloud of flies.

"Look at that, Sope!" -- His lordship's horrified expression told me something I needed to know. He had a soft centre. -- "I ask you, what animal would do such a thing? None! That's the work of a devil! There's no sense in it!"

"Isn't there then? You don't recognise the handwriting, that's all."

"And you do, I take it."

"Only too well and the address also."

"Which is?"

"It's a message for Wolf."

"I see. Well, if you've finished reading it, I think we'd better park further down. I wouldn't want Lady Victoria exposed to that after all she's been through, poor creature."

"You go ahead. I'll join you in a second. First though, I'm going to cut that poor woman down."

"Oh no, you're staying where you are!" [An athletic dive round the front seat and there I was, pinioned by the throat] "Forget the knife, you're not stabbing anybody else."

We parked out of sight of the hanging woman. It was one hell of a pity about the knife but at least Wolf would get the message. I found a maintenance manual in the door and, using it on the crankshaft for a pillow, resigned myself to inactivity -- maybe just as well. Quite apart from being screwed up about Victoria, the cumulative effects of all I'd been through were too much. "Just one thing, My Lord, what makes you so sure Zeb will bring her this way? He could easily choose another path or go off with her. She's worth a great deal of money."

"Apart from Wolf, no-one crosses Ready, least of all his own men. As for the way they come, there is some risk but I think it's a small one. This is the quickest way and he'll assume you've been taken back already."

"And what happens when they get here?"

"I'll do the same again, take over."

"There's another thing I don't understand. It's obvious enough why you're trying to get Victoria out of here but I don't see where I come into it. I really did lose the relic, you know."

"Oh that! I've no interest whatever in the so-called Christ phial and, if it comes to that, precious little in you either. You're only part of this because Lady Victoria said she wanted you around, back there in that awful bar. How long you stay will depend on her."

--- * * * * * ---

"Bring her this way. -- Are you alright, Victoria?" -- Lord Bertrand's voice released me from the nightmare in which I'd been struggling to gather up the remains of Victoria. She'd been guillotined and every time I took the head out of the basket, the executioner snatched it from me and tossed it back again.

"And who might you be?" -- Zeb's ugly voice was still about twenty yards off.

Lord Bertrand jumped out and went to meet them. -- "I am Lord Bertrand of Wells. -- What happened to the leg, my lady? What's this fellow been up to?"

"I haven't done anything to her. She's twisted her ankle, that's all. What's it to do with you anyway?"

"Everything as it happens. I've been asked by Captain Ready to take charge of her ladyship. Here's his memo confirming it." [Long silence as Zeb battled to understand the document] "Sure you understand what it says? -- You do? Alright then, leave her with me and get yourself back to Z-block at the double. The captain's waiting for you." -- I raised my head a few inches so I could keep an eye on things.

"And the boy, sir, what happened to him?" -- Zeb was looking around him. I ducked down -- too late. -- "There he is! The little bugger's hiding in your car! Not to worry, I'll soon flush him out of there. Wait here."

On my way to the floor, I had a fleeting image of Lord Bertrand as he spun round. -- "What the hell! -- No you don't!" [A rush of steps and the sharp crack of bone]

I looked out again. Zeb was sprawled on his face, Lord Bertrand standing over him and rubbing the side of his right hand. -- "Quickly, Victoria, into the car with you! We could be in desperate trouble now. Sorry, I forgot! Let me take the weight off that ankle."

"Sope!" -- Victoria looked down in fury as his lordship lowered her onto the floor beside me. "What were you thinking of! You stupid, stupid fool! They'll be here in a minute and it's your fault! Don't you think we're in enough trouble? Haven't I been through enough without you making things even worse? Just look what 's happened now!"

"Right now, the only thing I'm interested in looking at is you! I really wondered if I ever would again. When you're in a state to listen, I'll tell you everything. Such a lot's happened since you ran off and left me to it."

I watched Lord Bertrand gather up the body, jog back with it to the car and bundle it into the front beside him. -- "You two stay out of sight. -- I'll deal with you later, Sope. First though, we must get rid of this carcase. Christ, Sope, if you've brought the branch down on me, I'll see you're strung up if it's the last thing I do!"

We pull up in the middle of the iron bridge, where the water is deepest, and his lordship heaves Zeb over the rail. The splash is loud enough to carry for miles. Roar off again and park behind some trees. -- "Victoria, I only wish I could get the hood up but I can't so we'll have to take the chance and pray they don't notice you. See that rug under the seat? Kindly lie down on the floor and cover yourself with it, him as well. -- Here, take this and if the bloody idiot tries anything on, I don't care what it is, blow his head off."

Under the rug, the exhaust roaring only inches below and the antique springs flexing rhythmically, I was shocked at the state Victoria was in. Something very bad had happened to her since I last saw her running off. She was staring at me with a wild, terrified look in her eyes and the hand with the gun in it shook violently. -- "For God's sake, Victoria, you must try to calm down a bit. Lord Bertrand will have us out of here in a couple of minutes at most. There's no reason to panic! -- No, stop it, you mustn't do things like that with a revolver! Be careful, woman, it's going to go off! Jesus Christ!" [The barrel finally comes to rest against my throat] "What the hell do you think you're doing, woman? Put the bloody thing down!"

"Don't you woman, me!"

"It's going to go off! Put it down! If it does go off, you two will have more to worry about than I will." [Press, press] "Victoria, I'm warning you, take that gun away from my throat or I'll take it from you!"

"Shut up!" -- Her teeth were chattering. I grabbed her wrist. -- "Now you listen to me! You're going to get a hold of yourself and give the gun to me. If it goes off, apart from killing me and Lord Bertrand too probably, you'll bring the whole camp running and you know what that means. They'll take you back to z-block and that'll be it, you won't get out a second time. I promise you, you will not. Now, be a good girl and let me take it. Come on, I don't want to force you. Take your finger off the trigger."

She wouldn't let me take the revolver but at least the panic attack was subsiding. -- "Damn you, Sope! You don't know what I've been through!"

"You mean from Zeb?"

"Don't ever mention that name again! I don't want to hear it, ever! I don't want to talk about him or what happened! I never will talk about what he did to me, never! All I want is to get away from this terrible place and, if you do anything stupid again, I'm going to kill you!"

"And, if I do, you go right ahead. Look, my lady, I know it's difficult for you to get used to the idea but you really are safe now -- as long as nothing goes wrong, like shooting me for instance. Why don't you just hand the gun over to me?"

The car rattled over a rail-track and sped on toward the gate. -- "Let you have this gun! You must be mad!"

With all the excitement and the noise of the exhaust only inches away, we had been talking pretty loudly, more and more so. -- "No, Victoria, I am not mad, quite the reverse. What I'm saying to you makes a lot of sense. If things go wrong, at the gate say, Lord Bertrand will need me to cover him. I know how to use a gun. Come on, hand it over!"

"No I will not! If he needs any help, I can give it to him myself."

"And do you know how to handle a revolver? The way you're going on, I don't think you do."

"Oh that! There's nothing to it, just pulling a trigger and aiming at someone. I'm perfectly capable of killing someone if Bertie tells me to."

The brakes came on an instant. -- "He's right, Victoria, give him the gun. It's a very sound idea and I should have thought of it myself. Ok, now keep quiet and, Sope, don't you be in too much of a hurry, just be ready. The gates are coming up."

I keep watch from under the rug. The Bentley turns right, past administration and on toward the exit. Squint-eye view of open gates, the sound of what could be stones under our wheels or heels clicking. We accelerate away from the camp.

A couple of minutes fast driving on the open road and we pulled in under some trees, engine throbbing. Lord Bertrand flipped away the blanket and took the gun out of my hand. -- "Well done, Sope! Ok, Victoria, you're coming to join me in the front. Here, let me give you a hand." [The only woman I ever loved, gone.]

"And me?"

"You, Sope? You have my permission to make full use of the back seat till we've sorted out what to do with you."

"Frankly, I'd have thought it would be a whole lot safer for both of us to stay under the rug but you presumably know better, My Lord." -- I settled back to read the Bentley manual in wide comfort.

--- * * * * * ---

If it hadn't been for our situation, it would have been a marvellous drive, speeding along in such a car with the hood down, the soft buffet of breeze in my face, the growl of the exhaust and the cheerful whistle of roadside birds streaming past. However, it wasn't a joy-ride and though I managed to occupy my mind with the handbook for a while, the internal combustion engine and general car maintenance didn't present much of a challenge and the real question of the day soon took over.

"So, where are you taking us?" I asked the back of Lord Bertrand's head.

"I'm taking Lady Victoria to safety."

"Which is where exactly?"

"Can't say yet. It's still for Lady Victoria and myself to decide."

"So that's it! In spite of everything I've done, I won't have a say in anything from now on, is that right?"

"If we feel we really can't do without your advice, Sope, we'll ask for it, never fear."

"You know, that's more or less what Captain Wolf said to me back there in his office. Remarkable how like each other you autocrats are! Perhaps you'll be prepared to tell me this then, am I coming along with you or am I about to be ditched now that I'm surplus to requirements?"

"Don't compare me with Wolf again, Sope, there's a good fellow! Since you ask, I don't mind telling you that we're agreed you've paid the fare for a good few miles. After that, it will be entirely up to her ladyship. In the meantime, I think you'd do well to take in as much of this glorious scenery as possible. Who knows how much longer it will last?"

In no time, we were passing through the scented forest then out again among the sand-dunes and back onto the coast road. The tide was just about in, leader waves caressing the beach and clouds of gulls diving in the wake of a fishing boat. -- Could be he's right, I thought. This may well be the last chance I have of looking at a picture of the world as it should be and surely would be if only God's will were done on earth as it is in Heaven -- which it definitely is not nor ever will be.

"I must say, you're keeping very quiet, old girl." -- Lord Bertrand's voice brought me back to current events with a jolt. He sounded like he'd finally settled on his opening move. -- "Don't worry, I wouldn't dream of asking you about what happened. Suffice it to say that I'm very glad to have killed the swine. If only I could do it twice! Tell me, how are you feeling in yourself now we're on our way, happier?"

"You can say that again! I thought I was going to have a break down, especially when it looked like we were going to be taken again. It wasn't really Sope's fault, you know."

"Perhaps not. How's the ankle?"

"Right now, it's not my ankle I'm worried about. Like Sope, I've no real idea what's coming next."

"Then let's discuss just that, what comes next. You know who sent me after you, of course."

"I can guess but who knows, I could be wrong. There are so many possibilities after all! Just about everybody seems to have something to say on the subject of what I do with my life."

"Listen, Victoria, I'm authorised to tell you that he's still willing to go through with it in spite of what's happened."

"Is he really? That's very noble of him! What a fortunate baggage I am! My challis positively runneth over! Along with the rest of the human race, he does know I'm no longer a virgin, I suppose."

"He's seen the film, yes. It makes no difference, all things being equal of course."

"Ah yes, Mr Sope told me all about that! In Latin, it's called "cateris paribus". Sounds better in Latin, doesn't it? Not so threatening. Tell me, what things have to be equal if he's to go through with it in spite of what I've been through myself?"

"There's no need to be sarcastic, Victoria. It's only as you'd expect. Certain undertakings have to be entered into. That's standard practice."

"Oh yes? Undertakings such as what?"

"Oh, you know the sort of thing, religion, confidentiality, responsibilities, that sort of stuff. There are also some tests which have to be gone through of course. Once all that's out of the way, that will be the end of the past and the beginning of Victoria's fairytale future."

"I see! And what tests does he, or should I say his minders, have in mind for me? Not intelligence, I hope. As all the world knows, I'm not intellectually up to much. In fact, I'd be unlikely to score 100 let alone above it. -- Would he, I wonder?"

Lord Bertrand looked round at me. To all appearances, I was fast asleep. "It only has to be confirmed," he said very quietly, "that you're, shall we say, in the best of health. You know the sort of thing, I'm sure."

"No, as a matter of fact, I do not. You mean they want to check me out for foot and mouth or is it just my genes they're interested in, see what colour children I'll produce, things like that? My blood line's pretty good I'm told, at least as pure as his, if not more so."

"Look, I know you've been through absolute hell, Victoria, but please do try not to be so damned aggressive! All this is pure routine, nothing more."

"Aggressive!" -- Her voice went up a fifth. -- "You know what they're really worried about, don't you? They think I might have aids. That's it, isn't it?"

"I'm sorry but I refuse to carry on like this, old girl. Let's just say the tests have become established procedure. There's really nothing to get uptight about. Good heavens! Premarital testing has become commonplace among all classes of society from the top right down to the very bottom. It won't be in the least intrusive, won't take long to arrange and we'll have the results in hours at the outside."

"And will he be taking them too?"

"I wouldn't be in the least surprised. He's that sort, after all, a splendid, splendid man!"

"And that says it all, doesn't it? Tell me, if my results are positive, what happens to me? Do I get packed off to a nunnery or married to one of the tenants? There aren't that many options, are there? Perhaps I'll have to marry Sope."

His lordship took one hand off the wheel and patted her knee. -- "Do stop trying to provoke me, Victoria! As I know you understand perfectly well, the tests are just a formality, ninety nine percent certain. If the very worst were to happen, which it won't, everything would be sorted out privately and to your very great advantage. Now, come along, buck up and thank the lord it's all turning out so well after all. You really have nothing to fear and everything to gain. -- Talking of which, you've been anxious about your card, I'm sure."

"Yes, I have as a matter of fact. On top of everything else that's happened to me since I made my pathetic little bid for liberty, that Wolf creature confiscated my card. What's more, he took great pleasure in telling me that privileges can be taken away as easily as they are conferred. He even addressed me as Miss from time to time, pathetic little beast!"

"The same applies to him as well, of course. Not to worry though, the swine may have stolen the card but that's been remedied. Go on, take a look there, in the glove-box." -- He smiled triumphantly as she brought it out. -- "There you are! I went round and had a word with the governor of the central bank, good friend of mine from way back, and got you a replacement. There really wasn't anything to it."

"Bertie, darling, what a relief! You're too wonderful! I could kiss you!"

"Careful, old girl, you know what I'm like! -- Want me to look after it for you till we're right out of the woods?"

"No, I do not! I'll never let the beastly thing out of my sight, not ever! Now, I'm going to kiss you whether it's safe or not!" [Sudden swerve left, correct right, slow down, go on again]

I have excellent ears and a prodigious memory and all this conversation, especially the bit about her having to marry me, had been chiselled onto my brain as I sat there in the back with nothing better to do than listen and watch and every reason for doing both. – "Well," I told myself, "at least we know for certain where we stand now. I'm not giving up on her though, reluctant bride or not. As for Prince Charming, he may well scoop the pot this time round but the wheel has many turns to go and when it stops for good, it will be humble Josef Sope who breaks the bank."

--- * * * * * ---

Listening in on a conversation in which one has a deep and personal interest is a wonderful time killer. In what seems like minutes, the Bentley is swishing through the outer suburbs of the town. Hardly anybody about, some kids playing, the odd cyclist, a passing truck, one or two ordinary cars. We are approaching a bus shelter when it happens. One of those all-to-familiar motorbikes with two riders appears from nowhere. It is a big machine with yellow plates and as it draws level, the postilion turns his camera on us. Lord Bertrand's reactions are incredibly fast! -- "Not this side of Christmas, brother!" -- Slowing hardly at all, we swerve out and send the bike plus its riders flying. What a shot! The camera vanishes in a burst of splintering plastic under our wheels. [Piercing shrieks from Victoria] -- "Keep your hair on, old girl! It's in for a penny, in for a pound with scum like that. Don't weep for them! They'll soon pick themselves up and go scurrying back to their master, don't you worry."

"But Bertie, look, all those people running to see what's happened! There'll be more and more of them! We're going to be arrested, I know we are!"

"Wells," I chime in from the back, "You're a bloody idiot! I ask you, what a hare-brain thing to do out here in the open street! We haven't got a chance now. Why didn't you just put your foot down, for God's sake?"

"I'll put my foot on you if you don't shut up, Sope!"

"But he's right! In a car like this, we could easily have lost them, easily!"

"That's what you think! That was a branch bike, over a thousand ccs. Didn't you see the plates? There wasn't a chance of losing them. The only pity is I didn't run over them like the vermin they are. Still, at least we've gained some time, enough to fool them for an hour or two, maybe more. They won't find us hanging around if and when they turn up and they certainly won't guess where we've gone."

"What he says makes a lot of sense, Victoria. I didn't know about the plates."

"You surprise me, Sope. I'd have thought with all your experience, you'd know only the branch carry plates like those. Rather stupid when you think about it but there you are. I suppose it makes them feel important – or safe." -- He pressed Victoria's hand. -- "Anyway, let's forget about them, Victoria. What's done cannot be undone. I did what I thought best and there's no point in going over it. We must keep our minds focused on the job in hand."

We turned into the street with Teens and the massive police building. -- "Right," Lord Bertrand said, "I'm going to pull up around that corner. Sope, I want you to look after Lady Victoria for me. I have to drop a few words in someone's ear. -- Don't worry, Victoria, I know what I'm doing and you'll be perfectly safe. This won't take a second. I'll be back before you know I've left."

"But we can't stop here!" Victoria shrieked. "It's right on top of the police building!"

"She's right! What the hell are you thinking of? This must be about the most dangerous spot in the universe for us."

"On the contrary, right now, it's probably the safest."

"You may have your reasons for saying that but I know you're wrong. Whatever your business is, we simply can't take the risk. We must drive on!"

"Get this clear, Sope! You're the problem, you and only you. If it weren't for you and your impertinence, Lady Victoria would never have been caught up in this business. Just do me the kindness to stay put and behave like a responsible adult for a few minutes. I know you can do it, you've shown that once today already. Don't go to sleep or leave the car. We're all relying on you. If you should spot anything looking remotely like a special or a journalist, blow the horn and I'll come running. Now, pass me that briefcase, please, down there by your left foot. -- Right, here goes!" -- He jumped down from the car and disappeared round the corner.

"Did you hear that, Victoria? Try to behave like a responsible adult! Condescending fool! And to think I was beginning to respect the man! If there's anyone behaving irresponsibly, it's him! -- How about a drink? I could easily drop into Teens and get you something. Wouldn't take a second." [No answer] "What about a small screwdriver? -- Oh, as you like! I'm not going to be told how to behave by a stuffed shirt. I'm going to grab a beer and to hell with Lord Bertrand of Wells!"

Noisy as ever in Teens and I had to wait at the bar to get served. I was a bundle of nerves of course but my honour was at stake. At least, the area around the car had been deserted, not a soul in sight, let alone a policeman or a journalist.

Eventually, I got my order and started to stroll back. There was something I hadn't taken into account -- a vintage Bentley parked by the kerb with a beautiful girl sitting in the front will always attract attention. It had just started as I was coming up. Nothing to be alarmed about at first, people standing at a respectful distance, looking, then one or two going up and touching, trailing their fingernails across the radiator grill, feeling the leather upholstery, all trivial enough but it couldn't be allowed to develop. -- "Please don't touch the car." -- I climbed into the back.

A classical-looking child in a purple dress, her black hair braided and up to her nose in a cloud of candy-floss, climbed onto the running-board and thrust the stuff into my face. "Go on, Mr, have a bite!"

"Not now, thanks. Hey, be careful, you're getting that muck all over the place!" -- She returned the candy to her mouth, depositing a large helping on the back of Victoria's neck. -- "Now look what you've done, you messy brat! -- Keep still, Victoria, I'm trying to wipe the bloody stuff off and you're not helping!"

The child burst into tears and was immediately joined on the running-board by her dad. -- "What's up, love? What's he been saying to you?" "He says my candy's muck and I'm messy and I'm not messy, am I dad?"

"You'd better watch it, mate!" – The oaf glared at me as I dabbed away at the back of Victoria's collar. -- "Just 'cause you're a celebrity, riding around in an old crock with a high class bird doesn't mean you can dish up shit to ordinary, working class kids!"

"I wasn't aware I was dishing up anything. Now, please get off the running-board and take that child with you."

He didn't obey, of course, quite the opposite. He stayed right where he was, eyeballing me while the girl simultaneously wailed, stuffed candy foam and lathered her face with it. It wasn't long before we were joined by another man, then another till there were five of them on the running-board, one, in particular, taking a sinister interest in Victoria. He looked a nasty bit of work, greasy hair in a pigtail and skin so white it was obvious he spent most of the day hiding from the light. It started with him running his fingers through her hair. -- "The Queen of Hearts doesn't think ordinary folk are muck, do you, honey? You love us all and we love you. We read the paper plus we saw you on the films, we did, and blimey you're fantastic! Well, I'm looking for a bit of love and I don't mind if it costs a bit extra. How much for the round trip?"

"Leave her alone, Mr! -- Didn't you hear me? I said leave the young
lady alone."

One of Pigtail's companions started up a chant and soon they were all at it, singing out and rocking the car. "The Queen of Hearts, she's our old Dutch. She loves the people very much. The Queen of Hearts, she's our old Dutch. She loves …"

"Pack it in, you trash!"

Pigtail fired off a stream of obscenities and patted Victoria's cheek. "Her Majesty's not interested in the likes of you, are you, Queenie, my love?" [Pale fingers running up and down her face, her throat]

"Lean on that horn, Victoria!"

I leap out with the horn blaring [glimpse of a huge figure running] pull the shit off the car onto the road and kick him up the arse, once, twice. The shockingly muscular body twists around, pale face dancing inches away from mine, rush of tobacco breath. The sun goes out.

Chapter 12

When you've been beaten up a few times, you begin to lose your resilience and it takes more and more time to bounce back. For a good while, I couldn't make it. I just settled back in my seat, drifting in and out of consciousness to the rhythm of my chin bumping against my chest. Strong sun, the feel and smell of warm leather, conviction that my nose wouldn't blow ever again.

Suddenly, I became aware that we had stopped. The car was parked on the hard shoulder. -- "Then, for goodness sake," Lord Bertrand was saying, "tell me what you do want! Are you saying we'll have to drag him along right up to the bitter end?"

"I don't wish to discuss this any further, Bertie. I could never forgive myself if we did such a thing. Quite apart from the morality of it, the poor boy's in no state to fend for himself. Just look at him! It's at least twenty minutes now and he's still unconscious! That happened while he was trying to defend me, remember."

"And whose fault was that? It should never have happened, never! I told the blighter to stay put and, what does he do? He goes running off to that hole, Teens! I tell you this, Victoria, for two pins, I'd cut his throat. Just give me the word! And while we're on that, don't be misled by the way he looks right now. He's dazed, that's all. He'll come round again only too quickly. See those bushes over there? I could dump him behind them. They're not likely to think of searching away from the road. Ten to one, they'll take it for granted he's still with us."

"In that case, it wouldn't help us to throw him out, would it? They'll follow us anyway."

"But of course it would! Don't you see? It's not just what he's done, it's what he'll do next. That's the problem."

"You know, Bertie, you're making a mountain out of a molehill. Alright, he shouldn't have gone off like that but just think how he's stuck by me! Not to mention what he's been through himself! How could you ask me to get rid of him now? I owe him everything. I wouldn't be here now without him. I tell you, Sope is a good soul, the salt of the earth, and I know he would never knowingly let me down. I will not abandon him -- not without really, really good reason anyway."

"Victoria, I was hoping it wouldn't come to this but there's something you should know. Your Mr Sope is no ordinary man. I had a chat with a friend back there in police HQ and I'm convinced that what we've got in the back of this car is a fiend. He may seem more or less normal right now but that won't last much longer. In fact, I think the change has started already. At any moment, he could revert to his true, dark self and, when that happens, I tell you, Jesus himself will tremble! Really, my dear, Sope has a history so awful it gives me nightmares to think you've been alone with him all this while! If we don't get rid of him, he'll bring absolute ruin on us both. I'm certain of it."

"And you're always telling me I exaggerate! A fiend? Don't be ridiculous, there's no such thing. That so-called fiend of yours is, if anything, more like an angel. He's saved me from far, far worse than ruin, believe me. Who is this friend you've been talking to? Do I know him?"

"Sorry, I'm not in a position to answer that, not at this stage anyway. You'll simply have to accept what I'm telling you. Whatever Sope may have done for you, for both of us if it comes to that, he's no angel. He's a monster, a devil, and we have to cast him out or be damned along with him."

"Look here, Bertie! Sope has his faults, obviously he does. No-one could deny that. He tends to be arrogant and unpredictable but I'm positive that's because he feels under-valued and insecure. He's something of a revolutionary but who wouldn't be, the way he's been treated? He can certainly be extremely violent but then so can you. You're both prepared to kill if necessary and thank God you are! Anyhow, the point is, you've got him wrong. Sope is basically a gentle soul who wants to be loved, terribly trusting, easily led and faithful as a dog. He'd do anything for me, literally anything. I simply cannot take what you say seriously especially when you refuse to tell me who your friend is let alone what they told you.

"I cannot say any more, Victoria, not yet anyway. I gave my word. And, quite frankly, it's best you don't know the dreadful details at least until you're safely out of harm's way."

"But it can't possibly hurt to tell me who you've been discussing him with."

"Oh alright, I suppose you're right. The person involved is a very close friend of mine, Sir Percy Stone. you wouldn't know him. Suffice it to say, we've been friends for ever and I trust him and his judgement absolutely. Percy's one of us, very high up with enormous influence and profound inside knowledge, one of the very best."

"Then what's he doing in police headquarters? That's hardly the place I'd go looking for a close friend of yours. And since we're on that, I still don't understand why you had to go there yourself."

"I told you, I had to speak to somebody urgently. As for Percy, don't get it wrong, he's not in the police. He was there on business that's all and we just happened to bump into each other. No need to look so surprised! The political situation here's more complicated than you think. We have quite a few friends at police headquarters as well as enemies. And very useful they are!"

"I suppose you won't tell me what you and this person talked about."

"Not a chance!"

"Was it about me?"

"It's no good, old girl, I'm not saying any more. Just remember though that you're not the only problem on my plate, worse luck."

"Tell me this then, does your friend, Stone, have a position in the government by any chance?"

"As a matter of fact, he does, yes."

"Then I certainly wouldn't accept what he says about someone, especially if it's bad, without cast-iron proof. Everyone knows what professional politicians are like."

"How can you say that, Victoria! I work for the government, remember?"

"Ah yes but, Bertie, you're a diplomat. You're different. You're a genuine old-fashioned lord, a survivor from the age of chivalry. That's part of the reason you're so admired by those with eyes to see and no axe to grind. It's also why you have so many enemies, of course. By the way, in case you've forgotten, it's why I promised to say yes if you were to ask me a second time which, presumably, you won't, not now. It's alright, you don't have to answer. What you must do though is give me at least an idea of what Sope's supposed to have done that we should be so frightened of him. Well?"

"Don't give up, do you? Let me ask you a simple question. What do you think that mark is he carries on his forehead?"

"I don't have to think. I know what it is. It's a wound he received while rescuing innocent men, women and children, including me, in the arcade bombing.

He's convinced it's the mark of The Phoenix but that's only because he longs to be recognised as someone special."

"Sope is special. That burn of his is a brand, the mark of the beast."

Victoria blew out her breath in exasperation. "Look here, Bertie, I've had enough of this mumbo—jumbo! Either we take Sope with us or you go off on your own!"

"Victoria, you may be a very beautiful woman but you're one hell of a difficult one. -- Alright, if I agree to take him for a way at least, what about those tests? Will you go through with it?"

"Alright, where do I have to go?"

Lord Bertrand switched on the ignition and we moved off again. "We're going to a private clinic about ten miles from here. You'll be in and out again in around half an hour. The whole thing will be done by another old friend of mine, Dr McIntosh, a splendid fellow. He saw you in the police camp, remember?"

"And when do I get the results?"

"Oh, that won't take long. After the visit, we'll go straight round to one of my hide-aways, a little club in Chinatown. It's exclusive and very, very safe. We'll have something to eat and I'll arrange with McIntosh for the results to be telephoned through. Everything after that's already set up."

"And Fiend Sope, what about him?"

"No matter what he may have done for you, Victoria, we really must get rid of him as soon as possible. Any further sign of degeneration or of Wolf's closing in and I throw him overboard. Satan can take care of his own."

Silence, they say, speaks volumes. If so, we managed, front and back, to fill a public library over the next ten miles.

--- * * * * * ---

The Bentley came over a slow hill and began to drop down towards a deep water bay, on its Western side, a headland ribboning out into the open sea, to the East, the roofs and chimneys of a fishing-village. The tide was in and the salt spray smelled wonderfully liberating as we drove along the front and out into open country toward the clinic. I'd recovered pretty well by now and was feeling positively buoyant. What a stand Victoria had taken! Pity she had to be so bloody patronising about it but people in her bracket don't really know any better. Even more gratifying, I'd had further confirmation of what I'd known from the first. I definitely was somebody special, very special indeed, and I'd soon discover who that somebody was -- angel or fiend, it didn't matter which.

We pulled up a few yards from the sea wall and, with the braking, Lord Bertrand's briefcase shifted up against my leg. Normally, I would have pushed it back without a second thought but, on an impulse, I bent down and eased the catch open.

"God!" I said to myself. "What a pile of stuff this lord lugs around! -- Books, files, computer discs, palm-top, silver hip-flask, a mobile with camera, everything but a coronet! Hello, what's this, right down at the bottom? -- Heavens! What a lovely, little knife! Just like one of those daggers the Scots use. Oh, I do like this, so comfortable in the hand, such good, bright steel!" -- I stroked my throat with the delicate blade, shivering at its faint caress. "This is far too good for opening letters even if they do bear the royal seal! Right, a fallen angel must be prepared to fight for his rights so here goes!" -- I slipped the skean-dhu into my trouser pocket and felt a huge surge of self-love. In my experience, a good knife is the best aphrodisiac yet discovered. -- The rest of the stuff was dull in comparison but some of it might be useful. I stuffed the mobile into my pocket along with an address book and a kind of diary-come-log book. With luck, I'd be able to work through all that later.

--- * * * * * ---

"I hear what you're saying, Victoria," -- Lord Bertrand was talking in his no—nonsense voice. "but you're coming along with me. There's no need whatever to be anxious. As I told you, McIntosh will be there and I'll stay within calling distance all the time."

"But now we're here, I don't know if I can, Bertie! I've got cold feet. It's so soon after Z-block and afterwards! Frankly, I'm terrified!"

"In that case, all the more reason for getting on with it, old girl." -- Lord Bertrand sounded the horn long and hard. Dr McIntosh, accompanied by a muscle man in the short sleeved coat of a male nurse, came running down the steps. "Lord Bertrand! Good to see you, sir! And you too, my lady! -- Right, sir, what do you want Bossa here to do exactly?"

"I want him to keep an eye on the car, that's all. Any trouble, from any quarter whatsoever," [Meaningful look at me] "and he must do what I understand he's trained to do. If he can't cope, all he has to do is blow the horn. I'll be down in seconds."

If I'd been Bossa, I wouldn't have put up with that. Why should he be talked about rather than talked to as if to address him directly would contaminate his lordship's mouth? Not him, though! He just stood there, respectful and stupid, while the doctor repeated his orders just about word for word. What a goat! Apart from thanking Wells, the only words he uttered during the whole proceeding were "Bless you, my lady!" as Victoria descended fom the car to be led off like a queen to the scaffold.

"Look out! Mind the pussy!" -- My warning came just in time to prevent his lordship trampling on a feral cat as it crouched on the bottom step, dismembering a dove. He skipped over them both and the trio disappeared through the doors, leaving Bossa and me to our own devices.

--- * * * * ---

Bossa and I waited a while in silence, the breeze stiffening off the water and, about two thousand yards out, beyond the rocks, a white launch looking like she was heading out to sea. I waved, the way one does to boats at sea, but got no response. Otherwise, apart from one or two boats at anchor, scavenging gulls and the feasting cat, we were entirely alone.

I settled down to read through Lord Bertrand's address book. What a crowd of people he knew! Half a dozen royals, lords and ladies by the trolley load, sexy women, that sort of person, but also real VIPs, including ministers, civil servants and, most interesting of all, top military and police. One entry in particular hit me in the eye, Captain Franklin Wolf. Who could resist that? I dialled the number. -- "Captain Wolf? -- Ah, the man himself, brilliant! Recognise the voice? -- No, it's not. Try again. -- Not even warm, Wolf. It's your old friend and admirer, Josef Sope. -- Ah! Thought that would interest you! -- Where am I? I'm at the seaside. -- What any sensible person in a Bentley would do, sitting back and looking at the waves. Very pleasant! You'd never believe how bracing it is to breathe air free from corruption. Why not come and give it a try? -- Where exactly? Now, as if I would tell you that, you silly arse! -- No, she isn't. -- I can't tell you because, frankly, Frankie, I do not know or care. -- Why am I ringing? I want to make a deal, that's why. Interested? -- How generous of you! Ok, I'll give it to you straight. At this very moment, I'm holding a charming, little knife, double edged and ever so sharp and I want to remove your spleen. -- That's what I said, yes. You'd never believe it but I came across the knife in a condemned man's briefcase. -- Whose? Tell you later if you have a later. -- So, you've noticed! Yes, I do love them very much. In fact I prefer using cold steel to firearms whenever practical. I find the personal contact so satisfying. -- That's right! She was one of mine. My own work entirely! -- No need, I'll call you again when I've moved round the coast, Wolf, so keep those ears pricked! Grrrrr!" -- All very silly but worth it if only for the adrenalin rush.

I would have given Captain Ready a bell but decided it was too chancy. Instead, I went on hunting through the address book and there it was, an entry for Sir Percival Stone. He had four numbers, home, office, car and mobile. I muffled the phone in my cap and tried his home number, no good, office likewise. I dialled his mobile and he responded immediately. The background noise was exclusive restaurant. -- "That you, Percy, old man? -- It's Bertie. -- Wells, that's right. -- Really? You're clear as a bell. My battery must need charging. Look, old man, sorry to blight your lunch but I need something more on that Sope fellow. -- Sope! You know, Josef Sope. -- But you do! The man all the fuss is about, goes around with Victoria. He's very famous. Surely you remember! You were telling me about him earlier when I had to dash off. -- In police HQ, where else? -- What do you mean, you've never been near the place? -- No I am not and I find the suggestion offensive. -- True but I'm surprised and not a little shocked that you should bring that up now. I've got on top of it, hardly ever touch a drop these days before sunset, business lunches excepted of course. -- That's alright, let's forget it. Look here, maybe I'm a little confused about you and Sope. It couldn't have been in police HQ from what you say. Too much running around, that's my trouble. Anyway, I need everything you can give me on that character and I need it right now, the more negative the better. I'll put in a word for you at number 10, naturally. -- But of course it has to be the truth! -- Hello there! Hello! You still there, Percy? Hello!" [Din of restaurant-life then dialling tone] I put the mobile back into my pocket. Well, how about that!

I was working through the logbook when I became aware of body odour. Bossa was only feet away, piggy eyes fixed on me. My! He did look dumb! -- "What do you want?"

"Just looking, that's all."

"Then how about minding your own business and doing something useful? Go and see to that damned cat. I'm worried someone will trip over it or the remains of it's lunch."

"And what am I supposed to do about it?"

"Get rid of the bloody thing, of course. Go on, I don't care what you do, toss it into the sea, eat it if you want."

True to his goatish nature, the brute went off to do as he was told. I returned to the logbook but keeping one eye on events. Bossa was creeping up behind the cat, one hairy hand outstretched, when the animal spotted him and, taking fright, scrambled bloodily up his arm then streaked off, spitting like a firework. Bossa danced around a while, sucking the arm, then came back, obviously set on taking it out on me. -- "And what are you up to with that book, Sope?"

"Sope! Who do you think you're talking to? It's "Mr Sope" to you, nurse."

"Well, Mr Sope, I know that doesn't belong to you so why are you reading it?"

Bossa leaned into the car and grabbed at the book. I tried to fend him off but he was much too strong so I had to call on the knife. What a friend! Her wicked little point bit into the skin under his right eye, opening it up to the bone, sliced right down the cheek, over the jaw and a good way down the neck. There was blood everywhere. Bossa stood looking at me for a second, eyes wide in terrified surprise, then ran off screaming up the steps and into the clinic. Nothing more came of it so I carried on working through the book and by the time I'd finished the last entry, I knew quite a bit about Lord Bertrand of Wells including a few things he'd rather I didn't. In particular, I discovered that he hadn't been in the police headquarters earlier. According to the last entry, he'd stolen off to ring "the admiral" in private. Obviously, I must keep a closer eye on Victoria than ever. – "Thinking of which," I told myself, "I'd better go over and clear up those pigeon remains. We don't want her ladyship breaking that lovely neck of hers when she gets through with the doctor."

I strolled over. There was a ring around one twiggy ankle so I amputated the leg and popped it into my pocket for luck. Not that it brought me any. Charms are like religious relics, worthless except to the true believer.

--- * * * * * ---

The sea breeze was turning into a storm as I climbed back into the Bentley to wait developments. Wind-stirred waves thudding against the rocks, slapping them like the great potter with his clay, white horses leaping up, falling back, hissing, trying again, occasionally clearing the sea wall with a heavy thump and deluging the road. All at once, the engine noise of a plane flying at low altitude around the coast. As it passed over, I gave a wave and it replied by wobbling its wings. All quiet after that then the launch came back into view, heading straight for the bay. Something was wrong. In that sea, she was already far too close to the rocks for safety. I leaped to my feet, semaphoring danger. -- No response. The boat continued on her course, only about a hundred yards off the outer rocks now. -- "Good God! Look at that! It's the police and they're going to hit any minute. What a wonderful sight! Thank goodness I didn't go inside with the others!"

She was a real spunky boat, sporting a radio-mast and a pennant at the bow. I'm a lover of boats and it put me in quite a state watching her race toward her destruction like a bird, pitching, leaning over the water, her engines pounding. -- "Wow! They must be drunk or else their steering's gone! What can I do to help?" -- There was a magazine in the door-pocket. I furled it into a megaphone, raised it to my lips -- "Full ahead, there! Come full ahead! It's ok, you're clear of the rocks. Full ahead both engines, you lovely people!" -- The wind whipped my words away down the shore but that didn't matter because it was anyway too late. The launch's wild rush was about to come to an abrupt and well deserved end. She staggered once, twice, reared up on her stern, buried her bows in a timber-cracking smack among the rocks then, lying on her port beam, settled into her end.

"Alleluia!" I screamed through my megaphone. "Alleluia!" -- What a yell! Loud enough and wild enough to bring Poseidon running. It didn't waken the god but, as if in response, a blonde in police uniform appeared on deck and made for the rail. No mistaking her! -- "Jump for it, Stubbs, jump while there's still time!" -- I watched the bitch scramble over the rail, saw her slide down like a mermaid into the sea. She fought bravely for a minute or so but the waves over-powered her and her blonde head vanished. What a laugh! I gave a triple blast on the horn in triumph.

Chapter 13

Lord Bertrand came running down the steps of the clinic with Victoria close behind. -- "Sope! What's going on? Why were you blowing the horn? Where's the orderly?"

"See that over there? What do you make of it?" -- Both of them looked out to sea. -- "That, you'll be pleased to hear, is the wreck of Major Stubbs's launch. She was on her way to arrest us but I put a stop to that."

"Stubbs!" Victoria shrieked.

"The fiend herself! I lured them onto the rocks and there you see the results. The monster, Stubbs, is drowned and a good few other devils with her. -- Ok, it took you long enough to come, we'd better get going while we're still ahead of the hunt."

Lord Bertrand was standing looking at the wreck, his cheeks reddening as the full implications sank in. "Hang on a minute! If that's Stubbs's launch—it certainly looks like hers —they must know where we are."

"I'd have thought that was obvious, old man. Come on, don't dally, get those wheels turning or it will be too bloody late."

"But how did they find out? Either it was chance or information. They'd never have come round the coast on the off chance of spotting us so they must have been tipped off. What have you been up to, Sope? Where's that damned orderly?"

"We can go over all that later," Victoria said, climbing into the car. "Let's just get out of here!"

His lordship wasn't listening. "Well, Sope? I'm waiting. How did they find out where we are?"

"Oh alright, I'll tell you. It was Bossa. I'd been dozing and when I woke up, I saw him with a mobile. And guess what! He was talking to Captain Wolf."

"Bossa was talking to Wolf!"

"That's what I said. He was telling him where we were. He said you and my lady had gone into the clinic and he was out here keeping an eye on me."

"But I can hardly believe it! He's supposed to be one of McIntosh's best men. What did you do about it?"

"What would you expect me to do? I went for him, of course. I think I may have killed him but on the other hand he could just be wounded. He ran off screaming into the clinic. I can't think why you didn't notice him."

Lord Bertrand grabbed his briefcase. "One moment, Victoria, I'm going to ring McIntosh." -- He rummaged about for a few seconds. "Where the…? It's gone! Sope, how did Bossa get hold of my phone? You'd better be telling the truth!"

"I've no reason to lie, My Lord, none. It's obvious. He stole it while I was sleeping. Sorry about that but, as you know, I've been through the mill lately. Anyway, it's too late now. My lady's right, we're wasting time. Let's get out of here!"

He went to put the briefcase back and there it was, the address book lying open on the floor. "And how did that get there? I suppose you're going to tell me the orderly was reading it while you were fast asleep."

"There's no other explanation, is there? He must have used it to look up Wolf's number."

His lordship grabbed me under the armpit and hauled me to my feet. "If the orderly worked for Wolf, he would have known the number. Come on, fiend, tell me the truth! Where's my phone?"

"Oh alright, you win. Here, take the thing. The battery's flat by the way."

"You treacherous devil!" – He punched me in the face and swung me down onto the road. – "You were the one who rang Wolf, weren't you?" He shook me back and forth so violently I fell onto my hands and knees. The little knife clattered onto the road. "Good God! -- No you don't, Sope!" He was on to it milliseconds ahead of me and next thing, the point was pricking my throat. "Ok, what's the story this time?"

"I did not ring Wolf. After I'd taken the phone away from Bossa, I tried to find out about my background, that's all. I rang Sir Percival but he said he'd never heard of me let alone discussed me with you or anyone else. It looks like you've got some explaining to do yourself, doesn't it?"

"More to the point, how did you get hold of Sir Percy's number? From my address book! Out with it, Sope! What else did you tell Wolf?" [half kick, half shove with the boot] "Out with it, I said! What else did you tell your master?"

"I rang Sir Percy and no-one else. Among other things, he said he hadn't seen you for ages and had never set foot in police headquarters so how…"

The Bentley bursts into life, Victoria behind the wheel. Lord Bertrand vaults over the door and into the passenger seat. She pauses an instant and I manage to scramble into the back. Squeal of spinning tyres.

--- * * * * * ---

Leaving the bay with its wrecker rocks, we drive at furious speed along the sea road. For a good mile, the full tide has flooded the road and we might as well be driving in the surf, water roaring under the car and streaming out behind, but, in spite of calls to slow up, Victoria keeps her foot down. The Bentley is out of control, skidding about, her rear wheels spinning in the spray.

"Slow down, woman!" I shout again over the seat. "There's going to be one hell of an accident if you don't slow down!" -- Difficult to know if she's heard, eyes fixed straight ahead, both hands gripping the wheel. As for his lordship, he sits huddled in his seat not daring to look.

The coastline arches around to the South and over towards the horizon, rain clouds banking up like gigantic chef hats, one above another in layers of darkening silver. We get clear of the water without mishap but, as we come head on into the salt wind, things are happening under the Bentley's broad bonnet. It begins as we start going up hill, a rapid loss of power, the slowing rumble of tyres then, still a hopelessly long way from the top, death. [Victoria pushing the starter-button wildly but, apart from a mournful churning in the distant engine compartment, nothing]

"Now look what you've done, woman!" -- Lord Bertrand got out, unbuckled the strap over the bonnet and flung it open. I joined him, peering down at the magnificent array of sparkplugs, leads, filters and whatnot through a cloud of steam. -- "What's the diagnosis, My Lord?" -- He was wiping things seemingly at random with a silk handkerchief. I might as well not have existed. -- "If you ask me, you've got trouble with your ignition. The plugs aren't firing. Maybe there's water in the distributor." -- He continued poking about among the labyrinth of cables, adjusted a few screws, did something to the battery then went back and made Victoria shift over. The battery did its best for a good half minute but still no spark.

"Bet you anything you like it's the distributor," I told him.

"Stick to treachery, Sope, something you know all about. If it were the distributor, the engine would have cut out abruptly. The engine did not cut out abruptly. Therefore, it is not the distributor."

"But it wouldn't do any harm to take a look, would it?" -- He went back to wiping and adjusting things a while then, at last, unscrewed the distributor cap. The thing which sends the current round the sparkplugs was wet. He gave me a nasty look, lifted the part out and proceeded to dry it.

"I thought that would be the problem," I said. "When we went through all that water, that's what did it. Makes sense if you only think about it, doesn't it?"

Bang the bonnet down, buckle up again and Lord Bertrand walks stiffly back to his door. I follow. He tries the starter. The battery is desperately low.

"Looks like your battery's really flat now, doesn't it? It would have been a good idea to check the generator as well while you still had some power."

"Alright, Sope! I made an error of judgement. It can happen to the best of us, you as well."

"Better not make another then. Give it thought. If the battery's flat and your distributor's damp, you've almost certainly got water in your generator too. Look," -- I bent down in front of the car and pointed to a hole in the radiator grill. -- "When we were going through all that water back there, you must have picked up the spray through there. Isn't your generator in line with that hole?"

"You tell me."

"Well it is and there's your problem. The battery's all but finished because it's been pushing out current but receiving none."

"God! No wonder the governor wanted to get rid of you! How come you know so much about cars?"

"I don't. It's common sense, that's all -- plus I skimmed through the manual. You should study it. It's packed full of useful information."

He scrambled about under the bonnet for some minutes, got a duster or two from the car, wiped, blew, wiped some more then winded up pulling a starting handle out from under. -- "I take it you read how to use this."

"No but the principle's obvious enough. Want me to have a go?"

He climbed back behind the wheel and within seconds I'd got the knack. Heavy work but, after only a few tries, I was turning the huge motor over quite fast. The trouble was, it didn't bring quick results. Once, a solitary plug fired. Later, two or three and the engine did a lop-sided dance, very slow and depressingly unproductive. [death revisited] Increasingly desperate swings on the handle -- I was pretty well burnt out myself by now. -- And at last things started to happen. Lord Bertrand rammed his foot down and the engine roared into life.

"I've always believed that it's wise to make use of all information at one's disposal and you certainly had more than you needed on that occasion, My Lord." -- I pulled out the handle and sauntered round to my door but, before I could get in, the din of a police car approaching at high speed. No loitering. The old Bentley roared off and, if I hadn't been nimble enough to leap onto the running-board, I'd have been left to face the music.

The giant engine thundering ahead, wind whistling round my ears, just about stopping my breath and tearing at my shirt, we fly toward the top of the hill. [Terrific thump as Lord Bertrand changes gear] The disk of the sun in my eyes and the slipstream battering my face, fighting to loosen my grip on the side mirror, pushing me flat against the door.

"Be careful, Bertie!" -- Victoria's voice penetrates the wind blast like a panic whistle. "He'll be thrown off!"

"To Hell with Sope!" -- The curse comes zinging back. "He can take his chance! Tell the idiot to let go that starting handle!"

"The handle, Sope, drop it!" -- Victoria's shout crescendos through the hurricane.

I'm incapable of dropping anything. Hang on to everything with a dead man's grip! That's the only message my brain can send out. We breast the hill and plunge down the other side, the wind blasting oxygen into my lungs.

"Careful, Bertie, careful!"

"You silly woman! How the devil am I supposed to be careful? They're gaining on us!"

Round a bend and there, only a hundred metres ahead, a piece of agricultural machinery drawn out across the road, cops flagging us down. Lord Bertrand stamps on the brakes. The Bentley jammed, just about tearing my arms out, skids yards and yards, un-jammed, squeals into a spectacular emergency turn toward the grass verge and I'm suddenly flying through the air. Land on top of one special, likely killing him, leap up, hurtle through the rest of them, striking out with the starting-handle to right and left and, in the hollering hullabaloo, flash round the corner, up a narrow pavement by the railway station, round another corner and half jump, half fall down a flight of basement steps.

Chapter 14

"And where do you two think you're going?" I asked, coming up behind them on the platform as they were about to get into a first class carriage. "Not trying to shake me off are you?"

"Thank God! I thought you'd been killed!" -- Victoria was obviously relieved, albeit apprehensive at seeing me. She went to embrace me but, without saying a word, Lord bloody Bertrand of Wells hurried her on board and went to shut the door in my face -- some hope! I sprang into the carriage and settled defiantly on the red leather opposite.

"I suppose you thought you'd seen the last of Josef Sope, Wells, and by the laws of bodies in motion, so it should have been. It's a miracle I'm still with us. Roadblock or no roadblock, you might have stopped a second or at least slowed down so I had a chance to get in." [No answer, just a distant cough and flourish of a national newspaper. Opened up, it concealed their knees like a coverlet] "You said I should take my chance but you weren't prepared to give me one, were you, Wells? Don't bother to deny it. You thought I was asleep but I heard it all, word for word -- "I could dump him behind those bushes!", "I'll throw him to the wolves!". I heard everything, including all that bull-shit your friend, Sir Percy Stone, told you about me. Ha, ha! He didn't say a word of it, doesn't know me from Adam. He didn't seem to know much about Lord Bertrand of Wells either come to that, except that he's an alcoholic." [A savage look but otherwise nothing. Soft rustle of newsprint, sunlight flashing off Rolex watch] "Real, old-fashioned gentleman, aren't we, Wells? A survivor from the age of chivalry. Ha, ha! Lord Bertrand of Wells! Bertrand Haw-Haw more like, Lord of lies!" -- He worked his jaw muscles but still refused to rise. -- "Well, Wells, I taught the police a lesson and I may well be at your funeral too." -- Victoria brushed back her hair, sunlight ricocheting off my bracelet but said nothing.

"Honestly, Victoria, I'm surprised you're still with him after the way he behaved back there. Never mind what he did to me. He was so scared, I bet he soiled his noble pants. Go on, take a sniff!"

Lord Bertrand stood up. "You've gone too far, Sope! That was unforgivable! You're an evil swine and I've had enough of you! Get out into that corridor! You and I are going to settle everything!"

"Fine by me! Where's that knife you took from me?"

"Christ!" -- Victoria jumped up and stood in front of the corridor door. -- "Sit down the pair of you! Haven't I enough to cope with as it is without you two behaving like children? Come on, Sope, apologise! You too, Bertie!"

"You don't expect me to apologise to Wells, Lady Victoria! Everything I say is true. You know, I could have been on a slab by now! Or even back in Z-block!"

"And so could we! Anyway," [Operatic sighs] "Blessed be the peace makers!" -- She seized our hands and got us to link little fingers. -- "Bertie darling, just to please me, apologise for not stopping and for … and for whatever you might have said about him. -- And you, Josef, apologise for everything then sit down and stop feeling so sorry for yourself!"

Wells sighed heavily. "If you say so, Victoria. -- Apologies for any offence caused, Sope. I do in fact have very good grounds for wishing you ill. Even so, I forgive you for what you've been saying and will take the matter no further now. For your future health though allow me to remind you that it's on the whole best if men do not go through each other's private belongings. So there you are, dib, dibs!"

That was more than even I could handle. Ok, I'd been a bit silly but the boy scouts! Obviously, we'd plumbed the depths. I didn't bother to reply, simply leaned back and stared out the window while the two lovebirds smoothed each other's feathers then returned to their nest of top quality journalism.

--- * * * * * ---

In itself, it wasn't a bad journey, lots to look at, certainly. The train raced through old-fashioned countryside, fields with horses in them, cows grazing, isolated farmhouses, the occasional clump of trees, a deep cutting, the swift pulse of a bridge, more fields— one with a mobile home festooned with washing — another cutting followed by a sudden descent into darkness, sunlight bursting in again, flashing off Victoria's hair, glowing round the crown of Wells's straw hat, yet more fields, the occasional factory, warehouse, office block and soon slowing down as we entered the town, slithering through its suburbs, rattling the windows of rail side houses. A little boy with hair just like my own waved to us from an upper window, accidentally knocking a cage with two budgerigars in it off the sill and onto the track. What a wretched way to go, sitting on your perch with your lover one second then mashed under the wheels of progress the next! Poor little creatures, poor little boy as well!

"Wow! Either of you see that?" -- I had talked myself round into a conciliatory mood by then but it was no use. I was back in my kennel, waiting to be called while they'd become more self-centred than ever, sitting there with the paper spread out over their laps.

"It's a pity there isn't a dining car," I said a few minutes later, battling to attract their attention.

"Well, Victoria, it looks like we can breathe again for a while at least. They seem to have done a first class cover-up – worked on His Excellency, obviously. They've managed to keep names out altogether. That'll be Roland's work. Splendid fellow, been tipped for the Foreign Office. Well, he's got it in the bag now, I'd say. We're neighbours, you know, up in the Highlands, little place near Tomintoul, first class for shooting, fishing, golf, skiing, not to mention the old-and-bold of course."

"Tomintoul, you say? The family has quite a bit of land around there, I believe. But look at this for a weekend retreat! Vineyards always sound so delightfully self-indulgent, don't they?"

"I don't know about you two," -- I yapped soulfully on -- "but, frankly, I'm famished. -- Quaint, little town, isn't it? A bit like Sodom but not so picturesque. You two would barely have heard of Sodom, I imagine -- unless you've had it knocked out of you, that is."

"Not really."

"Mind you, it can be death setting up house together. Witness those two lovebirds back there."

"Bertie, let's turn the page. I'm tired of this stuff. Let's read the restaurant crits." [Much jollity, wrestling with noisy newsprint]

--- * * * * * ---

"It's not just the Percy Stone affair," I said later, as we sat around a drinks table in Lord Bertrand's club, waiting for lunch to be served. -- They were reading the international papers now. -- "It goes deeper than that, right down to the bedrock of human dignity, mutual respect."

Victoria scuffed her shoes on the expensive carpeting and shifted about in her red leather chair. -- "Not again! We've been over all that, shut up! We're reading."

"What are you reading about, then? Would you care to let me in on it? -- I am still part of the human race, I take it."

Wells groaned and curled his upper lip. -- "For the moment, you are, more's the pity. Why don't you get on with those peanuts and keep quiet? Lady Victoria and I are otherwise engaged."

"Reading the paper! Call that being engaged? Why the hell couldn't you take her somewhere else where there's music, dancing, people breathing maybe?"

"Because it's usually quiet here and the papers have to be read, that's why. Beside, I'm waiting for an important call. Now, kindly leave us in peace."

"I thought the whole point of having a mobile was being able to take calls anywhere you happen to be. How rude, incidentally, to tell a guest to shut up -- and without even taking your face out of the paper!" -- I brought my fist down with a wallop which sent the bowl of peanuts showering into their laps like confetti. -- "Or to sit and bloody well read when someone's talking to you!"

"Now I suppose he's satisfied," Victoria snapped, shaking nuts from her side of the paper.

"Of course he isn't, not yet." -- His lordship's noble face had turned prefectorial pink. -- "By the way, Sope, you're hardly qualified to give lessons in etiquette to us."

"But I could give you a lesson in something far more important, Wells, sensitivity. I'd have thought someone in your position would be more sensitive to the anxieties of others. Why don't you give your buddy at the clinic a bell? Obviously, Lady Victoria is anxious to hear. Beside, waiting around like this could be dangerous even if the police have been bought off for now. There's a war going on between the specials and security right at this moment, remember."

"Shush!" two elderly gentlemen hissed from their chairs by the library window and a thin man, who'd been studying the same page of an atlas since we arrived, looked up at us.

"Now see what you've done," Victoria whispered fiercely.

"Me! I haven't done anything yet. Your escort, or should I say companion, is the one who should be doing things. Those results must surely be ready by now."

"He's right there, Bertie. Why don't you ring up? I really would like to know."

"Shush!" -- The old men weren't reading, of course. They were reclining with their feet up on a shelf of the floor to ceiling bookcase, trying to snooze. At any moment, the gong would sound and it would be time for them to drag their arthritic bodies down to the dining-room. The thin man brought his atlas over to a table closer to ours.

Lord Bertrand bit his lip from irritation or nervousness and, cupping the mobile in both hands as if it were a secret device, got the number. Victoria and I leaned forward, ears straining. — "Bonjour monsieur," he whispered. "Ici, Wells. -- "En Francais si vous plait. Avez vous fini? -- Oh lord! Oui, of course, oui! I'll call again later, aurevoir."

"What on earth's happening?" -- Victoria's face was white. "Why were you speaking in French? Is something wrong?"

At that moment, a steward in black trousers and white tunic came over the Axeminster carpeting towards us. -- "Forgive me for disturbing you, My Lord. I regret to say that the manager has a small problem, sir."

"So do I, Maxwell. Can't it wait?"

Maxwell waved an ancient hand in my direction. -- "I do apologise, My Lord, but it is somewhat urgent. The staff are getting ready to serve luncheon. Will the young gentleman be at your table?"

"That was the plan, yes. Why do you ask?"

"He is not wearing a tie, My Lord."

"Then, organise one, Maxwell. Is that all?"

"There is also the question of a jacket, My Lord, and of suitable footwear."

Victoria's lips were quivering by now. -- "If you don't mind! What

Maurice Aldridge

did they say at the clinic? Is something wrong? Why won't you tell me? I must know!"

The thin man left off looking at his atlas, adjusted his watch then leaned his chin on his hand, pretending to study the carpet. Lord Bertrand swallowed hard and leaned close -- "I'm afraid there's been a bit of a hitch, old girl. It seems they're waiting for a second opinion. I'm reasonably sure there's nothing to worry about but, just the same, I'll get someone to talk to you as soon as possible. -- You still waiting, Maxwell! For pity's sake, use your initiative, man! Go ahead and fit the fellow out with whatever he needs. There's no need to bother me with trifles. I have far more important things to worry about."

Victoria looked as if she was going to faint but Maxwell soldiered on. -- "Would that it were a trifle, Lord Bertrand, but it is not. I regret to say there is nothing we could do about shoes even if we could solve the other difficulties. For you, I would normally be willing to lend the young gentleman a pair of my own but well you know, sir, there's always some risk, however remote, in wearing another man's clothes and, well, I wouldn't like to say his feet aren't well tended, My Lord, but…"

Lord Bertrand of Wells wasn't listening, he was glaring at me. -- "God! You're just one sodding problem after another, Sope! Clear off before I have you thrown out on your ear!"

"You know, I'm going to do just that and to Hell with the lot of you! Before I do, though, a few things demand to be said. My lady, don't allow yourself to become too stressed by what you've just been told. A second opinion isn't necessarily a sign that things are wrong. It could well be that the results look too good to be true. -- Now for you, Maxwell! You are an affront to the working class! It's sickening to listen to you, the way you toady on with your regrets and apologies, your 'Lord this' and 'Sir that'! Apart from your little manager, who cares a fig whether I'm wearing a tie and jacket or swimming trunks? As for borrowing a pair of your shoes, I wouldn't even if it meant going barefoot through dog's shit. -- And as for you, Wells, I'll spit on you in Hell!" -- So saying, I stood up, tipped my chair over and strode off, leaving them to clear up the emotional mess. The man with the atlas watched me on my way to the lift.

168

--- * * * * * ---

The lift operator, a pathetic creature in scarlet sash and racoon-tail hat, parted his latticework doors apprehensively and stood aside for me to enter.

"Entrance, comrade!"

Pulleys rumbling, the stretch and flex of cables, click, click, bounce and sway, doors folding back. I march over the Italian marble, past the porter's desk, punch the duty bouncer in his breadbasket and run down the steps.

For a good five minutes, I walked briskly down the pavement, muttering to myself and bearing down on people coming toward me, forcing them to give way. One couple stood firm at first but when I barked at them and made a rude sign, they fled. Wonderful how one's inhibitions vanish at times of bloodrise!

"And what the hell are you up to?" I bawled at a tramp digging around in some dustbins.

"He's looking for his credit card, Sope." A voice a lot like my own said behind my left ear. "You'd be doing the same if you weren't so scared of finding it."

"You're actually telling me," I said to the astonished tramp, "that I'm really goat flesh like you! You scum! I'm Josef Sope and I have friends in high places. I know Lord Bertrand of Wells and I've slept with Lady Victoria Hunter-Jones of Bingham Hall, often and often! What do you say to that?"

"Up yours is what I say, mate. You're bad news all round, you are. They should put you in a straightjacket -- and quick. -- Don't you dare touch me! I'll report you to Captain Wolf."

I grabbed him by the throat and shook him. -- "Will you now? We'll soon see about that. Sorry I haven't got a knife but this won't take long. Just try to relax." -- I forced him backward over the bin and strangled him. I was right, it didn't take long, two minutes at most, and could have been less if he hadn't thrashed about so much. When it was finished, I pushed the body into the bin and banged down the lid. The shocking thing was nobody at all attempted to intervene. They either crossed over the road or else just looked the other way. One or two tourists took a snap but that was it. There's modern civilisation for you!

Sad to say, my rant didn't last long after that. Generous dogs like me aren't built for sustained fury. Our guts aren't long enough. We tear out the liver, swallow without bothering to chew, crack open a few bones for a marrow-suck then subside into self-reproach and melancholy.

"Father! Why have you forsaken me?" -- The voice had rushed ahead and taken cover in the mouth of a pretty, little paperboy with a face like my own.

"What a hurtful thing to say! " Forsake" is not in my lexicon, my son." -- I gave the little fellow a pat on the head and the few pieces of silver I had left. -- "Behold, your inheritance! Go your way singing my praises and rejoicing!" -- He held out a paper but I declined. -- "Not for me, my son. That's the past and the past will be put right. Your father is about to take up his cross, turn the other cheek, go back and apologise. Never forget, it takes two to make love and two to fall out. -- Don't weep for me. If you prove worthy, I'll see you're with me in Hell." -- He didn't seem to understand so I kissed him on the left temple and turned back for the club.

It was pretty quick walking, still lots of people about but none of them bothered me. When I got to the dustbins, I took a look just to make sure everything was in order. The bin was empty. Had I made a mistake? One bin's just like another after all. I opened them all up but no, the body had walked off. -- Maybe, I thought, this is a good sign. If not, it's a very bad one.

Only about fifty yards from the club, I saw them coming down the steps to the pavement. Something was up. Victoria was sobbing and Lord Bertrand walked stiff as a heron, unsure whether to cuddle or peck her. They didn't notice me, just went across the road and turned right for the Chinese market. I ran, calling out, but they disappeared into the crowd.

Chapter 15

"House of The Harvest Moon" the sign above the restaurant announced in red lettering. I pushed open the door and entered. What a surprise! Instead of an oriental theme park drenched in the odours of chop suey, sweet-and-sour and jasmine tea, I found myself in a genuine Chinese eating-house, packed with diners, talking at the tops of their voices and clattering their spoons, chopsticks and what-not as if they were driving out the devil. A good-looking waiter came across, skinny as a Shanghai chicken and with a plait of spidery hairs dangling from a mole on his cheek. "I regret to disappoint you, sir. If it is for a take-away, we do not have them. I am very sorry."

"That's perfectly alright. I'm looking for acquaintances, An Englishman in a tweed jacket and there should be a beautiful young lady with him."

"We have many guests, sir. Perhaps you look for Lord Bertrand of Wells and his companion. They are at table number ten. Over there."

Number ten was a corner table, four chairs but set for two. Lord Bertrand was trying to get Victoria to take an interest in the menu but she sat opposite, frigid as a funeral orchid.

"May I join you?" -- His lordship flicked a frosty glance in my direction and retreated behind the menu. As for Victoria, though she said nothing, I could tell from the corners of her mouth she was relieved. I took the empty place next to her. -- "I'm sorry. I shouldn't have lost my self-control back there. I didn't mean to ruin the party." [No answer from him but, under cover of the enormous tablecloth, A gentle nudge from what I took to be Victoria's knee] "In spite of everything," I confessed, wallowing in the delights of self-criticism unwarranted, "I had no right to behave like that. A disgraceful performance! There was no excuse. I behaved like a ... well, I don't mind admitting it, like a revolting peasant. It's one of my problems, saying exactly what I think. I simply forget who I'm talking to. The truth just pours out. Please accept my sincere apologies. It's tough, having to battle for one's rights under what amounts to a caste system." -- Still no verbal response among the merry uproar of the restaurant but I did receive a playful tap on the ankle, followed by the pressure of a calf.

The waiter came over to take our order, mole-hairs floating. -- "Good afternoon, My Lord. It's a great honour to be permitted to serve you again, sir. Good afternoon Mademoiselle, Monsieur." -- I pressed my calf against Victoria's and whispered my thanks.

"What is chef's recommendation today?" Lord Bertrand asked, still acting like my chair was empty.

"As a starter, My Lord, most of the other regulars are having unhatched chicks but the cook has prepared his snake soup in case you should honour us."

"As you know, I prefer soup at the end of the meal but, very well, we'll start with cook's pride and joy. And bring over a half bottle of your finest Gao-lien-Joe. We'll choose the main course later."

"Thank you, My Lord. That's three snake soups and your usual gao-lien-Joe."

"Soup for two. And we'll only be needing two glasses."

"I'm doing penance at the moment, off liquids," I smiled to Hair-floater.

Moments later, a green bottle accompanied by two glasses arrived and, after it, two bowls of an ambiguous, yellow-brown liquid, steaming with the perfume of spices and herbs and with pieces of flesh lurking in the depths. It was all I could do not to dribble.

"Here, take mine," Victoria snapped, putting her bowl in front of me.

"Gosh, thanks! But aren't you hungry?"

"I've had all I can take of reptiles for one day."

I have to admit that, in spite of himself, Lord Bertrand acted with admirable restraint, tucking noisily into his soup and washing every other spoonful down with a gulp of Gao-lien-Joe. Victoria attempted the smallest sip from her glass, spluttered, drew in a raking breath and banged it down next to my bowl. Some fire-water! Having anaesthetized my larynx on one admittedly large mouthful, I banished the glass to a spot on the table's edge. Imagine my surprise when, looking up a few seconds later, I saw it was empty!

"Is My Lord ready to order the main course?" Hair-floater enquired softly.

"I am indeed. Fried gerr with the usual odds and ends, can cook conjure that up for me? You may tell him I would be particularly grateful."

"For you, My Lord, everything is possible. Will that be dog for three?"

"Have you chosen yet, Victoria? Come along, don't be anxious. Everything will turn out alright."

"Dog! You don't surely mean you're going to eat a dog!"

He shrugged his shoulders. -- "I most definitely am, yes. If you don't want to join me, I suggest you try the chicken and bean-sprouts with sweet and sour. It's not the usual Western junk, I can assure you of that. It's a speciality of the house."

"And the young gentleman?" -- Hair-floater looked slightly anxious.

"I'm sitting the main course out, thank you."

While we waited, I sat back and allowed the smells, the noise and Victoria's forgiveness to wash over me. -- "How were your results?" I asked Victoria, remembering how she'd looked coming down the steps of the club.

"Mind your own business, Sope!" [The first words he'd wasted on me!]

"No need to be abusive, Wells! I was only showing an interest. Anyway, I was talking to Lady Victoria, not you."

"Lady Victoria can do without your interest."

The atmosphere round table ten was positively Arctic. Having nothing to eat, I was left with nothing to do but watch how they got on. The chopsticks in The House of The Harvest Moon were not blunt at both ends, as is most common in China, but sharpened in the Japanese style to stiletto-points. Lord Bertrand was clearly a master in their use, spearing the roundels of dog flesh, swishing them around his bowl and transferring them to his mouth in delicate movements which made one think of graceful surgery. Victoria, by contrast, looked untypically awkward, picking ineffectually at her food as if she were trying to lance a boil without piercing the skin. I would have passed her a spoon but a peculiar thing happened. Wells was taking a gulp of fire-water when a hand crept onto the table on his side, slid swiftly across to his bowl, snatched a gobbet of meat and vanished. I gasped but said nothing.

"Here," Victoria said, interpreting my intake of breath as a sob of hunger and dumping a mound of chicken pieces in front of me. Well, perhaps I was hungrier than I'd realised. It's not unknown for a man to hallucinate when his blood sugar is at rock bottom. I seized a pair of sticks and, driving them into the meat, got to work. Barely half a dozen hunks down and it happened a second time. The hand crept up, slid crab-wise over the cloth, fumbled feverishly among My Lord's dog pieces then made off with one between thumb and forefinger. -- "Hell's teeth!" -- I couldn't hold it back.

"What is it this time?" -- he gulped down yet another glass of Oriental fire-water.

"There's someone stealing from your bowl!"

This was obviously not the first time Lord Bertrand had been robbed at table. No exclamation of disbelief or shock, he just dived under the table, howling with rage, Japanese chopsticks stabbing. A violent scrummage around my knees then a handsome youth in rags squirmed into the open, almost toppling Victoria off her chair. As he turned for the door, pigtail flying and bloody chopstick protruding from the right ear, I saw him tear the moonstone bracelet from her wrist.

"Thief!" I shrieked and leaped after him.

The pair of us tumbled out the door practically in tandem and I would certainly have brought him down if it hadn't been for the torrent of passers by. At that moment, the entire human race seemed to be on the move, surging down the pavement six deep at least and toe-to-heel. Thief dived into the flood like a rat plunging into sewage. -- "Thief!" I shouted in the bedlam and threw myself after him. For an instant, he disappeared in front of a square-rigged woman in a boiler suit and stiletto heels but I slithered round her and, reaching out, managed to catch hold of his trousers. -- "Thief! I've got you, you little bastard!"

Got him, I had indeed but bring him to a halt, I could not. Nothing could have stood in that heaving, shoving tumult. In Africa, wild deer used to gallop off in their hundreds of thousands over the plains to throw themselves into the sea as lemmings still do. It's much the same with the human race. If you're a little buck caught up somewhere in the middle, there's no opting out of the stampede down hill. That's certainly how it was for Thief and me. Humanity was on the move and we were swept along with it. I thought of the little princess rushing over the willow pattern bridge, leading her lover by the hand. Could Thief and I be crossing our own bridge? If so, the signs were not promising. The sights, the sounds, the smells, the very feel of experience had taken on a nightmarish quality. Everything seemed exaggerated, too big, too bright, too loud, too much like a horror movie to be credible yet too much of a nightmare to be wholly false. The windows of a live-meat-shop exploded into LSD proportions, bird cages leaning at odd angles, thinning and swelling into fantastic shapes. They were crowded with owls and golden pheasants and tiny feathered bundles which were, surely, never intended for the jaws of men. A pair of dogs, long haired and amber eyed, with tinsel round their necks, appealed to me from inside their steel traps, chests heaving, steam rising from lolling tongues.

"You bloody thief, stop!" -- He shouted something back but I couldn't make it out in the uproar. -- "Where the bloody hell are you taking me, boy, to life?" -- His shoulders flexed beneath their rags and the giant chopstick spurted blood like a harpoon in a sea monster's back. -- "You're not getting away from me, boy! I've got my hooks in you and I'm clinging on right up to the moment of truth." -- We passed a chemist's shop. In its window, a huge sign -- "Life-savers -- Beat the pill, for easy conception and safe delivery, guaranteed rubber-piercing and douche-proof."

Fruit and vegetables, carpets, a gunsmith's with grills on the windows and a security guard at the door, shops selling candles, spices, clothes and sacred books. More than anything, butcheries, butcheries and blood everywhere. I was towed past one, its open front exhaling the metallic scent of raw flesh and bone marrow. There were piles of meat on sheets of white and red paper, ribs, legs and shoulders, hands and feet. There were trays with tails in them, others piled with ears, dishes heaped with guts, a slab with tongues lolling side-along-side each other. A severed head, its eye sockets full of flies, gazed out from the shop's throat. Arranged round its neck, a garland of tiny hands and, scrawled on a board in red chalk -- "Unborn kids slaughtered fresh today!"

My part in the parade came to an abrupt end. We were passing a sumptuous-looking barbers, when Thief dropped the moonstone bracelet. It flashed among the moving feet and, bending to scoop it up, I slipped and he was gone, his arsehole wriggling down the throat of the crowd. As for me, I could do nothing in the forest of shuffling feet but curl up into the foetal position and wait.

--- * * * * * ---

"In here with you, Cheri!" -- A hand grabbed my collar and dragged me into the shop where I sat on the floor, trying to recover my senses.

"Where am I? Is this the finish or just the start? Is this what Hell's really like? God, I hope so!" -- The scene on this side of the frosted glass was a cross between the boudoir of a Mickey Mouse princess and a Parisian salon. Picturesque young women in billowing silks and youths in just about nothing, posed in deep sofas, chatting to clients, drinking with them, smoking, following their calling, all to the distant accompaniment of a heavenly harp. -- "If this is Hell," I said, looking around me in true delight, "Hell is where I belong!".

"The miracle is your young body wasn't crushed, Cheri," an electrifying, down-the-sewers-of-Paris voice said from behind me.

"Where am I, exactly?"

"Where you belong, Cheri. You're very, very special, not one in a million like you."

"You mean not one in a billion, woman! There's not another like me and at last I've come home! Fetch new robes and kill the fatted calf! Your master is returned!"

"First comes love, master. For you, I will do anything, anything you are capable of imagining." -- Her hand slithered into my waistband. -- "But where is it, master? Where is my pretty John Dummy? I'm coming to find you!" -- Her fingers curled around my testicles.

"No! It's still too early!" -- I sprang to my feet and bolted for the door, scooping up the moonstone bracelet as I went.

---- * * * * * ----

Back on the street, the human deluge had miraculously dried up and, in its place, the normal afternoon flow of traffic, city folk out shopping or on their way back to work. I walked slowly for a while getting my breath back and taking stock. Should I throw in the towel, head for the nearest police station and bring all this to an end, or should I make back for The House of The Harvest Moon? Obviously, things had not turned out well for Victoria and they would certainly go worse.

Chapter 16

"I'm looking for my friend," I informed the posterior of the waiter, who was on his knees, sweeping up broken crockery.

He tilted upright and turned his handsome head to look at me, the delicate hairs dangling from his cheek. -- "You ask for Mr Wells?"

"You just watch what you say! It's Lord Bertrand to you. No, I wasn't asking about Bertie. I'm looking for the young lady."

"I apologise, My Lord. Well, I'm afraid I can't tell you much. All I know is that the girl tried to go after you. Did you catch the beggar boy?"

"She's not a girl, my man! My friend is a young lady! Anyway, first things first. Where was she heading?"

"How can I know? When the rat-race gets going, hundreds of thousands, even the crème de la crème, are swept away and no-one hears of or sees them again or cares. Sorry I can't be more helpful! Now for my question, did you catch the thief, yes or no?"

"Hang on a minute. If you don't know where the young lady went, perhaps you'd be good enough to tell me where I'll find Lord Bertrand."

"As far as I know, he went the same way as your young lady. I tell you this, though, lord or no lord, he'll have the mother of all bills to pay if he puts his nose round this door again. Unless you, as a gentleman, care to settle on his behalf. -- You don't look too enthusiastic! I wonder why! In my experience, you upper class people are all the same, like crabs in a pot. You climb all over each other but you'll never help each other out. Oh well, that's the way the scum stays afloat, I suppose. Now, for pity's sake tell me, did you catch the little beggar boy? I need to know."

"Yes, I did. What's it to you anyway?"

His eyes filled with tears. -- "He's my youngest brother. What did you do, hand him over to the police? I must go and ask if I can bale him out."

"I thought about doing just that but, in the end, I let him go. The human race needs its drop-outs after all."

--- * * * * * ---

Not far from the House of The Harvest Moon, the stone wedding cake of St Martin's rose heavenward from a muddle of gravestones and monumental sculptures. The afternoon sun was glowing in its windows and, as I looked, the bells began to toll.

"Where is my lady?" the trebles rang.

"Waiting, she's waiting," the tenors sang.

"Where is she waiting?"

"Here in Saint Martin's."

Well, I thought, if it could happen to Jeane d'Arc, why not Josef Sope? The message seemed so clear and the bells repeated it so often, I had to walk across and check. It was possible, after all, that Victoria had been so terrified by the human tide as it swept past her that she'd taken refuge in the church. If that wasn't the way it was, so what? I had nothing to lose now -- except hope.

The church was packed except for the first two rows of pews which were pretty well empty. I made straight for them. How silly of me! I'd no sooner settled back than a stuffed shirt in a cassock came over and told me that the first two rows were private.

"Private? In what sense are they private?"

He looked startled. Serve him right! -- "Private? Well, private in the sense that they are reserved for VIPs, family, official guests and so on. Now, kindly move further back. I can't stand here talking, I've a great deal to attend to."

"But hang on! This is the house of God and we're all equal here, surely. I think you'd better tell me what all the fuss is about. Has The Minister died or something?"

"Is that supposed to be funny?"

"Not at all! Funerals aren't a laughing matter, especially when the deceased was a pillar of the establishment. How could the state continue to prosper without The Minister?"

He didn't answer, simply gave me an odd look, shrugged his shoulders and moved off to shake someone's hand. I did think about staying where I was but decided not to be provocative on this occasion and fought my way to a seat six rows back, right opposite the organ. Being for common mortals, it wasn't a comfortable stall and my view was blocked by several huge pillars but it would have to do. For a few minutes, I sat there, studying the congregation without bothering or being bothered by anybody but, as so often with me, that was to change.

"Forgive me, sir. Is there any news?" -- My neighbour, a rotund man in a dog collar patted my knee.

"Don't you dare do that again! If you have something to say, come out with it like a man."

"Oh dear! Please do forgive me, Your Worship. I didn't mean to be presumptuous. I only wanted to attract Your Honour's attention."

"As long as that's understood, fine. It's not necessary to go on your knees. What news are you waiting for?"

"I was wondering when we begin, Your Worship."

"I've no idea what you're talking about. Begin, what?"

The priest lowered his voice. -- "You are right to be circumspect, Your Worship. There are spies everywhere today, especially in this so-called house of God." -- He leaned closer to whisper directly into my ear. -- "What I want to know, sir, is when do we begin with the actual riot? The hold-up has worked well thus far. The people are growing more restive by the minute as they well might seeing that the ceremony hasn't even started yet -- a good hour late -- and I fear that, if we don't act soon, things could slide out of our control. To be frank, I'm only thankful you've come along to take charge."

"Take charge? I'm not with you. What is this ceremony and why should I have any direct interest in it?" -- I remembered Lord Bertrand's words – "everything after that has been arranged.". Victoria's marriage! My heart broke into a gallop.

"Come, come, Your Worship! You're teasing me! The minister knows everything there is to know about this so-called marriage service. Why! There can't be a single Tom, Dick or Harry in town who doesn't know who's to become who today."

"You don't say! Well, I, for one, do not. Whose marriage is it and why should The Minister be interested?"

"In operations like this, caution is obviously called for, Your Worship, but I'm amazed by yours! Presumably, you're testing me out. Very well, as you know only too well, we're gathered here today to witness the union -- excuse my smile! -- between Lady Victoria Hunter-Jones of Bingham Hall and the future king of Denmark."

By this time, my heart was pounding so violently, I could see it under my shirt. Could he? -- "I don't see how that can possibly be right. Are you sure you haven't got it wrong? Just look around you! A few private pews, just about empty, no courtiers, no visiting royals, no cardinals, bishops, politicians, no hangers on at all, not even one solitary TV personality! Just rows and rows of Mr and Mrs Joe Sope. Hardly the build up to a royal wedding, I'd have thought."

He went to pat my knee again, recollected himself, grinned knowingly. -- "I can't get over it, Your Worship! Butter wouldn't melt in your mouth, I swear it would not! As you must very well know, the official guests have been commanded to wait in the vestry until the problem has been sorted out. The minute that happens, they'll be processing in with all the pomp and circumstance we ordinary folk are so hungry to admire from a distance. However, it seems that the problem has not yet been resolved and, thanks to you know who, the press have been issued with guide lines and here we all are, not far short of a thousand clamouring for a command performance. The rumour is spreading that the Danes are in a state of shock and wants to cancel the whole show but that's next to impossible now. The people love their Queen of Hearts and will not be denied. If I may say so, The Minister is, as ever, to be congratulated on his masterful orchestration of events and I would be most grateful if you would pass that on, My Lord."

In spite of or perhaps because of the prospect of Victoria's being publicly humiliated, this had to be my call to greatness. -- "Tell me, priest, how did you discover that I'm on The Minister's staff?"

"Why, Your Excellency! For those who can read, your rank is emblazoned on your forehead. You carry his mark just as I do but at such an exalted level!"

"But how can you be sure of that? It could be that I'm simply carrying the scars of, shall we say, active service, something humble as that."

"There's absolutely no room for doubt, Your Worship. On your left temple, you carry the sacred mark of our terrible, all-knowing and soon to be all-powerful lord, the prince of darkness. His glorious name be feared for ever and for ever without end!" -- The priest crossed himself six times with the swastika. -- "You are in the service of Beelzebub as am I." -- He thrust his ugly head just about into my face -- "See? The mark of the beast, as the enemy call it, is on me also albeit at a most humble rank." -- There was a scar down the left temple but, next to mine, barely visible and crude. In fact, it was so unimpressive it could have been and probably was self-inflicted. The things little people will do to get a few inches up the greasy pole!

"Take your ugly face away! -- Lady Victoria, where is she at this moment, also in the vestry I presume."

"I doubt it, My Lord. I'm told she refused to be hidden away like some refugee waiting to be expelled. I understand she's waiting alone somewhere not far from the altar. She arrived nearly an hour ago with a wholly inadequate escort, just one admiral and a tall, superior-looking gentleman. Does Your Worship wish me to go and find out exactly where she is? It shouldn't be impossible."

The study of ecclesiastical architecture could hardly have been further from my thoughts as I sat there, tense as a piano wire, waiting for this weird character to come back but I'd noticed the odd person looking at me expectantly so I put on a show of being absorbed by St Martin's interior. The organ pipes were, in fact, quite inspiring, a double line of silvery tubes soaring into the high roof. I'd been craning my neck for some seconds before I spotted it -- high up under the ceiling, the inevitable camera disguised as a dove. It was leaning far out from its ledge, scanning the congregation. I looked carefully for the electric cable. The dove's eyes locked onto my face.

"I must warn you of something, Your Worship!" -- The priest's hot breath fanned my cheek. -- "You are being watched."

"I always am. It's one of those crosses I carry. What are you referring to in particular, the security camera?"

"Not just the camera, Your Excellency. Four rows back, some sort of tramp is getting ready to throw something. He's not one of ours."

I looked around and saw why the dustbin had been empty. What an ugly face he had, so swollen and scratched, not improved by the surgical collar. He was nursing something which could have been a rotten lemon salvaged from a dustbin but which could also have been a hand-grenade. -- "Scum like that are no threat to me, priest! What did you find out for me?"

Someone way off on my right started clapping rhythmically. They were joined by another then another till the slow clap had spread round the building.

"I can report that things are definitely coming to a head," the priest said. "Lady Victoria is standing alone behind a pillar near the altar. the admiral and her other escort are about ten feet away talking together. I couldn't get close enough to hear but it looked like they were having an argument."

As he was speaking, the admiral I'd spoken to at the Flight for Life Centre went hurrying by on his way out of the church closely followed by Lord Bertrand whose expression was a mixture of fury and despair. -- "Alright, priest, I want you to take charge for a moment. Stoke up that rumour about the Danes till it's ablaze. Don't let the hand-clapping peter out. Get some of your colleagues stamping their feet and shouting out for the Queen of Hearts. And, this is most important, do not start throwing missiles etc before I give the signal by blowing my nose!" -- I shoved the fool to one side and rushed down the aisle.

I found her without too much difficulty, cringing behind a massive pillar about ten feet from the altar-rail. -- "Good afternoon, Lady Victoria! I hope I haven't kept you waiting."

"Josie!" -- For a wonderful instant, I thought she was going to hug me. -- "Thank heavens! I'm feeling so upset and embarrassed standing here all on my own but what could I do? I can't let them treat me like an illegal immigrant or worse. God bless you! I've been praying and praying you wouldn't let me down and you haven't. What would I do without you!"

"Or I without you come to that! What's happening, where is this king of yours?"

"Josie, I don't know what's going on! It's so awful! Those results, they haven't come through! Bertie's been ringing and ringing! Now, he and the admiral have been summoned to the embassy!"

"So that's where they were going! What for, did they say?"

She looked as if she was about to burst into tears. I put my arm round her shoulders. -- "Don't worry, everything will be alright. I'll stay with you. We Sopes are with you always."

--- * * * * * ---

"How much longer can this bloody circus continue, for Christ's sake?" -- A priest came over. In drooping cassock and batwing collar, he could have been a balding House Martin. -- "I take it you're one of those wretched fans. How could you turn up here dressed like that! What would happen if the king saw you? Kindly go and hide somewhere! The royal party could arrive any minute!"

"What do you make of that, Victoria? The house of God turns out to be much like a gentleman's club! Not to worry, I'll be able to find somewhere close by and still keep an eye on you. The last thing I want is to cause you further embarrassment. You've been allocated more than your fair share of misery already. Who is this fellow, anyway?"

"Please don't go and don't mind him. He's just standing in for some bishop or other."

House Martin flushed. -- "Just standing in! If your ladyship had any idea of what I'm going through! You've no idea! The chaos and anxiety of it all! I tell you, this situation is rapidly getting out of control. If we don't get under way immediately...Thank God for that! His Lordship! About time too! But where is the admiral in the name of Heaven? I can't take much more of this, I truly cannot! What is going on? There are all those high-ups waiting in the vestry and I'm responsible! What is a mere mortal to do?"

Lord Bertrand of Wells was a changed man. Instead of striding along as if he ran the universe, he came down the aisle, hands clasped and eyes fixed on the flagstones like an undertaker's mute. He saw me, faltered a moment then stretched his lips in an icy grimace. -- "You again! It never rains but it pours! -- Well, Victoria, I've news for you at last. I'm sorry it's taken so long but it wasn't easy, believe me, even with your letter. They're so very strict when it comes to confidentiality!"

"Never mind about all that! Come on, tell me, it's alright, isn't it? -- Please, just tell me everything's alright, I can't go on much longer!"

Lord Bertrand took a deep breath as if he was about to dive into an ice flow. -- "I'm glad to tell you that you're in excellent health, my dear. Apparently, everything is going along splendidly."

Victoria gasped with relief -- "Then I haven't got aids?"

"Absolutely not."

"Then, what's the matter with you? Why are you looking like that, tell me!"

"Now listen carefully, my dear. What I'm about to tell you isn't bad news exactly but it could well come as a shock, at first anyway. I'm afraid to say you're pregnant."

Victoria sucked in her breath, went white then pink. -- "Pregnant!"

"I fear so. That's why there's been so much to sort out."

"Such as what, an abortion? I'm not sure I'm prepared…"

"It wouldn't help anyway. The marriage is off. The admiral and I did our best but the powers that be are already holding a press-conference. -- Come along. I think we should go somewhere quiet and talk this through. What you need at this moment is sound advice and I've been instructed to see you get it. You're very, very precious to us all and I'm determined to help, no matter what the cost."

"But what's going on here?" I demanded. "What could possibly be wrong with a young girl being pregnant? It happened to Our Lady after all!"

"Shut up, Sope! The last thing we all need right now is propaganda from you. -- Come on, old girl, take my arm. We'll slip out quietly."

Victoria was staring at him in shocked disbelief. -- "You mean all this has been for nothing? I'm to be publicly humiliated, sacrificed like a goat at the altar? You mean to tell me, all these poor, kind people have waited for hours just to see me shamed! It was supposed to be on television!"

I blew my nose. Almost instantly, someone in the congregation let off a firework. -- "Look, Victoria, believe me, I did my best. No man can…"

The missiles were beginning to fly and fireworks were going off all over the place, including a big rocket which made a direct hit on the pigeon-camera. -- "You and your lot are offal!" I shouted above the rising tumult and grabbed Victoria by the arm. "All that bull about fairy tale marriages and everlasting love or whatever it was and, the first little problem and it's cross the street and look the other way. Can't you see what it's doing to the girl? Why don't you marry her yourself, for pity sake? -- Look Victoria! Look at the idiot! He's embarrassed! If only I were good enough!"

--- * * * * * ---

"It would be best if you left as quickly and quietly as possible," House Martin shouted, waving his arms at the tumult as if he were conducting. "If you would follow me, we'll leave by a side door, out of sight and sound of the people and that hateful press. Oh God! This is so awful! This will go down in history and I'm standing in!"

Remarkable how resolute one becomes in a gathering riot. [Hymnbooks flying, fights breaking out to left and right, crack of fire-squibs, a heavy thud as from a hand-grenade, the organ belting out the national anthem, House Martin with his flapping gown trying to lead us off stage, Victoria looking up at me with death in her eyes, Lord Bertrand of Wells ready for a stroke] I gripped the Queen of Hearts' arm and, his lordship shambling in our wake, half walked, half dragged her back down the aisle and out of the deafening church.

--- * * * * * ---

"Hello, you three!" -- Captain Wolf was waiting for us with a gang of heavies as we came down the steps. -- "I do hope I'm not breaking anything up." -- There were rain clouds in the West, fingers of evening sunlight slanting accusingly through them. A stiff breeze rippling his trouser legs, remind one of a bad angel poised for flight. -- "What do you know?" -- He glanced up at the sky. -- "Sun and rain together! What say you, My Lord, there must be a Monkey's wedding going on somewhere, must there not?"

That should have been the last round for us but not with Lord Bertrand of Wells in the ring. Coming suddenly to his true self, he puts the captain on the pavement with a terrific right hook and, fists and boots flying, starts on the others. -- "Get her out of here!" he shouts, reeling from a heavy blow to the back of the neck then butting a cop in the guts, "You're a fine fellow, Sope!" [Thud] "I'll come for you," [Thud] "Victoria," [crack] "in Su."

Chapter 17

Throughout the rains of May, all is shrouded save the bridge at Seta Bay. [Basho]

A mad dash from the church, along the main street, up a side road, through a subway with the motorway roaring overhead, past what could have been a prison and round the corner with its traffic-island, the great bridge arching out of the town and across the bay, its support-towers fetlocked in spray, their heads soaring to meet the rain-clouds from the North. Victoria leads me over.

Once across the bridge, she swings off to the right, heading for the elaborate façade of a huge hotel. As she comes up, a black car rolls out across the pavement. The back door opens and Luigi leaps out, catches her in his arms and bundles her inside. The door slams shut and the car accelerates away at disaster speed, a posse of motorbikes in pursuit. I stand and watch, paralysed with grief, as the car and its cloud of camera flashing riders is swallowed up in the darkness of the future.

--- * * * * * ---

"That's the end of ambition for you," I told myself. "You've lost The Queen of Hearts and there's nothing worth being born for any more. Fiend or angel, what does it matter? In real life, you'll simply exist, Mr Joe Soap, the also ran. You might as well drop out of the human race right here and now."

I walk back onto the bridge, searching for a way up. Past the tollgate then begin to climb the maintenance ladder on one of the support towers. I pull myself rapidly upwards at first but I'm physically exhausted after all I've been through and by the time I've reached fifty or so feet, the strength has drained out of me. I try resting, crooking one arm around the ladder to transfer the weight from the muscles to the skeleton, then go on again but, after only twenty or so rungs higher, I'm as weak as ever. I have to rest again and again before I finally reach the cables and whistling wires at the tower's head. Rest there a good ten minutes, feeling the tug of the wind, hearing from far, far below the tiny sounds of police and ambulance sirens but not daring to look.

Eventually, start again, grab onto a heavy-duty cable running along at chest height and, feet balancing on a narrow strut, I begin edging out over the bay. Ten yards, fifteen maybe, a few more then my body abruptly refuses to go another foot and I'm stranded out there in the enormity of space. My body rests of its own accord but my mind cannot rest. Limbs need great energy to work but not the mind. The mind can run wild on the merest breath of despair.

"What's the matter, Sope, too weak to do even this? It's such an easy thing, to give in when there's nothing worth carrying on for. Go on, jump before you fall!"

"I will, I will! Just give me a moment or two to rest. I'm going to do it, don't you worry, but not from here. I must go further out, further out from the shallows to where those rocks are. It will be bloodier from there."

"Nonsense, you're just prevaricating! Get on with it, man! Stop thinking about her! She won't come back again. Jump! She was always too good for you anyway, a different order of being entirely. Hurry up, the wooden spoon's waiting and there's no other way but down. Jump off before you fall off!"

"I'm not listening! It's up to me where, how and when I go. Onto those awful rocks, that's what it will be."

The next tower looks no more than a stone's throw in the damp atmosphere though it must be at least a hundred yards. Above me, a large expanse of evening sky ringed by clouds, faintest silver of the moon. Truly, I am not afraid of what's to come but I have to give myself time to do it properly. After all, I did have some claim to greatness as Victoria's escort and I can't be expected to drop out without putting on a show. After all, this is my last chance to prove that I would have been a man of exceptional courage, prove it to myself if no-one else. All acts of self-destruction have the same ending but my performance must be exemplary even if there is no audience, no criticism and no applause either. Tragic, that, when you think about it. This is going to be the very last act Sope performs yet not a soul is here to see. Nobody will say "Bravo, Sope! What extraordinary courage he showed at the end!". There'll be just me, clouds, the dying sun and a sprinkling of stars.

It wasn't like that for Dido, stabbing her side again and again on the funeral-pyre, nor for Cleopatra pressing the snake to her breast. They were monarchs surrounded by courtiers, ambitious eyes applauding every thrust, each bite. There were tongues in plenty to wag for them, tell the world how wonderfully they'd died. Being who they were, they went down not just in gossip but in history. Greatness is enough to make self-destruction seem great. It was the same for Lord Brutus, miserable assassin! He had his armour-bearer standing there, holding the sword while he ran onto its point. Brutus, the murderer, becomes an icon, a symbol of extraordinary courage, because he has a pretty boy to tell the world how noble his end was. If he'd been a Joe Sope, he'd be remembered now, if at all, as a murderer, a servant who stabbed his loving master in the back. His end would be dismissed in a footnote as only what was to be expected from a criminal terrified of justice. It took mere rank to give friend Brutus great courage!

Too bad for the rest of us! I'll have to manage with only the heavens and myself to watch but I won't cheat, choose the easiest way even so. There's no self-respect to be won from that. And it could be so very easy! All I have to do is hang on till exhaustion makes me let go the cable. I'll look down automatically and vertigo will do the rest, take me off, dropping as a screaming stone. Not for me! That isn't good enough for the former Knave of Hearts. To meet my standards, it has to be an act of will, a triumph of despair, not an ignominious topple into oblivion. How then? To boldly fling myself out, lean backwards and push off from the bridge like a swimmer in air? Not for me! That would be like cutting your throat before the mirror with closed eyes. Simply turn around and step into the future. That has to be the noble way, the only way for the gentle Knave of Hearts.

Just one thing before I walk away, Victoria's moonstones. [I pull them out of my pocket.] What trash they are! How could anybody present these to a queen? How generous she was to accept them! Why! She clung on to them until that poor, little beggar boy tore them from her wrist!

Wait a moment, let's just think about that! Why should Lady Victoria Hunter-Jones of Bingham Hall go on wearing my miserable offering when she could have more precious jewellery than a strong man could carry? She must have had her reasons. Is it possible that Luigi could have won her body but not her soul? If so, there could still be a role for Josef Sope even now. Who can tell, perhaps this isn't her bridge to happiness at all. Maybe it was nothing more than an escape-route across the bay and there is still good reason to hope. Remember how she slowed the car, what she said at the altar, how she looked!

In a flood of emotion, I sob like a drunkard, sodden with relief at the possibility that Victoria still needed, maybe even loved me. -- "Victoria! I love you Victoria!"

--- * * * * * ---

The wind suddenly still and a silver curtain of rain advancing on the bridge like the broad panels of an angel's skirt, in its depths, a rainbow, perfect copy in watery colours of our willow pattern bridge, remote yet seemingly so close I feel I could thrust my hand into it with ease. I'm mesmerised, gazing like a child into the liquid light. -- "There's our bridge, Your Majesty! Wolf said there would be a Monkey's wedding. How blindly he sees!" -- I stretch forward and fling the bracelet out into space. It soars joyfully upward then down into the rainbow. -- "Victoria! Never stop needing me, Victoria!" [No answer, only chill rain wrapping the future in its silver shroud]

Chapter 18

One hour, more maybe, hanging in the rain, the light gone and my physical strength still not returned. The wind howling again from the North, shaking the cable, clamping cold cloth around my chest. -- "If I'm going to be any use to Victoria ever again, I must first find somewhere safe to sleep if only for a few hours."

The wind is in a fury and I find out that to descend a narrow ladder in the rain, all around shrieking struts and whistling wire and visibility more or less at zero, isn't as easy as it might seem, especially when you're physically exhausted and in an emotional shake. For a while, I manage ok, creeping cautiously down from rung to rung, but nerves, fatigue and gravity proved too much in the end. I was just above the lights of the motorway when my left foot slipped and I started to fall, slithering chest-on down the outer slope of the great leg, below the traffic and on, scrabbling at concrete, clutching wildly at passing bolts, rasping my toes and skinning my poor hands. Quite a fall it was and a painful coming down to earth.

"God!" -- I rolled onto my back. -- "What have I done to my hands? -- And my feet!"

I lay where I'd fallen for a while, feeling desperately sorry for myself, but it was no good. I had to sit up and take stock. Not everything, it seemed, was against me. The tide was out and I'd landed on a stretch of clear sand, well and truly bruised and shaken up but not one broken bone. -- "Well," I told myself, "things could have been much, very much worse. Someone, somewhere, is looking after me. -- Come on, Sope, up you get! If we're going to give the police a run for their money, we must be off."

I got to my feet and limped away without a backward glance at the bridge. Over in the West, the diffuse glow of city lights, remote and hostile in the rain. I headed North and, after about ten minutes plodding over the sand, found my way onto a road and open countryside. The downpour was beginning to ease and once, I could make out the shapes of cattle sleeping in the fields, their breath wispy-warm in the night air. Half a mile on, the fringes of a forest. I stumbled into the cover of the trees, across a clearing and collapsed in the shelter of a fallen elm.

--- * * * * * ---

I must have slept there in the shelter of the fallen elm for many, many hours because when I woke, most of my wounds had scabbed over and I was famished. In a forest, of course, it is always possible to find food and after a feast of nuts, berries, even a few innocent-looking fungi, I returned to the elm, more or les satisfied. It was evening and, standing in the lowering sun on the far side of the clearing, a great stag was stripping leaves from the trees. He was a magnificent sight and I sat watching him, watching and wondering as he browsed, flicking at clouds of flies or stamping them to flight with a hoof. Once or twice, I fancied he looked directly at me.

Now why, I thought, are you so bold? Even you should have the fear of Man in your heart. Either I'm such a sorry sight I don't frighten you or you can't make me out properly, sitting so still and with the trees behind. On the other hand, could be you're taking film. It would be the easiest thing to wire up a camera and what have you among all that antlery. -- I shook my fist at him. He stood an instant to stare then turned back to feed.

It took about half an hour before the stag moved out of the clearing carrying off the last drops of light on the tips of its antlers. That should have been my cue to leave as well and carry on walking in the cover of the trees or find somewhere safe to hide but my spirit suddenly rebelled.

"I've had enough of running away from trouble!" I said. "Let it come to me for a change. The police will run me to earth sooner or later and what if they do? I'll be able to take it and if I can't, it surely won't make any real difference to Victoria. There's very little chance, if any, we'll ever meet again. She's happy now in the arms of Luigi and if, for some reason, he's failed, there are all those other friends, not to mention ordinary good hearted men and women, hundreds of thousands of them, falling over each other just to wash her feet. The cruel reality is that, no matter what we Sopes would like to believe, none of us is indispensable, not even me. Let the police come and work me over if that's what they want! A few more torture sessions might not be so bad in any case. They might even do me good. After all, if it does turn out

I'm a child of Satan, which is not impossible, then I'm a child of the greatest sufferer in God's universe. Suffering must not repel me. On the contrary, it has to attract me. Without Victoria, suffering will be all I have, my reason for existing, and to suffer nobly, I must be strong as steel and steel is hardened on the anvil.

I dozed off again and when I woke, the full moon was sailing over the clearing, around her, the universe vibrating with countless stars. I stayed where I was to watch, watch and wait to be taken once more off the shelf. -- "I can't change what's coming so I may as well make the best of being out here under the moon. After all, the moon's not just a light to see by or hide from. She's the face of a girl in the sky, the mark of the lover's arrow flighted at the stars and, like as not, I won't be admiring her again, ever." -- It was so bright I could see right across the clearing from where I sat to the far side where the stag had been. Was that an owl, swinging down from the stars? Certainly, its flight made no sound.

"Hi there, Bubo!" I called. "If you've been sent by Captain Wolf to check up on me, tell him there's no hurry. Josef Sope won't be running away from anyone ever again. Tell him I'm waiting for him."

The owl came gliding across the open ground straight towards me, something sparkling in its talons. -- "What have you got there? You thieving sod! It looks like a bracelet!" -- I got to my feet and shouted at it, clapping my hands. -- "Drop that! Let it go, you lousy thief!"

The bird swung away, releasing its load. I ran over to look but there, instead of Victoria's bracelet, what looked like an oesophagus lying in the grass, aglow with rot. I kicked at it. -- "God! What a stench! There must be a dump for hospital waste round here somewhere. Surely, human flesh should never come to this. Made in the image of God! How abominable his works can become!" -- Kneeling under the moon, studying the oesophagus in the light, poking at it with a twig, my stomach heaved and I brought up.

Chapter 19

I was on my way back to the fallen tree when someone crept up on me from behind. -- "Got you!" -- Captain Wolf's muscular fingers clamped round my neck. "Where have you been all the day, sonny boy, sonny boy? Where have you been all the day, my sonny boy?"

"Let go, pig, you're crushing my voice-box!"

"The common man without a voice? The age of good government is come, at long last! Even so, we'll be needing a song from you in a while so I'd better let you relax." -- In one athletic movement, he had me on my face and his boot on the back of my neck. -- "Still hungry for spleen, Sope? Don't fret, I'll feed you some of yours if there's any left."

"I rather hoped we'd meet up again, Wolf." -- At least he couldn't read my expression with my face to the ground. -- "Terrific jaw-cage you're wearing! I barely recognised you. His lordship packs quite a punch, does he not?"

"Not any more, he doesn't. Would you like to see for yourself?"

At that moment, I couldn't have cared less about Lord Bertrand of Wells. What with being forced to lie face-down with a man's weight on my neck, the chill on the grass and the damp rising into my nostrils. -- "There's no future in torturing a corpse, Wolf. Wouldn't it be a good idea to let me up before I stop breathing?"

"Sorry, Sope! I was only being cruel to be kind. I wanted you to enjoy the cool while you can. After all, it won't be long before you're turning over and over in the kitchen." -- He shifted his foot to the base of my skull, bearing down so heavily I could make out the shape of the heel. -- "And thou shall crush the serpent's head. Get the connection, Sope? Of course you do, you're a fiend and so elevated! Christ! If you could have seen your face when my man told you that! You practically cried for joy. -- There's one thing I wasn't expecting though, why didn't you jump into the car with her ladyship? After all, it was your job to look after the poor thing."

"Wolf! Where is Lady Victoria? What have you done to her? Come on, tell me!"

"You mean you really don't know? Surely, you can't have been wandering about for all this time! It's been the only story in the media for the last four days and it's still top of the news."

"Just tell me, what have you done to Lady Victoria? Tell me for pity's sake!"

"Ah but I never do anything for pity's sake, never. But for law and order, now that's another story entirely. Maybe, I should let her tell you in her own words exactly what's been happening to her since you saw each other last. Now, there's a brilliant suggestion! I'll see if she's up to receiving visitors. -- That you, constable? This way." [Boots running heavily for some seconds then a gigantic figure standing next to me, ankles within biting range if only I could have freed my head] "See what I've caught, constable? It's our hero of the arcade, stunner of corporals, killer of women and courageous freedom fighter, Josef Sope. Looks pretty harmless right at this moment, doesn't he, like a badger with his head in a stick. Pity we didn't bring the dogs with us."

The constable knelt beside me as if he were short-sighted. -- "To be honest, sir, I'm a wee bit disappointed. I was expecting something out of the ordinary, devilish. This kid's no different from the rest of 'em."

"Ah but he's got a big, big ego and an enormous mouth," the captain chuckled, giving my neck a farewell press. -- "Right, put bracelets on him and check him out for knives. We'll walk him to the car. Watch out, though, with a full moon there's no telling, maybe he'll turn into a fiend." [Pinch of steel round my wrists, sweaty hands exploring my privates, a probing finger] -- Wolf looked on, his mouth twisted in amusement.

Wolf walked off and we followed him, me in front, manacled hands in the region of my throbbing member, the escort only inches behind. -- "Where are you taking me?" I asked him as we turned out of the clearing.

"Back to town, kid. It's not long in the car, half an hour."

"And what are they going to do, behead me or what?"

"Be'ead you? You'll be so lucky! Who do you think you are, king of England?"

"Then what is on the menu, do you know?"

"Well, that depends. As far as I'm concerned, kid, you are."

"You do know I've got aids, don't you?"

"So 'ave I, kid."

Thanks to Wolf's boot, my neck muscles felt as if they'd been shredded, darts of pain across my skull and down my shoulders. Even so, I screwed my head round to look and at such close range discovered the truth of the ancient saying, "ignorance is bliss". He was the squarest-looking beast imaginable outside a Holbein monster-graph. His head, face, eyes, nose and jaw were all square. He had square shoulders, a square chest and hands like squares of pork. Only the royal swell of his belly disturbed the symmetry. If he wasn't King Henry's recycle, he had to be a Russian bear. He even walked square. -- "Are you Russian?"

"Now, that's real good, that is! No, I'm not rushing. I'm walkin' nice and slow. Saving my strength to bite your head off for you."

"Christ, man! What are you trying to do? Back off, can't you? You're practically riding on my back." -- He was so close I could feel hot breath on my neck.

"My 'umble apologies, old boy! Am I buggin' you?"

I should have kept quiet. It's never smart to plant ideas in the brain of a bully. After that, Tank amused himself by deliberately knocking up against me, my heels, the backs of my knees and, of course, my arse. -- "Tell me, old boy, what was she like?"

"Just pack that in, you lousy pig! -- What was who like?"

"Your little aristocrat, the Queen of Hearts, of course. She looked fuckin' good in the movie, fuckin' wonderful!"

"You know something? I'm really looking forward to kicking your head in."

"Is that right? Funny but that's just what 'is lordship said and look where 'e is now. -- Come on, swing those 'ips. If you've got it, flaunt it while you still can. By the way, remember the tramp in the dustbin? 'Es got it alrigh'. 'E's workin' on 'er Majesty right this minute, lucky bugger! Says he's practisin' for when you arrive. Amazing little girl, that one! 'o'd 'ave thought she'd 'ang on so long?"

I turned on him, forgetting all about the cuffs. Tank's colossal fist loomed before my eyes like a battering-ram.

--- * * * * * ---

My memories of the car journey are confused and horrible. Apart from the blinding pain behind my eyes and terror over Victoria, they consist almost entirely of battling to keep Tank's paws off me. He already had my flies open when I came round and was mucking about in my pants. -- "You scummy bastard! Get off me! What the hell do you think I am?"

"Don't you worry, I know just what you are, kid!" -- His fumbling was beginning to inflict serious physical pain on top of outrage to what was left of my dignity.

"Cut that out, constable!" -- The captain didn't turn his head to look.

"It's alright, sir. I'm doin' anover body search, tha's all. Just checkin' 'e 'asn't taped a razor blade to 'is leg. Can't be too careful wiv kids these days."

Handcuffed as I was, it was fortunate that I'm something of a contortionist. Tank had just undone my waistband and was pulling my trousers down when I succeeded in wrapping my chain round his wrist and giving him a Chinese burn.

"Fuckin' 'ell! You wait, you'll wish you 'adn't done that, boy!" -- He withdrew, massaging the wrist.

"I thought I told you to cut that out, constable! Just leave him alone!"

"I'm not touchin' 'im, captain. The little bugger tried to bite me, that's all. I think 'e's gone off 'is 'ead."

Wolf gave Tank a straight look. He knew what had been going on, of course, but said nothing. I edged as far away as I could get and tried to make out where we were heading. Up ahead, the lights of the town and, soon, we were speeding through the outer suburbs, depressing streetlamps and block after block of high-rise hell, skirted open ground with trees, a park maybe, and pulled up outside a building with an imposing, magisterial facade.

"Well, Wolf, what about it? Is this where you're holding Lady Victoria?"

"This, Sope, is the Palais de Justice. Take a good look at the outside. It'll be the last you ever see of it."

"And Lady Victoria?"

"We'll have to see. But I'll tell you this much, her fate depended on you."

From the outside, the Palais de Justice was, indeed, an impressive building with its flight of broad, stone steps and massive doors fit for a cathedral or merchant bank. Not so its interior. The reception area! What a soulless, middle of the night place that was -- strip-lighting, walls in old cream, the floor covered in shabby lino, one tub with an anorexic palm sucking on the dust and, behind the duty desk, two cops snoozing. Wolf strode over, jaw cage glittering, and banged his fist down in front of them. -- "Rouse yourselves, you scum! There's work. One of you help the constable take this goat down to the cells. -- And go easy with him! The technical people want him fresh. Expect my orders any moment so watch you're awake!" -- He disappeared into a lift and I wasn't at all happy to see him go. We followed one of the sleep-walkers down a spiral stair into the echoing basement, along a passage and into my cell.

"Ok, kid, this is it, your own little place at last. We'll be nice and private 'ere, just you and me together. It's got all the mod coms. See, a bunk with 'and carved pillow -- you can 'ave that -- and, oh look! The piss-pot's only 'alf full! -- By the way, it wasn't too wise of you to skin my wrist back there." -- The other cop had deserted me and, in the cell, no more than six feet square, low ceiling and windowless, Tank was a colossus. His bulk crowded out the space and his voice boomed like a hog in a coalhole.

"So, it really hurt! What a shame! I didn't realise animals like you have feelings. Why don't you soak it in your urine for an hour? They say that works wonders."

He started pressing against me. -- "Come on now, kid, don't let's fall out. I just want to give you a cookery lesson while they're getting the oven ready. Ever 'eard of toad in the 'ole? I'm goin' to show you 'ow it's done."

"Don't forget the captain! He said to go easy on me, remember? The torturers won't like it if ..."

"And you know what you can do with Fancy Frankie! Don't worry, I'll go easy. Come on, drop those pants! You're goin' to 'ave a cookery lesson."

"Hang on! What would it be worth if I play along?"

"Listen, comrade Sope, you ain't in a position to bargain. Drop the bloody things or I'll tear them off you!"

"Ok! What about a kiss first, just to make up?"

"Now, that's more like it! There's my lovely Joe! A bit of oral just to get my mouth ready! Ok, open up!" -- He lowered his monster face but, quick as a ferret, I wrapped the cuff chain round the neck and snapped his head down, bringing my knee up into his mouth. -- "How was that for a sexy ride, fat arse?"

Tank staggered back, more surprised than hurt, slab hands over his face, giving me the all clear to ram his genitalia. The combat which followed was noisy, brutish and deeply repulsive. Twice, he all but succeeded in raping me, the first time on the floor, the second up against the door, and I knew it would not be long before I was forced to yield. We were about to engage in a bout of wrestling, me squatting with my back to the wall, Tank leaning on me like a Sumo wrestler, when a third body burst into the cell, emitted a savage yell and dropped him with a combination right cross to the ear and upper cut.

"Wow! Am I glad to see you, K-O! The bugger just about had me!"

Friend O'Toole was standing astride the unconscious Tank, breathing heavily, his eyes horribly bloodshot and cheeks livid. -- "How long's this been going on, Ducky? Did the arsehole hurt you?"

"It was nothing compared to what you've done to him. Thank God you turned up! How did you manage it? I didn't expect to see you ever again."

"I'm not surprised after what you did to me. I'm up for letting you go, been in this hole for days. Luckily for you, they're pretty slack about locking the cell, seeing I'm still supposed to be one of them."

"I'm truly sorry about the stun gun, K-O. Hasn't messed up your heart, has it? You don't look too good."

"You're the one who messed up my heart, Ducky. We were going to stick together, remember? -- What are you up for exactly, murder or what? They've got the girl, you know, been working on her for some time. I don't know if she's still going but it really would be better for her if she just gave up the ghost."

"Working on her! Christ! So it wasn't just talk, they have actually started! Where is she right now, for God's sake, in this building? You must take me to her, help get her out! We must! I'll do anything you ask, literally anything!"

"It's like in Z—block, isn't it, Ducky? You can't do anything much with those cuffs on."

"I know that, you simpleton! Get the bloody things off me, can't you? Come on, hurry up, pick the locks or something!"

"I seem to remember you got me to do that last time. And now I'm a simpleton! Well, maybe I don't know how to pick locks. On the other hand, maybe I do. You'll have to wait and see. First, though, I'm going to paralyse your new friend. Looks like he's coming round. Move back over there and keep out of the way."

I stood obediently in the corner for the first few kicks but K-O's breathing was so laboured and the gasps he made as he heaved his boot in were so alarming I had to intervene. -- "That's enough! You're overdoing it, man! Come on, quit kicking him -- or what's left. I don't want your heart packing up on me while I'm in this mess!"

"Simpleton! Don't" [kick] "call me names ever again," [kick, kick] "and don't interfere in what you know not of, you simpleton." [kick] "When it comes to this game, I know every bloody thing" [kick] "there is to know." [terrific kick]

"Cut it out, you fool! At this rate, you'll have an attack before we've got this bracelet off me!" -- I grabbed him by the shoulders and struggled to pull him off the battered Tank. -- "Didn't you hear? Stop I tell you, stop! Come on, leave him!" -- We were engaged in a curious little dance toward the bunk when he started to buckle in a series of rhythmic groans. -- "Christ, K-O! I told you not to overdo it! Here, lie down. Please, please don't go yet! There's so much to do!"

I managed to get him onto the bunk, where he lay, groaning rhythmically like some weird breathing-machine, sweat pouring off him, eyes closed, fingers massaging his left breast. Suddenly, he sat up, stared at me with wild eyes, tried to reach forward to take my hand then passed out. -- All of which, of course, left me as good as helpless, still in handcuffs, the remains of one cop on the floor and what looked like the corpse of another on the bunk. -- "Bloody Hell! There's nothing I can do, nothing! I'll just have to wait here with them both."

--- * * * * * ---

"Do you mean to tell me you're responsible for all of this?" -- Wolf's voice was falsetto as he stood in the blood spattered cell, surveying the carnage.

"I suppose you could say that, yes, but quite innocently. What's more, I can't say I'm sorry because I'm not. Right now, I may be the whipping-dog but, even so, I'm not prepared to be buggered without putting up a fight."

"Are you being serious? They try to bugger you and wind up like this?"

"Not the one on the bunk, no. He's innocent as a babe."

"Wait a minute!" -- He bent over K-O. -- "This is O'Toole! What on earth was he doing in here?"

"I suspect that, like the rest of us, he was looking for company. He must have missed you, I'm sure."

"And what about him?" -- Tank's bottom teeth had been driven into his upper gum, wrinkling the lip and nose into a dreadful smile.

"Tank? You should know all there is to know about him. He was your best friend or so he said."

--- * * * * * ---

Marched from the cell, a heavyweight on either side, up the echoing stair and into another cell with padding on the walls. They laced me into a straight-jacket, chained me to the bunk, turned the regulation white light into my eyes then left, all without a word.

I have to say that, in many ways, the change of cell was for the better. It was quiet, clean and, best of all, I was on my own. The trouble, as so often, was in the mind. I simply couldn't lie there, the light glowing pink through closed lids, and wait without worrying about her. – "What in Heaven's name are they doing to Victoria at this very minute? What are they making her do? Can she say anything at all, still make sense of what they're saying? Of course she can! They'll make sure of that, they're after information -- or are they? I've seen torturers working solely for the thrill, often and often, play with a piece of wire, push it slowly into their victim's body, their ears, through the windows of their eyes! Right at this moment, that tramp with the surgical collar, he's working on her. While I'm chained down here in the silence, that hideous creature's crouching over her, laughing while she begs for mercy! How long before I'm forced to watch?"

Horrific thoughts, scenes, images of Victoria's torture kept creeping in and sidling around my mind. I began to hear voices in my head. -- "For Christ's sake, God," -- I put my hands together. -- "don't let them go on torturing her! Don't let them do anything to her at all, please! Do what you want with me, anything, anything at all but in the name of Mary, holy mother of your only son, leave Victoria, the best and loveliest of people, in peace!"

Maybe God was listening, maybe he wasn't. I seemed to lie there for ever, muttering away while my imagination remorselessly tortured me. Inside the jacket, my body ran with sweat and in the trembling silence, I learned that the knees of the terrified do indeed knock.

--- * * * * * ---

It's a relief when the two porters come back for me. -- "Hi there! Brought any news? Hang on! What's that pole for? -- No, not this! I can walk, I can walk!"

The two men hoist the pole onto their shoulders and carry me off, swinging between them like a stuck pig. -- "Where are you taking me? Please tell me, where?"

Through set after set of swing-doors, dull clunk and thud as they close behind, buffeting the heavy air, building up wave upon wave of heat. -- "At least give me an idea of where we're going! Surely you can tell me that much!"

Push ahead through a final door and swing along a stone passage running steeply down into the stifling bowels, monstrous cobwebs, bare bulbs lighting up the hot air. We come to an iron grille reaching to the roof and forged for eternity. I see an inscription high up but upside-down, can only guess at what it says. The gate's clatter behind us, locks close with teeth of iron. -- "Please, please let me walk! Please don't carry me like this! Please, I beg you! Have mercy on me!"

Through a fire door and on down a flight of steps, descending into the heat, past two, three furnace rooms, the air throbbing with the smell of iron close to melt down. -- "For God's sake, I can't breathe with my head hanging down like this! I can't breathe, please let me walk!"

Through a waiting room, people chained up like dogs, moaning to themselves, some rocking back and forth like they're at The Wailing Wall, not one calls out as we pass. There's an Italian girl near the back with an Afro hair do, bottle blonde looks so great frizzed out, defiant. -- "Keep it up, signorina! Have faith! The master has not abandoned us yet!"

The next few moments, I cannot bring myself to think about. The shrieking hell of a long room with unspeakable contraptions in rows like the beds on an accident and emergency ward, the atmosphere thick with bone-sawing and the stench of bodily fluids. In the far corner, half in the shadow of block and tackle, the remains of a beautiful face, blonde head cradled in blood. Those eyes! –I lost consciousness.

Chapter 20

Ragged feet shuffle across the frozen river. From under the ice, hair streaming in the current's flow, anguished faces beseeching mercy. Through the great gate of lead, above in black -- "Abandon hope all ye who enter here!". Emerge in the narrow street, push through the crowds of people staring up into the gorgon's eyes, transfixed for eternity. We go by the river of fire, a host of politicians straining to drink from a pitcher of cold water. Above us on the road, an emaciated girl toils at pushing her countless children up an endless hill. In the market square, men and women with porcine faces battle over troughs filled with pieces of gold.

The palace is majestic but deserted and ice-cold. Down corridor after corridor, walls hung with scenes from Dante, all utterly without life. Enter the throne room. The darkness is not of midnight, not of closed eyes. It is the absolute negation of light. There is no sound, not even the pounding of my heart. I fall to my knees and a cold breath flows into my nostrils.

--- * * * * * ---

"You have a visitor," the duty torturer said, spraying me and the rack with aerosol then drawing the sheet up under my chin. "Mind you be polite, don't speak except to answer questions and don't complain about me, the other operatives, the machinery, anything at all."

The white light which had been blazing into my eyes when they strapped me down and was still there each time I was brought back to consciousness abruptly went out, leaving the walls bathed in the soft glow of comfort lights. The door opened and a huge man in the robes of a cardinal strode down the ward toward me, in his train, a flock of hangers on, Captain Wolf and the governor among them. —"Well, well!" -- He leaned over me, icy breath fanning my face. -- "So this is Josef Sope, the renegade who refused to get into my car! I take it he is conscious, nurse. It's hard to tell with him lying so still and the face blown up like that. -- He is, you say? That's as well because you'd have to revive him otherwise and time is not with us. -- Can you hear me,

Sope? Nod your head if you cannot speak or you're too overawed to do so."

"I hear you."

"Well done! Now, let's see how much you still understand. Where are you at this moment?"

"I'm on the rack."

"And do you know why you're there?"

"They say I'm on the rack because I need straightening out."

"Quite right! You do need straightening out but, apparently, the treatment isn't working. In fact, I'm told you're as deformed as ever." -- He took a chair alongside my head. -- "This mark, here on your left temple, what do you suppose it signifies?"

"I only wish I knew. Some say one thing, others another."

"Then I shall tell you, myself. That mark is the badge of Beelzebub. You are — or were once — a high ranking officer in the service of the prince of darkness, one of the so-called damned. Can you appreciate what that means?"

My heart leapt for joy. "A high ranking officer!"

"See that everybody? His eyes light up! Promising! -- Tell me, do you have any notion who I might be?"

"The prince himself?"

"The prince himself!" -- He beamed down at me. -- "Alas no. I have no claim to that eminence, at least not yet. I am the spirit in command of the police and popularly known as The Minister. And why do you suppose I've come here tonight?"

"I hope you're here to take over the supervision of my torture, Your Highness."

The minister's laugh was angelic. -- "And why should I do such a thing, you naughty boy?"

"Because you want results and the hospital staff just aren't up to the job."

"My opinion precisely! Obviously, you and I will have to teach these fools how it's done, Sope. We'll sort everything out together." -- He turned to the duty torturer. -- "Pass me his case-notes, nurse."

When The Minister is reading, nobody, it seems, dares to breathe. Even the groans and curses of my fellow sufferers ceased while he studied the file, turning each page with a crack of disapproval. -- "I have to say,"-- He snapped the file shut. -- "that's one of the poorest case histories I've ever read! Haven't you studied my handbook on torture therapy, nurse? You can't possibly expect to bring this particular patient to his senses with a regime like this. Look here," -- He flipped the file open again and stabbed an angry forefinger at the first few entries. -- "all this could have been thought up by a child! Look at it! Totally bereft of imagination! No psychological preparation to speak of, no investigative torture, nothing! You simply move into physical procedures as if he were a side of pork! Just look at it! Prolonged traction, thumb screws, severe shocking, acid, ice blocks, … and so it goes on and on, a ragbag of bone-headed operations, all of them physical and all extreme! Weren't you informed of his background?"

"No, Your Eminence, I wasn't told a thing. I was only given the list of objectives and told to get on with the treatment."

"But you only have to look at him, for God's sake! What's that on his forehead, a love bite? That alone should be enough to tell you that he must have a phenomenally high pain threshold. Christ, man, he's all but one of us! I want him to recover and, for that, he needs carefully selected treatment, not this butchery. Why didn't you probe his weak points first and work on them? It's all there in my handbook, including an introduction to psychological torture, a chapter on initial compliance routines and a reader-friendly appendix on technological advances in physical procedures. What the hell made you decide to ignore all that excellent advice? Do you think you know better than me or what?"

The duty torturer could hardly wait to defend himself. -- "The captain told me I was to dispense with compliance routines, Your Eminence. He said he wanted results in minutes, not years."

"Captain Wolf said that, did he?" -- Wolf's face was ashen. -- "And what happened to the psychological component? The mind is this patient's weakest organ, for God's sake! Are you telling me Captain Wolf told you to ignore psychology as well as everything else I discuss in my book?"

"May I say something, Your Eminence?" -- Head down and shoulders hunched, Frankie Wolf had physically shrunk.

"No, you may not unless and until you're told to! --- Well, nurse, what were your instructions regarding psychological torture?"

"I was told to skip it and get on with the serious stuff, Your Eminence."

"Is that so? Then, you'd better tell me this -- what action was taken on my memo regarding the Hunter-Jones woman?"

"I'm afraid my secretary failed to pass it on to the staff, Your Eminence." -- Wolf's intervention was barely audible.

"I see! So it's your secretary who's to blame, is it? -- Nurse, clear that equipment and bring it alongside Sope's rack then go and fetch the woman. -- Hell, Wolf, no wonder you lost your command! And after all I've done for you! I'll have something to say to you! What on earth were you thinking of? Sope, here, is crippled, crippled with love for Hunter-Jones. That's why I sent you the memo, for your personal and urgent attention! Hunter-Jones must be tortured where he can have sight and sound of everything. I guarantee, he won't last more than a few minutes. -- Well, nurse? Why are you standing there gawping at me like Lot's wife?"

"The woman is already beyond further torture, Your Eminence. We finished working on her a full three hours ago."

"Say that again! You've finished with her?"

"Completely, Your Eminence."

No sound except the scrape of The Minister's chair as he turns right around to stare at cringing Wolf. -- "Get yourself down to my office immediately and stay there until I come!" -- My mind was paralysed by the news of Victoria but, even so, it registered a flicker of compassion for Frankie Wolf as he shuffled away out of the watching ward.

"Well, Sope," -- The minister turned back to me. -- "it looks as if I come on the scene only just in time. Your case has been appallingly mishandled so I shall have to take it over myself. Very well, let us assume nothing and go back to the beginning. You say you need straightening out. Tell me, where do you think you went wrong?" -- I tried to speak but no words would come out, only dry air.

"Didn't you hear me, Sope? I asked you where you went wrong!"

He waited, everyone in the ward waited. -- "I'm too late! Too late!" – I heard myself howling like a tortured dog.

The minister of police watched me with obvious satisfaction. --

"Take note, nurse, and learn! It would have been so very easy! -- That's enough, Sope! Enough, I said! I'm waiting for you to answer my question. Where did you go wrong?"

Eventually, my voice came back, a voice from the dead. -- "I… I didn't go wrong. They say I'm lying. I'm not lying. I didn't hide the relic. I lost it."

"Ah, but that's what he was told to say, Your Eminence!" -- Like almost all in his profession, the duty torturer had a one track mind. To him, the possibility that a victim could be innocent was inconceivable.

Not so, his eminence. -- "What he says may very well be true nonetheless, nurse, and, if you'd studied my book, you would recognise that. Sometimes, we have to accept that we are being told the truth and, when that happens, we do well to abandon that line of enquiry and look around for another, then another and another until the entire range of interesting possibilities has been exhausted. It's obvious that you and Captain Wolf have been wasting valuable time and effort in flogging a dead horse when you should have saddled another. -- Very well, Sope, I shall accept that you are telling the truth and that you simply lost the relic. Why was it entrusted to you at all, do you imagine?"

"Because I was the only Joe Sope around at the time, I believe."

"The Hunter-Jones woman told you that, didn't she? And she was right, absolutely right. What a long, long way you've fallen, Sope! To think that one of your standing should accept such a ridiculous commission, guarding a little bottle of scent! What possible honour could that bring? The so-called Christ phial was of no significance whatever! It was a cheap fraud, utterly worthless!"

"The importance of a relic is in it's influence over the credulous, not in its being genuine. Throughout history, far more wars have been fought over foolish beliefs than over truths. The Christ phial was revered by the followers of The Phoenix and therefore represented a threat to the state. As we all know, faith can be exploited in many ways, including as fuel for the furnace of insurrection."

"So endeth the first lesson and delivered with such engaging pomposity! What a splendid bounce back from utter despair! Really, Sope, I could weep at your loss! At the risk of provoking more sermonising, were you happy to follow The Phoenix' orders or did you do so in spite of your better judgement?"

"I didn't and still don't accept that the end may justify the means, that the innocent may legitimately be slaughtered to win the victory."

"And there you see why, in spite of your distinguished rank, you're classified as a miserable goat. You are on that rack not just because you lost a bottle of scent, not even because you refuse to remember anything that would help to find it, but because your personality is flawed, perhaps fatally so. Carrying that mark, you should be a man of great distinction, perfect in evil. You should be at the side of evil in its battle against good. You should love evil with all your heart and with all your mind even when it seems to be directed against you. On receiving the Christ phial from the terrorist's hands, your only thought, your instinct, should have been to give it up immediately to the security forces or, if that proved impossible, to destroy it. The evil course should come automatically to you as does the downward slope to flowing water but it does not. When an opportunity to aid the cause presents itself, you are as likely to do good as evil because you are not psychologically consistent. Your character seems to have been corrupted by goodness, making you unpredictable and therefore unreliable. Now," -- He lowered his voice to barely a whisper. -- "I'm going to tell you something. We in the ministry at one time believed in you completely. In light of previous performance, we thought you capable of breaking free of the animal chains of humanity. You, we said, could become a great fiend, a leader of devils. All that was necessary was for you to undergo trial by ordeal harsh enough to purge you of one or two foolish notions which had crept in and hardened in spite of the governor's efforts. On my instructions, you were classified as a goat, a nobody, so that you should be fully motivated to lie, cheat, steal, murder your way back among the sheep where you had formerly belonged. But what do you do? You fall in love! And, being weakened by love, you begin to vacillate, bend this way and that, here and there perform little acts which our enemies would applaud. I'm told you even prayed! Truly, it looks as if you are all but lost in spite of our efforts. You are already far along the road to becoming a typical Mr Average, neither wholly evil nor thoroughly good, an incorrigible nobody. Tell me, does that prospect appeal to you?"

"No, Your Eminence, it does not! It's intolerable!"

"That is exactly what I hoped to hear and as long as you continue to feel that way, I am happy that the work on you should continue. Who knows, you may rise to greatness yet. Certainly, we in the ministry will do everything in our power to help you realise your evil potential so that you can take your rightful place among us. -- Now, let us quickly resolve this little problem of the so-called Christ phial." -- His mobile rang. -- "Well, what is it? -- You're not interrupting me, Captain Ready, on the contrary, you arrive at an excellent moment. Bring it in to me immediately."

Captain Ready, dark suit and tie and looking very pleased with himself, came bustling down the ward. The minister took a document from him and skimmed through it. -- "Well done! This should settle the matter and take up no time at all. Just to make things easy for friend Sope, kindly summarise in broad outline The Phoenix problem and your excellent proposal for its resolution."

"Your eminence," -- Ready fixed his pale eyes on my face as if I were a complete stranger. -- "on your instructions, the committee of public security, of which you recently appointed me chairman, is currently engaged in sweeping away the many thousands of legends and myths surrounding the infamous lie of the so-called Christ, son of God, which have grown up during the last two thousand years and continue to warp the human intelligence. Among these myths, that of The Phoenix, otherwise known as the fire bird, is scheduled to be discontinued from 24 hours next, that being the end of its current five hundred year cycle. It is by no means a vigorous myth at present but it has the potential to do the cause great harm and must be eradicated entirely. We are, therefore, engaged in destroying all relics associated with the fire bird. As part of that operation, the security forces, now under my command, have been involved in cleaning-up operations, including the capture and elimination of the terrorist who calls himself The Phoenix and his gang. Regrettably, it has come to light that twelve terrorists, not two as reported by Captain Wolf, my predecessor, escaped capture and have set up an underground network dedicated to the conversion of the masses. Among the many ridiculous claims they are making is that The Phoenix will return among them through the blood shed by the so-called Christ and preserved in the phial. Unfortunately, the phial, which was passed on to Sope for safe keeping, cannot now be traced. The problem is minor and could have safely been ignored had not an interested party from outside the ministry exploited it to create difficulties. The argument is that, unless we can produce proof positive that the phial no longer exists, we cannot prove that The Phoenix will never return and so the legend must be allowed to continue. My committee's recommendation is, therefore, that Sope sign a declaration that he wilfully destroyed the phial -- which is what I would have expected him to do in any case."

"Splendid! -- You satisfied with that, Sope?" -- The minister was, evidently, more than satisfied. -- "You see now how easily this little affair can be resolved. You have only to put your signature to a formal confession which will enable us to wind up an ancient and thoroughly misleading myth. -- As if a true son of God would permit himself to be represented by a fowl! -- I should say, in case your own situation has not been fully explained to you, that you have failed to qualify for reincarnation and that the recommendation of both the governor and the police is that you be thrown into the everlasting fire. Since talking with you, however, my faith in you has to some degree been renewed and I am inclined to be lenient provided, of course, you are cooperative. How do you respond?"

"May I have an hour to think it over?"

"No, you may not! Quite apart from anything else, we do not have an hour to spare. The interested party, a wayward and thoroughly disreputable spirit who occupies a ministerial position elsewhere to which he is no longer entitled, is insisting that, since the rebirth of The Phoenix is due to take place at midnight, the matter be resolved before then. Agree now or abandon hope for eternity."

"You say, if I sign, you'll be lenient. What would that mean in practice?"

"It means you will be taken to a spot some miles from here and dumped. Rather than being committed to everlasting fire, you will be allowed to take your chance with the worms. There have been those, I'm told, who have come out of the experience reasonably well and gone on to achieve a successful birth even if their lives have been wretched. However, as I've indicated, I have from the first taken a personal interest in your case. Should you survive, which is quite possible given your background, you may come back and put yourself under my personal care. As a sign of my favour, I shall, myself, supervise your treatment. Everything possible will be done to smelt that wretched streak of goodness out of you and, once that has been achieved, it should not be long before you are ready to take your place as one of my deputies here in the ministry. Does that answer your question?"

"Just one more question, what about Lady Victoria? If I am to be given a chance to escape the everlasting flames, she must as well. That's what our contract requires."

He snorted. -- "Oh that! Surely, after what's passed between us, you're not still clinging onto that childish fantasy! -- The Queen of Hearts' knave!"

"But a contract is a contract. I swore to serve her to our journey's end and I cannot possibly break my word, not in my present state of health anyway."

"Tell me, nurse, are the woman's remains still in the building?"

"I believe so, Your Eminence. They certainly were when I came on duty an hour ago."

"Then they should be still. Very well, Sope, since it will cause you infinite pain, I grant your request but be advised that it represents yet another example of weakness on your part and will have to be paid for in the future. Your baggage will be travelling with you as will the remains of a great many of your fellow patients. -- Chairman Ready, the papers for signing, if you please."

"And will I have the option to be reborn along with Lady Victoria?"

"As you once again demonstrate, every fool makes his own Hell. Put your mark here." [Frosty fingers guiding my hand.]

Chapter 21

"Well, at least they didn't leave my face on you!" I said, looking down at the severed head as we rattled through the side streets in the back of the garbage truck. I'd managed to get into a sitting position half way up the load of rubbish and the head was cradled between the bars of an iron bedstead, entangled by its hair. -- "You must have been quite striking once. Even now, you have the look of the master about you. Never mind me, what a long way The Phoenix has fallen!"

The head spread its lips in a bloody smile. -- "At least you still recognise me, Sope. Thank God for that at least! The Phoenix is fallen, yes, but only to rise again. You'll see. Now, get on and start digging me out of here!"

I went down on my hands and knees. The face was horribly mutilated, cut and bruised, streaks of blood and the teeth shattered but the eyes looked straight into mine with the cold authority of the true fanatic. -- "Am I hearing voices again," I said, "Or did you really speak to me?"

"You heard what I said, Sope, get on and dig me out! Hurry up, we don't have much time!"

"It's still talking! Jesus Christ! I'll soon put a stop to that! Shut up, you! Shut your bloody mouth!" [Kick, kick]

The head screwed up its eyes as if trying to ward off the blows. -- "Stop, Sope! Stop kicking me! Pull yourself together, man! I'm your master and I order you to dig me out! Use your hands, anything. Hurry, hurry!"

"But I must be mad! You were severed from your body! I saw it happen with my own eyes!"

"Sope, you must get a grip on yourself. I wasn't beheaded! I'm just buried up to the neck in all this, this offal. Get me out! There isn't much time left!"

"But I saw it happen! I'll never forget the sight of you swinging by your hair. You spoke to me!"

"Sope! All you saw was a series of images, crude propaganda on state television. I can't believe you could be so gullible. You're supposed to be intelligent yet you're taken in by a horror film put out by The Minister of police! I ask you, who but a simpleton would trust their ears or eyes when what goes into them is controlled by the state? It's all propaganda! Every word, just about, every image on the screen is there to control the people, tell them what to think, what to say, who to praise, who to condemn, what cause to support and which to oppose. This place is run by a gang of dictators and, to the dictator, the only acceptable thoughts are his own. That's why there can never be free speech here, because there is no freedom of thought."

I sat there a while, staring at the head. How right he was and how stupid I'd been! Of course the film was mere propaganda. I knew that at the time for God's sake! My face on a severed head! What the hell had they done to my mind? I'd have to sort this one out. -- "I don't need you to tell me what goes on in a police state. Propaganda doesn't fool me. It's just that I was traumatised by the sight and sound of you and no wonder." [A silent stare]

It was hard work and I had to battle for some time before I finally got The Phoenix onto the surface. He'd been put in a body bag and I had to cut it open with a broken bottle. Even after the torture hospital, the smell of burnt flesh was nauseating and the sight of those maggots! There were thousands of them crawling up and down! -- "And I thought I'd suffered! What on earth were they trying to do? I'm almost too scared to brush these things off you. Your flesh, it's like charcoal!"

"That's what most of it is, pretty well. The fools thought they'd humiliate me with red-hot irons but I survived the ordeal and, in the end, they had to admit defeat. Praise be to God! It was a great victory he gave me and now everyone will know exactly who I am. I am The Phoenix and woe betide my detractors, especially those who are right now trying to persuade the people that I'm just a lunatic, a sick-minded troublemaker like any other who dares oppose this regime."

"One thing I have learnt, friend, and that is, too much self-esteem is a kind of blindness. -- Well, now we've got you more or less clear of maggots, where do we go from here?"

"Unless I ride on your back, Sope, I won't be going anywhere. In case you haven't noticed, I'm totally paralysed."

"Totally! You really mean to say you can't move at all?"

"That's what I said. From the throat on down, I can neither move nor feel. Made a fine mess of me, didn't they? Cut my spinal cord. And for what? Nothing! My courage wasn't consumed by their fire, it was nourished by it. It was my body which failed. Those fiends were the ones to be humiliated, not me. I succeeded, they failed. I shall go on to greater and greater victories in the service of the risen Christ. They must go on their bellies to their master to be whipped. I'm beaten in one thing and one thing only, thirst. How I thirst! There is nothing in my mouth but dust. It feels like I'm reduced to ash, hot, dry ash. How I long for drink! The first thing you must do is get me something, a few sips of water to wet my throat. "Water", what a wonderful sound that word has! If you can't find water, bring something else, I don't care what it is, vinegar, blood even, anything to break the drought inside me. Dear God, how I thirst!"

"But there won't be anything fit to drink on this truck. Still, if you're that desperate, I suppose I should take a look. By the way, you're not the only one who's suffering. Maybe you should be grateful you've only got yourself and your ambition to burn over."

As I expected, there was nothing. Plenty of slime, weeping flesh, the hindquarters of a dog, but for drinking, nothing at all. I returned to the terrorist. -- "As I told you, it's no go. There's nothing here, not one drop of fluid to take away my own thirst let alone yours, not even a drop of vinegar. What I'd give for a sponge of that myself!"

"Then there's nothing else for it. When did you last go?" -- It took a second for the shock to subside. He meant it! -- "There's no need to look so horrified. Your water isn't of any use to you in the bladder. To you, it's just a waste product, something to be got rid of, but to me it will be as a gushing stream. Hurry, I thirst!"

"But I can't do a thing like that!"

"I don't see why not. It won't be the first time after all. Remember the desert? We managed to survive there for forty days. Hurry, I thirst."

"Hang on a moment! Survived in a desert? When, where, what desert?"

"So, they did that, did they, wiped your memory clean as the proverbial slate! That's really ominous! They always leave something if only as food for nightmares. I'll have to give that a lot of thought. Meantime, do as you're told and get on with it, for the sake of your soul, start pissing!"

214

--- * * * * * ---

"Where do we go from here?" I asked. The Phoenix was lying helpless among the rubbish, trying to blink away a persistent bluebottle.

"You might ask! Where do we go? If you hadn't lost the phial, it would have been easy enough for me at least but thanks to your negligence, I will have to find my way back to life without the blood of Christ, something that's never been attempted before. Why the hell did you have to go and lose the Christ phial? -- If you did lose it, that is."

"Who told you I'd lost it?"

"You did. You were screaming it out for hours on end. -- "I don't know where the phial is, I lost it! Please, you must believe me, I lost the blood of Christ and I don't know where it is! Please stop, please!" I doubt there was anyone in the Palais de Justice who didn't know that you'd failed me. Let's just hope the enemy don't find it! Then at least there'll still be hope for the cause. The regime will have severe problems convincing the people I'm finished. Beside, I have one ally in particular who will stand by me. He'll find a way round. Of that, I'm certain."

"I hate to tell you this but he's already failed. They have all they need, a confession."

"Confession! What are you saying, Sope! What confession?"

"I … I signed a scrap of paper. It said I'd destroyed the phial myself, which is, apparently, every bit as good as handing it over. I should never have done it, you'd say, but I did and that's all there is to it. Who knows, it could turn out for the best in the end. We'll just have to wait and see."

"But I don't understand! Why on earth would you do such a thing? It may well have undermined me and our cause completely!"

"Your cause, you mean, not mine. I didn't ask to get involved in all this in the first place. Still, I suppose you could say I made an error of judgement and, if so, I suppose I'm sorry. The thing is, at the time, The Phoenix myth really didn't seem all that important. As things turn out, it may well have awful consequences for me but it didn't look that way then. The point is, there was no malice in what I did, none. His Eminence, The Minister, came to see me and … Oh hell, why go on?

After all, if I hadn't signed the bloody thing, I wouldn't be here to look after you now, would I? Nor would I have a chance of saving anyone else. -- Here, let me get rid of that fly."

"Holy mother of God, what a sly creature you've become! You Judas! What did he give you? Not silver, surely! That wouldn't tempt even you here. I suppose His Eminence, as you call him, flattered you, told you how special you are, how important to him, how great you once were and would one day become again. Flattery, that's what he showered on your head, empty words, hardly a good return for betraying your master!"

"There was no betrayal in it, I've told you that once already. But you are right in one thing, His Eminence did say something of what he plans for me. And why shouldn't he? Is it so ridiculous that Josef Sope of all people should be honoured? Am I not as good as anyone else, completely worthless? Not to you it seems, not when there's no-one else around to lean on. I tell you this much, holy as hell you may be but The Minister beats you hands down when it comes to personal relations. He isn't a bit like you, abusive, over-bearing, self-satisfied and oh so patronising, with the skin of a rhinoceros. He didn't call me names and treat me like cannon fodder. On the contrary, he showed me some respect and actually went out of his way to set out my past and future place in the scheme of things which, if I take it -- I repeat if -- will be a place of great distinction. Take note of that, great distinction! This mark that so disfigures my face, do you recognise it by any chance?"

"You know the answer to that perfectly well."

"Yes, I believe I do now. For a time, I actually thought it was yours, the mark of The Phoenix, but I know better now. That's no ordinary shrapnel wound, the sort of meaningless scar any old Joe Sope picks up as he's blown up by one of your mines. My scar's something special, the mark of the prince of darkness! Not a common foot soldier, mind, mine is the mark of one who was once highly honoured among the ranks of the damned and could be so again if he chose."

"I am impressed! And who interpreted the mark for you, His Eminence?"

"There have been others but yes, The Minister confirmed it himself."

"You pathetic, little man! What would you want with such honour?

Don't you realise that Satan and his followers exist in a state of the profoundest despair possible and will do so till the end of time? How could you be so very desperate to be loved! The minister sees your weakness plainly enough and, of course, he would talk that way, wouldn't he? Words are cheap, they cost nothing and his especially are worth nothing. Your friend, The Minister, fed you with fine words, pretty flies for a little fish to bite at, and how you gulped them down! What marvellous bait to draw you into sin! All the torture in the universe fails but a little praise, an empty promise of greatness and you leap to betray the cause like the Judas you are! You always did have a touch of the night about you, Josef, and once again it comes out. You're a common traitor, not some great fiend whatever His so-called Eminence may tell you. You've betrayed your saviour, me, and all your former comrades. You deserve to be in the legions of the damned! Well, at least I know now why you remember nothing of your life with us. If only there hadn't been one! Anyway, it's too late to go back now. I'll have to make do with you as you are, not as you should be. As for you, you'll have to go down on your knees and beg for mercy then do whatever penance is required of you. It isn't going to be easy and you may well fail yet again. Just think about it! Because of your weakness, I'll have to take the hardest road of all, blind faith, and that may be too much even for me. I forgive you, of course, but I'm going to be hard on you, very hard right up to the bitter end. So be warned, once we've been dumped, I'll be riding on your back for God knows how long."

"Hold it there, you! There's something we must sort out between us. Either you stop calling me names or I'll leave you to fend for yourself. Judas! Who do you think you are? You talk about me leaping about but I think you're the one who's doing the leaping, leaping to conclusions. I don't know that I want your forgiveness and as for carrying you on my back for God knows how long, I haven't agreed to carry you anywhere and I'm not sure I'm going to. Judas! How dare you? With the possible exception of myself, I've never knowingly betrayed anybody, certainly not you or your cause. How could I? At the time the relic was foisted on me, I didn't know -- or at least I didn't remember – anything about you or what you stood for but you certainly thought you knew a lot about me. Ok, maybe it's true that I do have a flawed character. Maybe

I am incurably good natured and loving. You were quick enough to take advantage of it, that's for sure. Talk of kettles calling pots names! You're every bit as bad if not worse than you claim His Eminence is! "Ah," you said "Joe Sope's our man! Dumb ass, he'll stick his head into any yoke you like to shove in front of him! If there's no other way, load the blood onto Mr Everyman's back, let him carry it like the beast of burden he really is." That's what you said. Well, I didn't owe you anything then and I don't owe you anything now. In fact, you're the one who's in debt -- to me! Even a Joe Sope is worthy of his hire so, if you want to ride on my back, you'll have to pay the going rate."

"And what do we use for money, promises, flattery, is that it? Now, there's something you really value! So be it! In return for your labour, I'll dress you up in fine words, give you a few dozen titles as well, make you a prince, a cardinal if you like. I promise to shower you with empty praise and false promises till your ego bursts. You can have more of that from me than you even got from your friend, His Eminence, The Minister of police, and look what you did for him!"

"The fare I demand is simple, Mister. I'll carry you and help you without reward for myself. I only require that you allow me to lay what remains I can find of my mistress, Lady Victoria, alongside you if and when you burn in the fire of life, so that she can live also."

That shook him! If he could, I believe The Phoenix would have hugged himself. -- "So there is a little spirit left in you after all! What a blessing that you should have the chance to serve me in spite of everything! Praise be to God! I grant your request. So as to try your courage and frustrate the cause of evil, Lady Victoria may enter the fire with me as may you also if you qualify for life by then. It's not going to be easy though and your first difficulty looks like being a purely practical one. You'll have to find her. Where is she, where among all these remains are we to find your so-called Queen of Hearts?"

"Where indeed! Look at them all! How on earth am I to tell which bag she's in! There must be the remains of hundreds here, bag after plastic bag full. Obviously, His Eminence was having a laugh at my expense. Well, it's one he'll very much regret in due course."

--- * * * * * ---

The truck swung through a tight corner, almost pitching me onto my face in a mess of leaking bags, changed gear and accelerated along a street of sky-high warehouses. -- How serene the moon looked sailing through the distant sky, another existence out there if only we could reach so far! -- Leaving the town, we rattled out onto the broad expanse of moonlit plain, distant shapes of refuse dumps, lakes of chemical waste, everywhere a green glow and, on the flyblown breeze, the pungent odour of decay.

"One thing I can tell you," I said, "where-ever else they've sent us, it's not to Golgotha. This is never the place of salvation, the merciful alternative to everlasting fire! We've arrived in the bowels of Hell itself. How lenient his eminence turns out to be – and how lenient I shall be to him when my time comes!"

"Ah but you haven't experienced one iota of his mercy yet, that I can assure you! Anyway, you're right, this isn't Golgotha but neither is it Hell. It's the city rubbish dump, your future home and, if I fail, your last stop but one."

"You know, either you're suffering from megalomania or you're wickedly trying to provoke me. I'm Josef Sope, remember. I represent the soil of common thought myths and legends feed on. I'm perfectly capable of surviving without your help. The question is whether you can without me. Without dumb animals to drive and slaughter, the goatherd is irrelevant and that's an invaluable truth fanatics like you would do well to ponder on."

"And you might benefit from the ancient saying -- he who sups with the devil had best use a very, very long spoon."

Winding in and out of the hills of waste brought back memories of the drive in the police car with Victoria. I could feel the tears running down my cheeks as I thought of her and what she'd been through largely because of me. The Phoenix noticed and, of course, seized the chance to show how strong he was. -- "Emotional nonsense like that won't help, Josef, quite the reverse. It will only sap your will and weaken you even further. Learn by me! Love, unless it is purely spiritual, is a luxury which has no place in the revolutionary's heart. In order to overcome the enemy, one must be disciplined, totally committed to the struggle and, above all, completely without fear. But fear is at the heart of love. Love makes a man fearful for the one he loves and so it weakens him. We will try to save Lady Victoria Hunter-Jones -- if such a thing is possible-- but we must attempt it in order to test your strength and to frustrate the enemy, not because you're in love with the victim. Love your God, his only begotten son, Jesus Christ, and your duty but no other. If you're to be saved, you will have to free yourself of love for Lady Victoria completely. As I've told you before, the need to love and be loved is a serious fault in your personality and, if it is not corrected, it will one day destroy you. She doesn't love you in any case and never will -- not in the way you want."

"I don't think you'd recognise true love if you got into bed with it! How could you possibly know how Lady Victoria feels about me?"

"Because I was in the equipment next to hers in the torture ward for a while, that's how I know. The Romans used to say that wine unlocks the truth. As you must know, terror does the same thing but even more so. Lady Victoria didn't call out for you once, never so much as whispered your name. Back there in the ward, all she could say was "Luigi, Luigi, please help me Luigi!"."

"Maybe it was like that, maybe it wasn't. I can't believe you heard absolutely everything she might or might not have murmured in that Bedlam. As for my need to love and be loved, that's exactly what His Eminence said, more or less. How alike you two are, extremists both! The difference is, you're wrong and he's right. It's perfectly possible for a saintly man to love another human being but for someone who is wholly evil, any love is impossible even self-love. I don't claim to be perfect yet either in goodness or evil. As for Lady Victoria, it doesn't matter how she feels about me. As you of all people should know, love is in giving, not receiving, and she needs my love more than ever now."

--- * * * * * ---

Half a mile or so and we draw up beside a hut at the foot of a hill of cast-offs, rusting cars, dead refrigerators, mysterious fragments of machinery, a skeletal crane over head, three bodies hanging from hooks in the jaw. One of them was stripped to the waist. Before he'd been winched up, Captain Wolf had been scourged to the bone.

The truck keeps up a violent shudder as a voice calls up directions, faint scent of tobacco, then off we lurch, skirting the outer dumps of the plain before finally pulling up on its North-most border. Here, the tip is still relatively young, not rising in mounds but spreading out in a lake of glowing refuse punctuated by shadowy trees and, everywhere, the flies. Brakes spitting, the truck reverses and avalanches us with the rest of its load into some bushes before it bounces away, farting diesel.

I was right, this isn't Golgotha!" I spluttered, struggling to get a foothold in a muddle of collapsing bush and hospital waste. The Phoenix was sprawled close by, face down.

"That blind faith of yours," I said, "will have to work miracles all on its own. I can't see myself doing much and there's no chance of Christ walking out over this lake to save you! Just look around, smell, feel! The whole place's heaving with maggots! They're crawling all over me already! Ugh!" [Panicky brushing of legs, arms, face, neck, slapping and flapping, all to no avail]

"It's idle to blaspheme, Josef! Christ will save all who truly repent. As for me, I don't need to be told what it's like here. I can smell and taste only too well. In case you haven't noticed, I'm in distress. How long must I wait for you to come over and do something about it?"

I went to his aid, each step sinking to the ankle-bone, the stench stomach-churning. It took a whole lot of struggle, argument and blaspheming before I could even get him onto his back. -- "And what do you need your slave to do for you next, oh leader of men?"

"Get me up on your back, of course. Don't stand there thinking about it, hurry up, time's running out! You only have to midnight."

"You mean, you only have to midnight, comrade! I could well be here a little longer." -- I do my best, heaving and pulling, getting him half up, falling on my knees, starting all over again and again. It's a waste of time and effort. For one thing, being paralysed, he can't hold on and, when I wrap his arms round my neck, the hands won't lock. -- "I can't manage! Sorry, I must take a rest for a moment. -- Maybe," -- There was a low tree fairly close by. -- "Maybe, I could drag you over there and somehow wrestle you onto a branch. It might be possible to get you down onto my back from there."

In this hell, things are always even more difficult than they look. I manage to get him up onto a low branch but he slides over the other side into a thorn bush. -- "Christ, this is horrible! It's become farcical, a black farce!" -- The thorn bush is deeper than it looks and, armed with terrible spikes, quite impenetrable. The Phoenix looks like he's reclining in a barbed wire hammock. I settle down a few feet away to brush off maggots and take a rest. Some rest! Not creeping things only, of course, in seconds, I'm flapping at swarms of flies, hundreds of bluebottles and queer, little black devils with a flesh tearing bite and eyes bright red in the night. Needless to say, no angel from on high swoops down to set things right. In the uproar of insect wings, only the flap and shrill of vultures descending to feed.

"I appreciate that you're incapable of doing much for yourself," I said after a few minutes, "but you've simply got to do something. This isn't going to work unless I have some help. Why don't you pray to your master? Perhaps he'll set you on fire with a bolt of lightening or something. After all, you didn't lose the Christ phial, that was my doing. In any case, I'm sure it couldn't matter less to God whether we still have the thing or not."

"There you go again! Of course the phial matters to God! It contains the blood of his only begotten son and nothing can make up for its loss, nothing but faith, faith pure as fire and unquestioning as a babe in its mother's arms. That's the faith I hope to achieve and I pray for it constantly. I haven't stopped praying for faith since I first took up arms. How else do you think I was able to come through trial by fire? My faith confounded my enemies then and it will do so again. I will succeed, I will, I will, no matter what the odds! All I require of you is that you give me what aid I need in my struggle. Come, wake up, bestir yourself and set out on your own road to redemption by getting me out of these thorns."

"You know something? If words were deeds, you'd be in paradise by now!" -- We start all over again and eventually, he's flat on his back in the open, staring up at the moon, his forehead lacerated to the skull by the thorns. -- - "It's no good trying to get me up on that branch again! You'll just have to think of something else."

"Such as what, for God's sake?"

"Well, you obviously lack the strength to lift me so there's nothing for it. You must cut off my head and carry that. -- Now what's the matter? Don't you have the stomach to carry out work the common butcher performs time and again each working day? This isn't the moment for squeamishness!"

"Carry on, mock me as much as you like but I won't do it! It's no go, I refuse!"

"Well, it's that or nothing and surely you don't want to be doubly damned! It was an evil hand, yours, that brought me to this state. Now let's see if you can use it for good. Cut away my head and, I promise you, your burden of sin will be the lighter. Hurry now, do it!"

Looking at The Phoenix as he lay there, his face a mask of maggots, I was overcome with pity in spite of my dislike for him. Cut off the poor creature's head? Surely I could attempt it at least.

--- * * * * * ---

Who'd have thought it would come to this, a great fighter in the army of God lying on his back, impatient to be butchered, while the poor fiend hunts miserably around for a kitchen knife or something? – "Let me see, the load we were in is concentrated in this area more or less. I'll start here."

In a pile of domestic waste, nothing, not a thing remotely suited. Further away, a huddle of body bags. I take a look while I'm passing just in case but there are no identifiable remains. Later, a bit of rusty tin but still no good. – "I'd never get through the spine." -- Several tool-like objects fashioned from stone but without sharp edges. It's like that, search after search, the same fruitless variation of trash. – "If only I had that lovely, little knife!"

Suddenly, something yielding under my foot. An ear-splitting yowl and a long-bodied cat sinks its claws into my ankle. -- "Blast you! Let go, Hell-cat! -- Here, haven't I seen you before?" -- Grab the beast by its tail, swing it round my head in spitting circles once, twice, three times, let go. It flies away, shrieking into the dark.

Reaching down, I discover what the cat was doing, chewing at something in a bin-liner. I thrust my hand in. Cold flesh! Something touches the back of my hand then clings delicately round my wrist. -- "Jesus! What's this?" -- A brief resistance then it begins to yield and the moon is suddenly bright.

"Victoria! Victoria, my love!"

There should have been dancing under the moon, caressing, kisses of love, but, with midnight rising, there was no time for rejoicing. I tied the mouth of the bag and lifting it onto my shoulder then started back for The Phoenix. What a small weight she was to bear!

"What's that you're carrying, Sope?" [The body revealed] "So that's it, I knew you would let me down in the end. You've been away for ages and what have you been doing, looking for something to help me? No, you squander precious time in searching for the remains of a woman to add to my load. So be it! My trial will be doubly hard now and your own suffering also. Once again, I forgive you. You may leave her on my chest where I can watch her while you go off again and look for an axe or something."

"Not likely! For a while at least, Lady Victoria belongs to me. She's mine and she'll stay with me until it's time to do what I have to."

--- * * * * * ---

In the end, the best I could find was a bottle. It was heavy glass and I had to try several times before it shattered. The jagged edges sparkled in the light and, kneeling beside the terrorist, I saw my hand was shaking. -- "This isn't going to be a clean job but I can't help that. It was all I could find. If only I had a good knife!"

"Don't waste time! Get on with it!"

"Still, if only I could get my hands on a saw or something! A meat-cleaver, that would be the thing. Ok, I'm going to start ... right ... now!" -- The glass tears the skin just above the throat and I see his eyes screw up. I can't hold onto the neck of the bottle and have to stop, my hands shake so. -- "Sorry, I'll try again. Ready?" -- The glass bites into the flesh and begins tearing at the sinew. I fling the bottle from me. -- "It's no use, I can't do it! -- Don't look at me like that! I cannot cut off a head with a bottle. It's not in me. Don't worry, though, I'll be back."

--- * * * * * ---

I go with Victoria to the hut where we stopped for directions. Close by the Crane dangling its human fruit, I can hear Captain Wolf's Tongue moving. The poor sod is still not quite dead. -- "God have mercy on all of us, captain, especially me!" --I clamber up on a box and manage to get the hook out of the jaw. The body falls to the ground, knocking me over. Even so, I'm happy I weakened.

Creep round the wall of corrugated iron to the open door. Thin sound of a disc-player, odour of tobacco smoke and methylated spirit. Bowed back of a young man sitting at a table looking at a sex mag. Opposite him, the butt end of a loaf of bread, the knife stuck into it. I place Victoria on the threshold, slip into the stuffy room and fling myself onto his back, hand stretching towards the bread.

"The lord be praised! At last I have a knife! I should be able to make a civilised job of it now. -- As I leave, I prize a cigarette lighter out of the corpse's fingers then remember Wolf. I lift Victoria onto the table. -- "Wait there a moment, my lady, I'll be right back."

Frankie Wolf is where I'd left him, lying on his back. Through the layer of moving maggots, I can see he is not dead even now. I slice through the up-turned throat and watch his eye-lids flutter. The lips attempt a smile. —"Let that be my last bout of mercy!"

Back in the shed, there are already rats running over the feet of the corpse and several are swarming up the leg of the table where Victoria is waiting. I let the first one reach the top then chop it in half and feed it to the others. I seize my lady and we leave without looking back.

--- * * * * * ---

"It's still no good," I told him, hands trembling more than ever. "I thought I would be able to do it but, even with a knife, it's still not in me. If only you could struggle! Anyway, you can't so that's an end of it. I'll just have to carry you as you are, there's no other way for me."

"If you don't even have the strength to behead me, I doubt you'll carry me far, especially with that woman as well. To decapitate what is virtually a corpse with a bottle would have been difficult but with a bread-knife! That's a cripple's work! You'll never be able to carry her and me plus what I have to bear. You'll have to leave her behind."

"Or you."

--- * * * * * ---

We're ready to set off, Victoria in my arms and The Phoenix hanging down my back like a human cloak. I'm bending beneath the weight and his hands, tied under my chin, press hard against my throat. -- "Which way do I head?"

"The middle of the dump. See that clump of trees? I'm sure that's where I'm fated to burn. -- Watch where you're walking, you fool!"

"I can't keep watching my feet! Your angels will have to do that for us. I must lift up mine eyes unto the hills."

For some distance, only the crunch and crack, slip and slide of my steps and rasping breath. [Caterwauling from the direction of the trees] We move slowly in a pillar of flies under the yowling moon.

"I still think you should get rid of the woman, Sope! You're never going to make the trees with both of us to bear."

"I sure as hell won't make it without her to give me hope!"

Another five minutes, The Phoenix heavier at every step, my spine so bent I must soon go on my knees or fall. -- "How can you weigh so much? The weight of you is pressing me into the earth! I can barely keep up my head to see."

"It's not me, it's her and it always will be her. Forget about love and keep fighting, I can see the trees just up ahead. We're nearly there."

Fifty, sixty more stumbling steps, the burden of love in my arms and the weight on my back increasing as I move closer. -- "I can't go any further, Phoenix, you're breaking my spirit! I can't go on! Please, fall from me, I'm not strong enough for both of you!"

I collapse under the colossal weight but, his hands tied under my throat, The Phoenix rides on me. "Only yards to go! Crawl on, Joe Sope, crawl on! It's now or never again for the three of us!"

Crawl along under the weight of love and the suffering of The Phoenix towards the future, the mass of the world bearing down till my arms give out and I have to inch forward a foot at a time, dragging the body bag. Suddenly -- "Look up, Josef, look up!"

Three trees standing apart and, unless I'm dreaming, the middle one holds its branches outspread. The great yew rising from the glowing corruption, majestic, its limbs shimmering in the moonlight.

"That's it," I call out, "the tree of life, and we're going to reach it in spite of the past! Praise the gods, the loss of the relic was nothing! It's pure love and faith alone that count! There is rebirth after all!"

As we approach the base of the yew, I feel the strength surging back into my limbs. The wooden pitons are still there, rammed into the holes in the trunk and, straddling the cross where I had perched, a chaotic nest of rushes spread as an open grate. Blithely, I carry my burdens up, stepping from one piton to the next, a young lover, bridegroom full of hope. I set Victoria and The Phoenix down on the rush grate, take the lighter from my pocket and apply the flame. As the fire begins to dance, The Phoenix revives, arms opening, lips spreading in wings of flesh. I delay a moment, watching the first buds of fire exploding round the terrorist's lips, roses of flame spreading over the body, blossoming in feathers of flame, the great yew rising toward the moon, its head a billowing crown of fire. Flames are all over the tree, fire dancing on its branches spread like massive wings against the sky. For a few seconds the flames ignore Victoria then wrap around the bag and she explodes into joyful life.

For Josef Sope, there is nothing left. I must turn away and begin my descent from the tree of life. It is going to be a long and most dreadful road back to the prison. -- "I loved you, Victoria! I loved you!"

Maurice Aldridge